VIETNAM BLUES

D. R. VAN WYE

THACKERY-STERLING
chatham, ma

First Edition: April 2019

Cover Design: Wicked Whale Publishing

Library of Congress Cataloging-in-Publication Data

Van Wye, D. R. / Vietnam Blues, Pages: 312

Summary: In the final years of the Vietnam War, American military advisors and their Viet Cong adversaries struggle with doubts, fears, loss, and despair as grim events unfold to an unexpected conclusion.

ISBN-13: 978-1-7336384-0-1

THACKERY-STERLING
chatham, ma

Published in the United States of America

For all those who serve.
With kind remembrance of
TM 88, Kien Hoa Province, RVN

NVA/VC Regimental Positions in Military Region IV
April 1972

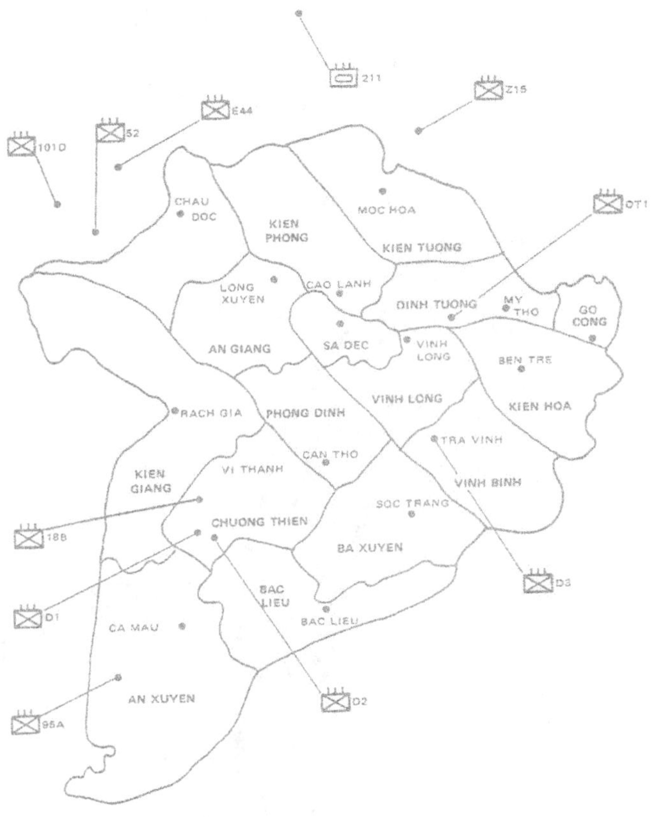

The Easter Offensive of 1972, Lt. General Ngo Quang Truong, U.S. Army Center of Military History, Washington, D.C. 1980.

Sketch of VC Island

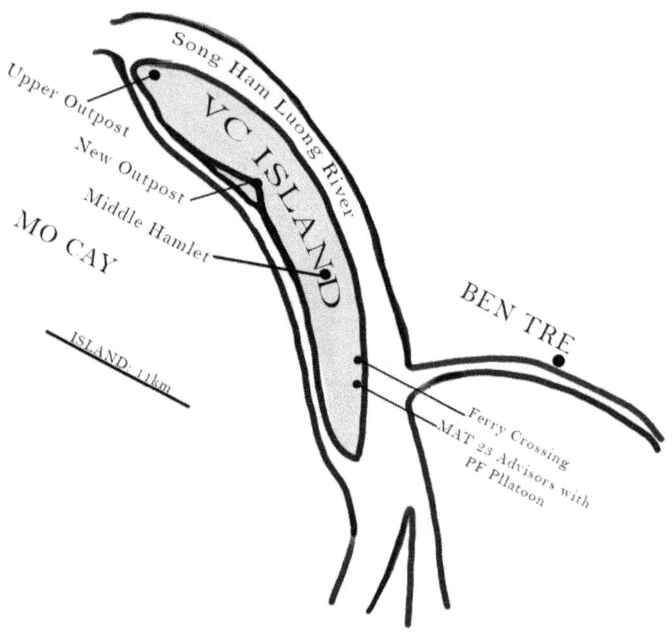

Table of Contents

QUOTES

"The war in Vietnam was not lost in the field, nor was it lost on the front pages of the New York Times or the college campuses. It was lost in Washington, D.C., even before Americans assumed sole responsibility for the fighting in 1965 and before they realized the country was at war; indeed, even before the first American units were deployed."

    -H.R. McMaster,
    <u>Dereliction Of Duty</u>, 1997

"There never was a time when, in my opinion, some way could not be found to prevent the drawing of the sword."

    -Ulysses S. Grant (1822-1885)

"Surely it is the right of citizens in a democracy, especially citizens of military age, to ascertain that the great decisions of war and peace are made with care and deliberation."

-J. William Fulbright,

The Arrogance of Power, 1966

"…What you don't like done to yourself, don't do to others."

-The Analects of Confucius (Translation by A. Charles Muller)

Acknowledgments

Ben Tre Province in South Vietnam is known as "the cradle of insurgency," with a history of resistance against colonial powers. It was renamed Kien Hoa by former President Diem in an effort to quell Viet Cong insurgency. The name Ben Tre was restored after the country was taken over in 1975 by Communist forces.

In addition to my own experiences in Mo Cay district of Ben Tre province, I have relied on the works of other authors to establish an accurate context for the story. A very helpful book to develop a deeper understanding of the insurgent's point of view is the memoir, No Other Road to Take, by Mrs. Nguyen Thi Dinh, who was born in Ben Tre province, led a popular uprising in Mo Cay district in 1960, and became Deputy Commander of the South Vietnam Liberation Armed Forces in 1965. Another useful publication to understand the VC perspective is A Viet Cong Memoir, An Inside Account

Of The Vietnam War And Its Aftermath, by Truong Nhu Tang, the Viet Cong Minister of Justice and the highest official to defect to the West after the war. A U.S. Army report on The Easter Offensive of 1972, written by Lt. General Ngo Quang Truong is also very helpful, along with several Rand reports from the era. Additionally, captured documents housed in the Texas Tech Vietnam archives are helpful in verifying enemy activities in the area where the story takes place.

One of the most compelling books about the war is A Bright Shining Lie, John Paul Vann and America in Vietnam, by Neil Sheehan. It provides insights into the people and history of America's involvement and is well documented and researched. A book by Frances Fitz-Gerald, Fire In The Lake, The Vietnamese in Vietnam, provides an extraordinary in-depth view of Vietnamese culture, history, and politics before and during the American war. Special thanks to Dr. James A. Robinson, M.D. for sharing a collection of newspaper and maga-zine articles published in Hanoi and acquired from medical colleges in eastern Europe. Other useful resources regarding the broader aspects of the war and the chronology of events are Vietnam at War by Lt. General Philip Davidson, and Vietnam, A History by Stanley Karnow.

Many thanks to my wife, Elizabeth, an accomplished news writer and editor, for reading early drafts and providing constructive suggestions. My thanks also go to Peter Ericson and Brian Van Wye who read drafts, and provided thoughtful comments and helpful suggestions. Finally, the useful suggestions and insights of editor Kat Szmit were very helpful in the completion of the manuscript.

ONE

Screaming in Mo Cay

It was a terrible year. In 1959 villagers in Mo Cay district, Ben Tre province, South Vietnam had not recovered from the French occupation before they were pressured to choose between allegiance to the revolutionary Viet Cong or the brutal and repressive government of South Vietnam. In May, the regime of President Ngo Dinh Diem enacted a law authorizing military tribunals to impose a death sentence on anyone belonging to the Viet Cong.

In the village of Than Ngai a crowd gathered around a respected teacher in the late afternoon. They were tired from a day of work in the hot sun and humid, ninety-degree heat blanketing the rice paddies and orchards surrounding the village center. Now, under the cooling shade of coconut palms they waited eagerly to hear the latest news from the teacher, Le Thai Tong. He was seen as a wise man of the village and also known as a prosperous farmer descended from rice and fruit growers going back beyond recollection.

Tong looked furtively at the faces of villagers around him in the center of the sprawling village, just down the path from his ancestral home. His eyes searched beyond the small clearing to a crescent of thatched houses. He thought, *government spies will report dissenters to Diem's henchmen. I see my usual followers. I see others eager to hear about the latest government brutality. But, who else watches?*

He cleared his throat and in the same clear voice he used as a school teacher he said, "A friend told me what happened there. I can picture it now: worried villagers squatted with shoulders hunched, crammed into the square, looking fearfully at dozens of government soldiers surrounding them. A line of yellow bulldozers and other heavy equipment idled further behind the soldiers."

Tong paused, then continued, "Captain Huong was in charge. You remember him. He is the heavy one with the swagger stick and the big belly. He looked down at the huddled people and asked why they were only women, children, and old men. But, he must have known. No doubt the young men had fled into the jungle to avoid recruitment into the South Vietnamese Army, or they had left to become Viet Cong."

The villagers in front of Tong nodded with knowing looks in their eyes.

Tong looked at those nearest to him. "Remember," he said, "the government thinks Ben Tre province, what they call Kien Hoa, is full of Viet Cong. They say we protect and hide insurgents." Some in the crowd murmured their agreement.

Tong raised his voice slightly, "There is more. Captain Huong told the villagers, 'President Diem declared you will move to the agroville. You will give up your houses. Here, in Mo Cay District the VC make trouble. You must move to the new village of Than Thoi to be protected from the insurgents.' But, my friends, we know that no one in that village wanted to leave their ancestral home."

Tong held up his hand, palm out toward the crowd. He said, "We know that weeks earlier, these same villagers had been forced to build the new government village, the agroville. They said it is ugly. The men were forced to do hard labor. They suffered days on end of clearing land, digging ditches and wells, and fortifying the perimeter around the agroville. The government would not pay them or even feed them. Their families had to bring rice from home and help with the work."

Tong shook his head and looked down. With anger in his voice he said, "People do not want to leave their homes, away from their land and the graves of their ancestors. But what did Huong do? He shook his swagger stick and claimed that a month earlier he told the people to dismantle their houses and take down their fruit trees. He said the enemy feeds off the land and shelters there. He said the people disobeyed the government."

In a lowered voice Tong continued, "The people

were afraid. No one dared a reply to Huong. But then, he pointed his swagger stick at an old man and told him to get up and come over."

People leaned in toward Tong. Some shuffled closer. He cleared his throat, "The old man didn't move. He only shook his head from side to side, looking directly at the swagger stick on the out stretched arm of Captain Huong. Huong took one step forward, pointed the stick at the nearest soldier and said, 'seize him up.' The other villages had fearful looks on their faces. They all hung on the moment to see what would happen next."

Tong drew a deep breath as he looked around at the faces in the crowd. He could see they were eager to hear what happened. He said, "Captain Huong looked at the old man stooped before him. He asked, 'Why have you people defied the orders of your government? You were told a month ago to be ready to move, to tear down your houses, and to destroy your crops?' With a faltering voice, the old man said, 'Captain, sir, many here are troubled about leaving our homes, the lands of our ancestors. We need them. We need our land to survive. The coconut trees and the orange trees give us fruit to sell at the market. Our paddies will soon be ready to harvest. We have nothing in Thanh Thoi. It will be too much work for our tired backs to make a new life there. It is easier here where our ancestors have shown us how to grow things and make a living.'"

Tong nodded his head, as if in agreement with the old man's words. Others around him also nodded. "Then," said Tong, "Huong's face turned red. He said,

'I should have you beaten for defying your government. What you say makes no difference. We will deny the enemy a place to get food and shelter here. This whole village will move to Thanh Thoi immediately. But, I will be lenient today to show you I know this is not easy for you. You will have one hour to gather your possessions, your pigs, your chickens and other livestock. Then, you must get on the path to Thanh Toi. You have one hour. Then we will bulldoze your houses and your trees and flatten this land so no enemy of the government can make use of it. Now go.'"

Tong paused again. He looked at the somber faces before him. He said, "At first, the villagers did not move, as if immobilized by shock and fear. They wailed. They cried. They screamed. But then they hurried to collect what they could before the bulldozers plowed away their heritage."

Tong looked into the faces around him. People shook their heads. They muttered, "Very bad. Not right."

Tong responded, "This is true. When we defeated the French in 1954 at Dien Bien Phu we thought we were rid of imperial invaders in all of Vietnam. But now in 1959 things are worse than ever, at least here in Mo Cay. Now we have the Vietnamese tyrant Diem and his American advisors. Peaceful villagers are caught between them and the VC. The government rules by day and the VC rule by night. Both the government and the Viet Cong do harsh things. Now there is a law, Law 10/59, that military tribunals can order death for anyone they think is VC."

Heads nodded. People shifted their feet.

Tong lifted his gaze and said, "I tell you this because I hope we can keep up a good face to both sides and keep our homes from being bulldozed. You know me. You know that I do not take sides. Yes, I was Viet Minh fighting the French, but now I am a teacher and only want peace for my family. I hope we have a peaceful village. I want my family to live here and not go to a government village, an agroville. If we are forced to leave our ancestral homes, then we will no longer be who we are. We will lose our souls. We must save our way of life." Some in the crowd nodded their heads. Others looked at Tong with sad eyes.

A MONTH LATER, IN THE MIDDLE OF THE MONSOON season, three dozen government soldiers arrived on foot in the village of Thanh Ngai. They came up the narrow cart trail from the river where they had jumped off sampans powered by little motors with long propeller shafts to churn the muddy waters. Their boots were covered with the thick, slimy muck of the river bank.

The Vietnamese lieutenant in charge of the govern-ment troops walked up to one house where a man sat under the thatch porch sharpening a rice-harvesting sickle. The man looked up at the officer and nodded, with a slight smile on his face. The officer stood with thumbs tucked in the front of his web belt, a U.S. Army .45 caliber automatic pistol in a black holster at his side. The other soldiers walked between the houses deliberately searching for someone or something.

"Good morning Le Thai Tong," said the lieutenant.

"Good morning lieutenant. What brings you here again?" *I know why you are here.*

"We are looking for signs of the enemy," replied the lieutenant. "The district chief says that there are troublemakers in this village, and you have been stirring people up again, too. You are on the list of questionable people. The village chief reports that you have been speaking out again, complaining about many things."

"Is it wrong to complain about excessive taxes, and control of our lands by rich land owners?"

"Taxes? No one likes taxes. But President Diem needs your taxes to protect you from the insurgents and to keep things safe."

"There is no safety for us," replied Tong. "The government replaced our traditional village elders with appointees who are corrupt. They don't protect people from the communists, and they force our sons into the military. They come to our homes and drag away people they suspect of being enemies. Ever since Diem proclaimed the To Cong anti-communist program innocent people get hurt, and their families suffer. People are beaten, tortured and murdered. We had this under the French, and now we suffer the same! The government is even killing the former Viet Minh, the very people who defeated the French and gave the government a chance. This is hard to believe lieutenant!"

"Yes Tong, I know these things can be upsetting. But, they are necessary to secure our country. We know the communists in the north want to take over our country. Sometimes harsh measures are necessary."

"Yes, but you do not protect us from the insurgents. You're here in the day and VC come in the night to threaten those who cooperate with you."

"We have a plan to protect you, the agrovilles. We will protect you in a government village."

"Yes, this is Diem's plan to make life miserable. He wants to uproot people from their traditional lands where their ancestors are buried and make them move to another place that the government chooses. They live under crowded conditions with little chance to make a good living. They have to leave the lands they worked hard to make productive for rice, for fruit and livestock, and live under worse conditions."

"It is for the best. You must give it a chance," replied the lieutenant.

Tong could feel the rising heat of anger. His stomach tightened and the muscles in his shoulders tensed slightly. His senses became more alert. He made a conscious effort to stay calm. He said, "We've heard what happened to the people in other villages. The government forces them to labor on the agroville without pay, then bulldozes their houses, knocks down their fruit trees and bans them from their lands. How is that better?"

"Tong," intoned the lieutenant, "You are a respected elder in this village. You teach in the village school. You are a successful farmer. You have seen many things. You must use your experience to persuade the other villages that the government plan is good. Do not speak out any more, or things will get bad for you. I have seen that you are a man of conscience, but do not let that lead you to trouble. My superiors see you as someone who takes sides against them. To them, it is simple. Anyone who speaks up is seen as the enemy."

Just then, Tong's daughter, Tu, came around the corner of the house carrying a basket of fruit from the orchard She was only fifteen but clearly becoming an attractive young woman. Her dark, shoulder-length hair framed the delicate, youthful features of her wide face. Upon seeing the lieutenant, she stopped abruptly and looked down. "Hello Lieutenant Thach," she said.

"Ah, Tu," said the lieutenant in a very pleasant tone with a broad smile. "It is good to see you. I remember seeing you the last time I was here. It was a month ago."

"It seems so," replied Tu. "Was your journey difficult?"

"No. It is easy for us soldiers. We are used to going through the countryside."

"I see that you are talking to father. Would you like an orange?"

The lieutenant took one as Tu held out the basket. He smiled alluringly as he looked into her eyes and said, "Thank you for being so generous. An orange would be good on this hot day."

Tu smiled timidly and entered the house.

This young man likes my daughter, thought Tong. *Perhaps that is why he is warning me and not doing worse.*

Lieutenant Tach looked back at Tong, sighed with a little shrug of his shoulders, and said, "You have a nice family, Tong. I hope they do not get caught up in the difficulties we have around here. It is best if you keep quiet and do not get caught up in disagreements with the village government appointees."

"I see," replied Tong.

"Anyway," said the lieutenant, "This village may not move to an agroville yet since we are not ready to build a new place." He nodded at Tong and said, "Until next time."

THAT NIGHT, LE THAI TONG, HIS WIFE, KIM, SON, Nha, and daughter, Tu sat on benches around the cooking fire. Water bubbled in a covered pot over the wood embers. Rice bowls soaked in a bucket of water on the hard, earthen floor. The family sat quietly, looking into the fire, and enjoying the fullness of a meal.

Kim broke the silence, softly saying, "It is dark tonight, and the bugs make a steady chorus."

Everyone nodded and there was a unanimous but soft "uh hum" from the other three, as if no one wanted to break the quiet moment around the fire.

Tu spoke up, "Father, that lieutenant comes back

again and again with troops to poke around the hamlet. He always acts suspiciously and disapproves of what you say in the village."

"Yes," said Tong, "but did you see the way he treated you?"

With a grimace, on her pretty, round face, barely discernable in the shadowy light, Tu replied, "Oh...yes. Oh...if it means he won't bother you, father, then I can live with his attention."

Observing the discussion with interest, Kim interjected, "Sorry I missed this. But, Tong, I am worried that the government soldiers keep coming back and they single you out. They must suspect you of being against them."

Tong looked at Kim. He nodded his head slightly several times, tight lipped, then glanced at his two children looking up at him apprehensively from their stools. Just then, they heard a quiet voice outside: "Tong... Tong, are you home?"

Tong recognized the voice. He rose from his stool and took a step toward the door as he answered, "Yes, we are home, Tra. Please come in."

Tall and thin, Tran Van Tra appeared to be even slighter when framed in the doorway. He nodded toward Tong and Kim, glanced at the children and said, "How is your lovely family, Tong?"

"We are well. Thank you," replied Tong, thinking, *the Viet Cong must be visiting the village again*. He asked, "Will your entertainment troupe be singing and acting for the villagers tonight? They learn much about the virtues of liberation."

"Tonight, we have more serious work. Now, would it be possible to speak with you in private, Tong?"

Kim's eyes fluttered as she gave an anxious glance toward Tong. He nodded several times with an assured look and said softly, "Don't worry."

Tong looked at Tra and said, "Yes Tra, it is a warm evening and we can enjoy it outside."

The two men stood a few paces away from the house under a coconut palm tree. Tong said, "Tra, are you here on another Viet Cong visit to recruit our young men?"

"Yes, we have several who may be joining our forces, in spite of the government crackdown with their To Cong campaign. If only we could get an old Viet Minh fighter like you to join with us!"

"I'm proud that I fought against the French. I'm glad those imperialists were finally forced out of our country. Dien Bien Phu was a great victory. It showed those tyrants they weren't as good as they thought. But I have no thought to join again."

Tra noded respectfully. "It was a great victory for our independence. We revere old fighters like you, but it would be better if you would join again and speak out in our favor. You are a respected man in this village. People listen to you. More of them would join our forces."

"Yes, but I think they listen more to me when I don't take sides. Oh yes, I speak against bad ideas, but I prefer to remain neutral. I want peace in my homeland. I saw too much fighting against the French. I have scars to prove it. If only this government weren't so harsh on our people. Maybe Diem will be overthrown by some faction and things will get better without fighting! It's too bad the Americans are helping Diem."

"Yes, the Americans," replied Tra. "How can they support a tyrant like Diem when they had to fight for their own independence? I admire the principles in their Declaration of Independence. Our people in Saigon worry that the Americans will get more involved. That is a force to be feared. Or, maybe they will see things as they really are and help liberate us from these fascists."

"It would be nice to see such a power on our side, but, I am afraid they have been fooled by Diem. They have gone too far in supporting him."

"You may be right my wise friend. Time will tell," replied Tra.

"Tra, old comrade, it's good to talk with you about our troubles, but why did you come to my house tonight?"

"We heard that Diem's soldiers were here today looking for weapons and supplies and stealing chickens from the people. The lieutenant was overheard bothering you about your talk on those stupid agrovilles and the harshness of the government."

"Yes, Tra, that lieutenant did speak to me."

"Did he threaten you?"

"It was more like a warning. My daughter, Tu, came

by while he was there, and he became very pleasant. I think he likes my daughter."

"Yes, Tong, she is a beautiful young woman, and smart too. Did you know she is interested in the resistance?"

"What?" exclaimed Tong.

"Yes, she talks to the women who follow Nguyen Thi Dinh, our beloved revolutionary of 1945. She wants to know more about what the resistance is doing. She even knows that you were a brave, Viet Minh fighter against the French. You can't keep these things from your children."

With some alarm in his voice Tong said, "If the soldiers find out she is talking about this, it's bad. They already suspect me."

"Yes, my friend," Tra replied. "She is learning that feelings against the government are growing in many provinces. Many recognize that our political efforts must combine with military action to be effective. The rice pot is beginning to boil. The soldiers will begin to suspect more of us."

"But, I don't want my children to get caught up in this."

"Talk to your daughter. Tell her to keep her enthusiasm quiet. Tell her to watch out. She may think she has fooled the soldiers, but they could turn on her or you overnight. They have abused and even raped women in other villages."

"They have not done that here because they think they can control us," said Tong.

Tra's shoulders stiffened and he said, "Yes, but as the resistance builds they will get more suspicious. I will tell you that Madam Dinh had to retreat to the swamps many times to be safe. She was almost caught several times. The soldiers can surprise us and sweep through a village without warning. They pull people from the fields and their homes and take them to the district prison. People are beaten and tortured. Some are never heard from again. Some wind up in Poulo Condor prison."

"I have seen some of that and heard the stories. I fear for the people here. The soldiers do what Diem wants them to do and he is a tyrant. He says he hates communists. I think he just wants to control everything. The soldiers are his puppets and his appointed village officials are corrupt. Too much land is still held by rich landlords. People have to pay too much in taxes. I fought the French to be free of this oppression and now it is happening again."

"Yes, my friend," said Tra. "That is why we are here tonight."

Tong looked Tra in the eyes. His eyebrows were raised in a questioning expression. He said, "I thought you were here to recruit fighters?"

"Yes, and we have justice to mete out too. We are pulling the village officials out of their houses and putting them on trial for the injustices they have done. Come and see."

Tong followed Tra to an open space in front of the village chief's house where Tra's fighters had gathered several prisoners. Tong saw the village chief, the assistant village chief, and the clerk. Dozens of villagers were gathered in a semi-circle around the three men who were on their knees with their arms bound behind them. Tra strode to the front of the gathering where several Viet Cong fighters held rifles pointed at the prisoners. Other fighters stood further back behind the crowd.

Tra stood straight, shoulders back, his tall thin frame like a pillar of justice in the dim light of a half moon. He pulled a paper from his pocket, cleared his throat and said, "Ngo Dinh Thieu, you are accused of being a traitor to the people of Vietnam. You have joined with the tyrannical Diem regime and have been appointed by them to take the place of the village chief elected by the people. You have accused villagers of subversive activities and had them arrested and imprisoned where they have been beaten and tortured. You have given jobs to your cronies. You have taken government money intended for village projects, and stolen funds to put in your own pockets. There are other crimes you have committed that we need not enumerate here. How do you plead?"

By this time, Thieu was shaking with terror. He knew what happened to corrupt officials accused by the VC. The crowd was quiet with only a few low murmurs. He said, "I only do what I am ordered to do. The district chief forces me to do these things."

"So," growled Tra, "You admit your crimes?"

"I was forced."

Tra looked out at the crowd, with a stern countenance. The he looked down at Thieu. "If you admit your crimes you will not have a painful death." Thieu rocked on his knees, with an anguished look on his face. He said, "No, no, I don't deserve to die. Yes, I did them. I admit it. Give me mercy. Please give me mercy."

Tra shook his head. He said, "Does anyone here think this man is innocent of his crimes against the people?"

No one spoke.

"Ngo Dinh Thieu, no one speaks for you. We are here to protect the people from tyrants and cheats like you. You have spoken against you neighbors and have caused them imprisonment and pain. You have taken from their livelihood for your own gain and you have been unjust in your dealings with the people. Justice must be done in the name of the people. The movement sentences you to death. Because you have admitted your crimes you will be given a swift death. You will be taken to a designated spot in the jungle and beheaded." With that, he signaled to his men. Two fighters grabbed Thieu by the elbows and dragged him off to the side away from the gathering.

Now Tra turned his attention to the other two kneeling prisoners. "You two have been accused of helping the corrupt and traitorous village chief commit crimes for which he will punished by beheading. Do you admit your crimes?"

The two nod their heads vigorously.

Tra turned to the assistant chief and said, "Nam

Hiep, you are accused of working efficiently for the government and abusing your power. You stand by while the chief extorts money from innocent villagers. You willingly work for the government and take satisfaction in serving the Diem regime. You are also accused of arrogance in dealing with the people. You will be taken away to our reeducation camp and then brought back to confess your crimes to the people to see if they will forgive you. If you lie about your crimes or the people do not forgive you then you will be punished severely." Tra looked over to his fighters and nodded. They quickly pulled Nam Hiep to his feet and dragged him off.

Tra again looked out over the crowd. He said, "Good people, we know you have suffered from the crimes of these officials. We are here to protect you from mistreatment by an unfair and cruel government. You can see we are fair in seeking justice for the crimes of these officials. The movement is fair and compassionate to all in the name of the people." His inner voice said, *we cannot kill all the officials, or the villagers will think we are too violent and unjust. They may think some of the accused are innocent but won't speak up out of fear. Better not to turn them against us.*

Tra turned to the kneeling clerk. "Tran Van Ban, you are accused of serving the government efficiently, but arrogantly and standing by while the village chief extorted bribes from the people. You are also accused of flirting with the women of the village and using your official position to gain favor with them. Now you must confess your crimes here in public. If you lie or try to conceal your crimes the people will judge you harshly." Tra thought, *this pathetic man's behavior is petty and laughable. It will be enough to reduce his prestige and what little power he has.*

Still shaking, with a faltering voice Ban said, "I will confess my crimes against the people. I have served the government for two years as a clerk; I have seen the chief accept bribes from villagers to get favorable treatment in receiving government supplies and building materials; and I have been arrogant in my treatment of people in the village. Also, I have used my position to meet women and flirt with them." Scattered tittering and a few uh-huhs were heard from the crowd.

Capitalizing on the crowd reaction to increase his victim's embarrassment, Tra asked Ban, "How many women did you flirt with?"

With a guilty expression on his face, as if he had been caught in the act of a crime, Ban looked up and stuttered, "I…I am not sure. Perhaps many. I…I can't remember them all." More laughter arose from the crowd.

Tra said "You must be accurate if justice is to be done. Now tell us how many women you flirted with."

"Yes," said Ban. "It was nine. It was nine, no eight, eight." A few people in the crowd said, "Uh huh, Uh huh."

"Did any of these eight women return the favor?"

"No…I don't know, maybe one."

"So, you were harassing innocent women on official business and wasting their time?"

"Yes, please forgive me. I won't do it again!"

Tra looked out to the crowd and raised his hand. "Should he be forgiven for his crimes against the people?"

At first there was silence. Then a few women said, "Forgive him. He is harmless." A few men followed the example and echoed the women.

Tra nodded. He looked at Ban and said, "The people have saved your life, but the movement cannot ignore all of your crimes. Your life will be spared but you must show more respect for the people in your dealings with them and you will show more consideration for the agents of the movement in your official duties. If we suspect you of being a spy for the government, you will suffer harsh justice."

Ban gasped with relief. The fighters stood him up and untied his hands. While rubbing his arms he looked at Tra and said, "Thank you, thank you."

Tra nodded at Ban and then turned his attention to the crowd. "Good people. Tonight, you have seen justice done by the movement. We will watch out for you and make sure the tyrants of the Diem regime do not abuse you. We will let the government soldiers think they are in charge here, but we will be back at night to set things right. Meanwhile, as we leave, my fighters will be happy to collect your donations of rice or piasters to help in the cause."

As the crowd started to disperse Tra looked purposively at Tong and said, "Good night old friend. Next time we meet I hope you'll join the movement. You and your daughter will be most welcome. If she's like her father she will be very persuasive in recruiting the reluctant young men. They will be ashamed to see a young woman fighting in their place. Your proven capabilities with the Viet Minh will be valuable in training new recruits."

Tong replied, "You flatter me, my friend. Remember, by remaining neutral I can be more effective in helping people see what is happening to us. But, for now, your spies should keep an eye on that clerk, Tran Van Ban. He is as slippery as an eel."

Tra waved to Tong as he walked away into the night.

Thoughts of Tu raced in Tong's mind as he rushed home. He loved her deeply, as with all of his family. *If she is already allegiant to Nguyen Thi Dinh, a most wanted woman, then her life is in danger. She must learn to be more careful.*

TWO DAYS LATER ARTILLERY SHELLS STARTED landing around the village. At first, they hit the jungle areas around the rice paddies where insurgents might be hiding. People ran to hide in the dikes around the paddies or to go home and hide in underground bunkers that had been built long ago to protect against French artillery.

Tong and his family hid in a dark, shallow shelter built right under the floor of their house. The bottom was covered with mud from the wet of the monsoons, but they sat on crude benches and trusted in the thick layer of hardened earthen floor above to protect them. In the dim flickering light of an oil lamp made out of a tin can they could see the sticks and boards which held up the cellar roof.

Kim said, "Something is wrong. They haven't done this for years!"

It was well known that Diem's army would shell any area they suspected. News had traveled throughout the Delta about the slaughter of people and livestock in many villages. Fruit orchards had been blown to bits and even family graves had been upturned by exploding artillery shells throwing the earth in every direction. The government didn't care who was killed in its merciless pursuit of the Viet Cong or their supporters.

"It will pass," urged Tong with a hopeful voice. "They will tire of loading the heavy shells in their big guns. They must've heard about the village chief being overthrown and beheaded. I fear that the soldiers will come and take prisoners. Keep the children out of sight."

"Yes, Tu is the age of many girls who have joined the movement," answered Kim. "They might suspect her."

Tong nodded slowly, his lips clenched flat. Their son, Le Thai Nha, followed their conversation with his eyes wide open. He was only twelve, but he knew what was going on. Tu sat, staring forward, as if seeing images in her mind.

After a few moments of silence Tong peered at Kim in the near darkness and said, "Maybe that snake, Ban, ran to the authorities at district."

"I hope not," Kim replied.

After a while the shelling stopped. "Wait here," said Tong. "I will go see if it is safe to come out." Without waiting for a response, he crawled to the entrance way and slid open the wooden hatch on the floor of the house.

Seeing his house was still intact, Tong looked over at the house next door. It was still clouded by dust where a wall had blown down. *Are my neighbors harmed? That is where my daughter's best friend, Chi, lives.*

He turned his head and yelled down through the trap door, "Our neighbor's house was hit. I'm going over to see if they're all right."

He ran over to the fallen wall and saw the neighbor's trap door. It was not scarred or broken. Voices came from below as the door started to open. His neighbor pushed the door back, poked his head out, and blinked his eyes in the strong light.

Tong asked, "Are you alright?"

The man looked up at him and, after a muted laugh, said, "They didn't get us this time!"

"We worried when we saw your house."

Just as the neighbor was about to respond they heard a recognizable voice booming through the village. Almost in unison they said, "It's Captain Huong!"

The two neighbors exchanged looks of alarm, with expressions of shock and fear on their faces.

Tong shook his head and grunted, "Agh."

In a loud voice Captain Huong ordered, "Round up the people." Soldiers went from house to house barking commands at villagers still shocked by the blast and destruction of the artillery shells. The people hung back to see how their livestock and other possessions survived the onslaught. The soldiers yelled impatiently at people to move to a clearing near the old village chief's house. Sometimes they pushed villagers on the shoulder or brandished their rifles.

Captain Huong stood in the center of the clearing, arms folded tightly across his chest, glaring at the villagers. A wooden and steel contraption had been placed in the center of the square. People stared at it with dread and looked around nervously. They knew about the violence of the Diem regime in punishing suspects, but this was the first time many of them had seen a portable guillotine, a carryover from the days of French oppression and ruthless enforcement of their dominance.

After the shrieks and protests over the rough treatment, the crowd quieted down under the domineering presence of Captain Huong. Several soldiers stood behind him. Lieutenant Tach and a platoon of soldiers stood behind the crowd.

With a stern look on his face Captain Huong said, "This village harbors insurgents. Communists are among you. They were here the other night and killed your village chief. This cannot be tolerated. The government will not rest until the communist menace is gone! We will punish anyone who gives safe haven to communists. If you denounce the communists who are here or tell us where they are, then you will be rewarded." He held up a leaflet. It showed the picture of a woman. He read aloud, "'Reward of 10,000 piasters to anyone who can apprehend Nguyen Thi Dinh, an extremely dangerous Viet Cong female.' Does anyone know where she is?"

Huong cast his eyes over the crowd. Farmers in loose fitting, black clothing, the usual aobaba, looked down, held the hands of their loved ones, and said nothing.

Huong waited. Then he said, "She is just one of the communists in Kien Hoa Province. There are others and more rewards. You must cooperate with me to get rid of these people!"

Again, no one spoke.

Huong handed the leaflet to a soldier. He raised his voice, "The body of your village chief was found in the river. His head had been chopped off. You see how harsh these Viet Cong are? We know they were here the other night. They accused your officials of crimes and punished them. This will not be tolerated!"

There was an uneasy stirring in the crowd, as if they suspected what might come next.

Captain Huong straightened up and, in a sharp, loud voice said, "Bring me Le Thai Tong."

Several soldiers grabbed Tong by the arms and

thrust him into the center of the clearing. Tong resisted slightly. There was no way to escape.

Captain Huong asked "Tong, where is your family?"

Tong look to his side and replied, "I don't know. I haven't seen them since the shells fell on our village." *I hope they are safely hiding.*

Using his swagger stick, Captain Hoang struck Tong on the side of the head. He staggered under the blow. Blood oozed from his temple.

"Tong, your family is acting suspiciously." Seeing no response from Tong, the captain continued, "You were seen talking to a known VC leader just before the attack on village officials. Do you deny that, Tong?"

Rubbing his jaw Tong spoke, "I deny that I and my family are VC! I was talking to a man the other night."

"What is his name?'

"I can't say."

"Say his name," demanded Captain Huong. Hearing nothing, he struck Tong again with the swagger stick. Tong held the side of his head with one hand and groaned an "aghh."

"It was Tran Van Tra wasn't it? I know it was him. Don't deny it."

"I have done nothing wrong," shouted Tong. *I hope he vents his anger and stops this.*

"Where are they, your fellow VC?"

Tong shouted, "I am not a VC! Not a VC!"

"We have orders to execute any VC who commits crimes. We will make an example of you," said Huong.

"This is not just," exclaimed Tong. "You have no

proof that I am a VC. The VC come here because you do not protect the village. Your soldiers don't stay at night."

Upon hearing this accusation, Captain Huong stiffened and fumed, "Who are you to tell me what is right and criticize my soldiers? You will pay!"

Tong looked at Captain Hoang. The look of disbelief on his face turned into a grimace. There was profound sadness in his eyes.

Captain Huong gestured to the soldiers. They held Tong tightly by the arms. Hoang pronounced, "Le Thai Tong, you have been seen conspiring with the VC before a murderous attack on village officials. You have had a role in the abduction of the assistant village chief, and the intimidation of the village clerk. All of these officials were duly appointed by President Diem. This constitutes insurrection and criminal conduct as an enemy agent. In addition, members of your family have been observed associating with VC suspects or sympathizers. You and your family have been acting suspiciously. Under the authority of President Diem's To Cong campaign, you are sentenced to die by guillotine. Immediately!"

Tong reeled. *This can't be true. I won't see my family. I hope they are safe.*

Soldiers half walked, half dragged Tong to the guillotine in the center of the clearing. The crowd stood back numbly. There were wails of protest from a few. Others stood immobilized in shock. Tong's arms were tied behind his back. His head was thrust over the block. The blade had already been lifted into its striking position. The soldiers stood for a moment waiting for a signal. Captain Huong swept his eyes over the crowd. He paused, lifted his chin, then nodded forcefully. The blade smashed down with a rush and a thump on the block. Blood spurted. An anguished moan arose from the crowd. People shrieked. The air was filled with a chorus of screams.

There was screaming in Mo Cay that day. There was crying in Mo Cay that night. From deep in their souls, people felt their ancestors screaming for all victims of injustice in Mo Cay.

TWO

Captain Hoyt - 1971

Sergeant First Class Fowler and Specialist Chovinowski waited at the small dirt airstrip outside of Ben Tre. A cloud of tobacco smoke hung over them in the hot, humid air of the monsoon season. Between drags on their cigarettes, they glanced up at the clouds in the sky. They heard the familiar drone of engines before the aircraft appeared. Each knew what to expect. All of the pilots liked to come in fast and low to minimize exposure to the enemy. The noisy, twin prop plane swept over the tree tops and dropped down over the airfield in a gentle swoop that placed it right over the runway. The engines reversed thrust with a roar and the plane stopped in a short distance.

The rear ramp of the plane dropped down. Fowler and his sidekick watched a man with an expanded midsection and large sweat marks under his armpits and down the back of his fatigue blouse struggle to balance a duffle bag over his shoulder. As they walked toward him he announced, "I'm Captain Hoyt."

Sergeant Fowler gave a nod and said, "Welcome to Ben Tre, Sir." Chovinowski simply nodded.

Hoyt said, "I know we don't salute in the field in Vietnam, but thank you, men."

"Yes Sir," replied Fowler. With a knowing chuckle he said, "We wouldn't want to identify you as a target, sir, if there're any snipers in the tree line."

"Er, thank you sergeant."

"Well sir, it's not really that bad now. After all, it's 1971 and after all these years of war we have a well-established US military advisor team here in Kien Hoa. Team 88 is the command group and there are Mobile Advisory Teams , MAT teams, in many districts. That holds down VC attacks."

Hoyt's face puckered a bit. He thought, *just how bad is it here?* Then he responded, "Glad to hear that, Sergeant Fowler."

"Yes, sir. Now sir, me and Chovinowski are the only supply guys for Team 88, so if you would help us load up the truck with these supplies from the plane, we would be most obliged."

Captain Hoyt looked around, as if trying to find someone else to do the work. After a moment he said, "Ah, okay sergeant."

Fortunately, the loading only involved a few crates and boxes. Hoyt took his time and provided only symbolic help as he let the enlisted men sweat through most of it in the hot, humid air. They piled the load into the "deuce," a two-and-a-half-ton truck. As Fowler drove to Ben Tre the other two stood in the truck bed behind sandbags with their M16 out, watching for attackers.

After a short ride the truck pulled up to a cement-walled compound on the bank of Ben Tre River. The compound contained several one-story cement buildings with tin roofs, and a large pavilion. The roofs were covered with several layers of sandbags. Hoyt thought, *those sandbags must be protection from rockets and mortars. This is the real thing. I'm really in the war zone.*

As Hoyt jumped down from the back of the truck, Sergeant Fowler pointed to a gate where a Vietnamese guard stood with an M1 carbine fitted with a long banana clip. "Welcome to Team 88 headquarters, sir. It's the Colonel's Headquarters overseeing all the Mobile Advisory Teams, or MAT teams in province. You will need to report in to Captain Baker, the admin officer."

"Thank you, sergeant."

Hoyt found Captain Baker in the main building of the compound at a desk in one of the small offices partitioned out of the staff room. Baker looked up as Hoyt knocked on the door frame.

"Captain Baker?" asked Hoyt.

"Yup. You must be Captain Hoyt. We've been expecting you." Baker stood up and shook Hoyt's outstretched hand.

"Great to be here."

"Good," said Baker. "We have a slot open for you so there won't be any delay in your assignment. I'll give you a quick briefing and you can bunk down for the night in the transient room. The old man wants to see you tomorrow morning."

Hoyt wondered, *what kind of assignment will I get? Maybe a nice staff job? After all, I'm a captain. Rank has its privilege. The compound looks like a nice safe place to wait out the war. I just want to get some Vietnam time on my record. That would help for a promotion back in my Ohio reserve unit.*

Baker gestured to a metal folding chair. "Have a seat. It won't take long to brief you."

"Great," said Hoyt with a touch of enthusiasm in his voice. "I want to unpack my duffle bag and get settled."

"You might not need to do that," said Baker. "You won't be here for long."

Hoyt slumped slightly as his countenance drooped to a momentary frown. *Maybe I won't get a staff job?* He forced a smile to cover his disappointment and answered, "Oh. Right."

"You're going to a MAT team, MAT 23 in Mo Cay District. Major Crane is the District Senior Advisor."

"OK," responded Hoyt tentatively.

Baker continued, "MAT 23 just came out of the Huu Dinh Forest, north of here. They had a couple of months working with a Lien Doi. That's an infantry battalion. Charlie was lobbing rockets on this compound and the old man wanted that stopped."

Hoyt said, "Sounds serious." Hoyt knew that "Victor Charlie" referred to the Viet Cong and was a slang term that stemmed from the use of phonetic alphabet letters for V and C in radio talk. The term was one of several used to refer to the enemy, including Mr. Charles, Chuck, and Cong.

"It was," replied Baker. "So, they went up there and cleared Charlie out of the jungle and set up some outposts to keep an eye on things. Only thing is, they had a tough time - lost their team leader, Captain Blake. John Blake. He was a really good guy, a good team leader."

"Sounds like they got into it," commented Hoyt. He was thinking, *they hit some bad stuff. I don't want to get zapped, too.*

"Yeah, but they're good soldiers. The team kept at it and they captured one of the VC leaders. After that, Charlie's resistance kind of faded and the battalion was able to clear the whole area in a few more weeks. It's a good team you're getting."

"Yuh." *I want that for my own career advancement,* he thought. *They're already seasoned and know what they're doing. I'll just have to let them know who's the boss and get them to make me look good.*

Baker paused as he looked at the green-eyed, jealous look on Hoyt's face. He cleared his throat and said, "There are four men left on the MAT team: Lieutenant Van Howe, Sergeant First Class Bradford, on his second tour, Sergeant First Class Clarkson, also on a second tour, and Staff Sergeant Jackson, the team medic. They're all good and you're lucky to have 'em."

"Yes, very good," said Hoyt. "What's our mission in Mo Cay?"

"The colonel will brief you on that tomorrow morning. Right now, I'll give you some background highlights so you'll be ready to talk to him." Baker pointed to a map of Vietnam on the wall behind him. "We are in the IV Corps Tactical Zone, basically the Mekong Delta. It's one-fourth of the South Vietnam territory and has half of the country's population. It's a strategic, fertile, rice-growing and agricultural area interlaced with streams and canals, interspersed with forests, swamps, and jungle. You'll see a lot of flat land with rice paddies and jungle areas around the waterways and villages. Hoyt responded, "Okay," in a flat tone.

Baker rocked back in his chair as he continued, "Down here in the Delta, if we go by land it means walking on paddy dikes, which the VC booby trap, or sloshing through the paddy water which slows us down, to get to a tree line where the VC take cover to fire us up."

Hoyt said, "Uh huh," and thought, *this sounds dangerous. How did I get into this?*

Baker saw the look of extreme disenchantment on Hoyt's face. With a commiserating tone he said, "It's not all like that. Sometimes there are choices. There are roads. But they are mostly dirt so the VC bury road mines. We try to clean 'em out by day but the VC put 'em back at night. It's a little better on Highway 4, the one paved road we have. The VC may take a few pot shots from a distance where it's hard to get a good aim.

Of course, if you stop too long you could become a mortar or rocket target. They might even try an ambush on the road, but that's usually a bit too risky for them."

Hoyt nodded his head slowly with a slight grimace and said, "Not too easy here."

"Yeah, said Baker, "but the good news is we have lots of waterways. There are 2,400 kilometers of navigable waterways and 4,000 kilometers of manmade canals. That makes for easier travel if you can avoid the Rocket Propelled Grenades, or RPGs. Unfortunately, the waterways make it easier for the VC to move supplies and get around. You'll be seeing lots of water."

"So, it's name your poison on choosing how to go somewhere," Hoyt declared.

"Yup," replied Baker. "On the other hand, the VC can't be everywhere, so you just have to make the right choices." Baker lifted his chin, held up his index finger, and in a slightly raised voice said, "Oh yeah, the other thing about traveling is to deal with the high temperature. You can sweat to death with ninety-five-degree heat and high humidity. It's like warm soup! Take your salt tablets on those days so you don't pass out."

"Yuh. I'll do that," Hoyt said glumly.

"That's my basic spiel on the area," said Baker with a positive tone. "But keep this in mind: This province is one of the richest for rice, fruit, and coconuts in the whole country and Charlie wants it real bad. Matter of fact, it has been a major food supplier for the insurgency, going way back. So, be ready for anything."

Hoyt rubbed his chin and uttered, "Oh boy."

Baker nodded, "There were no US ground forces here until '66 when the 173rd Airborne Brigade kicked VC butt in Operation Marauder, but before that the US Army 13th Combat Aviation Battalion out of Can Tho provided support to the ARVN. You know that ARVN means Army of the Republic of Vietnam, right?"

Hoyt nodded and proudly said, "Of course."

Baker resumed, "After that, the Navy and Army Riverine Task force was formed in 1967 to patrol the coast and rivers. The Army part of that was the 2nd Brigade of the 9th Infantry Division. Later, in 1968 the whole 9th Infantry Division set up a base in Dong Tam, five miles west of My Tho, so all three brigades were in the Delta. One of their big goals was pacification of Kien Hoa Province. That's what we call it. The VC call it by its original name, Ben Tre."

Hoyt leaned forward in his chair and intoned, "Right."

After clearing his throat, Baker said, "The 9th raised hell and racked up high body counts. Some of the advisors thought the civilian population suffered badly. Lots of innocent people were killed or injured. After that, the 9th was sent back to the States in August of '69. About the same time the Navy finished turning things over to the Vietnamese. Now, in 1971, with Vietnamization, it's mostly advisors like us and special operations groups like the SEALS supporting the Vietnamese. There are three ARVN divisions, the 7th, 9th, and 21st. Plus the RVN Navy operates several assault groups covering the Delta."

"I see," said Hoyt while rubbing his chin.

"Well Captain Hoyt," Baker said, "unfortunately what you see in the Nam ain't what you get. There are layers and layers. The history is long and deep. The culture is complicated."

"Oh?" muttered Hoyt.

"Yeah. It's not easy to sort out what's going on in Vietnamese heads. You will find Confucianism, Taoism, Buddhism, Catholicism, Protestantism and various sects. Most people venerate their ancestors and believe their souls continue to live on and coexist with the living. Families are patriarchal with strong ties and women are held in high esteem. Polygamy had existed but was outlawed in 1959. A lot of families have ties to the old Viet Minh or the VC. So right there is a pretty choppy mix to keep in mind."

Hesitatingly Hoyt said, "Right. Right."

"But," Baker stated, "There are some everyday facts. Rice, pork and fish are a big part of the diet. You will hear about nuoc mam, or fermented fish sauce. You won't mistake its sharp smell in rice bowls."

"Yeah. I heard of that stuff. Rotten fish smell," said Hoyt.

"Well, the Vietnamese love the stuff. Better watch not to insult them. We're trying to build rapport with them 'cause we have to get along to do our jobs. Matter of fact, if they really like you, they may offer you a chicken head to swallow with your rice."

"Whoa!" exclaimed Hoyt.

"Yeah. Well. That doesn't happen so much anymore.

That was back in the early days before they knew advisors were not too keen on that honor. Good thing they're polite."

"That's a relief," Hoyt responded.

Captain Baker took a deep breath. "OK, that's about it for right now. If you don't have any administrative questions, you can get some hot chow in our mess hall. It's small, but we have a good cook and it almost tastes like home. My clerk, Specialist Adams will show you to the bunkhouse."

"Thanks. Thanks for the info."

"Good luck in Mo Cay!"

THE NEXT MORNING, HENRY HOYT STOOD BEFORE the door of Lieutenant Colonel Michael J. Cartwright's office. The door was open, but Hoyt hesitated before presenting himself to the man who would write his officer efficiency report. After a moment, he knocked on the door frame.

Colonel Cartwright looked up from the map on his desk. With a deep voice he said, "Come in."

Hoyt made two strides to stand in front of Cartwright's desk. He stood firmly at attention and snapped a right-hand salute. "Captain Henry Hoyt reporting, sir!"

The colonel sat up straight and returned the salute. Then he stood up and extended his hand to the captain. "Welcome to Ben Tre, Captain Hoyt."

Hoyt grasped the outstretched hand and returned a firm shake, firm but not aggressive. He saw that Colonel Cartwright was taller with a thin, wiry build. The colonel's narrow, tight face was topped by tightly cropped, sandy brown hair. Hoyt thought, *the colonel looks very fit, like he could lead every man here in a five-mile run and a tough obstacle course. I hope he doesn't think I'm too flabby. I don't want to make a bad impression on this obviously capable career military man.*

"Thank you, sir," replied Hoyt. "I'm glad to be here."

"Good, good. Have a seat captain," said the colonel gesturing to a metal folding chair across from his desk.

"Thank you, sir."

"Captain, it says in your file that you have been in the reserves for nine years, including your first active duty assignment in Germany."

"Yes, sir. Out of college ROTC I was assigned to a one-year tour in Germany. That was after a short state-side tour at Fort Hood with the First Armored Division."

The colonel shifted a bit in his seat. "How is it that a tanker wants to work as an advisor to the Vietnamese infantry?"

"Well sir, after active duty I was in the reserves for seven years. With the war going on I wanted to get involved so I applied for active duty in Vietnam. They told me there were not enough slots for tank officers, but I heard that MACV was looking for officers in any combat branch of the service."

"True enough, true enough. You heard right. Still, I am surprised that a man in your situation with a safe reserve assignment would risk coming over here."

"Well, sir. That's how soldiers get promoted," said Hoyt sitting up straight in his chair. He thought, *Its just same old, same old in my reserve unit. I was stuck in a sideline job as battalion administrative officer, as if my commander didn't think I had the potential to take command of a company, not that my performance as a platoon leader in Germany was very stellar. Plus, I'm happy to get away from my wife and two daughters who seemed to enjoy shopping more than doing anything with me. Back in the states I felt like just another cog in the machine.*

"Right," said Cartwright. "It seems you have some ambition, captain. You'll have a chance to prove it with your assignment." Colonel Cartwright paused and looked directly at Hoyt.

"Yes sir, that's just want I want."

Cartwright nodded and cleared his throat. "You will be joining MAT 23 as the senior officer and advisor to the local village-hamlet security forces, part of the Mo Cay District security plan, under Major Crane. He is running a good show in the district and you will take direction from him. The main mission for MAT 23 is to pacify what's called VC Island."

"Right, sir. VC Island?"

"Yeah, when you go across the river, called the Song Ham Luong, the ferry lands on what is really a big island. Your team is at the ferry landing with a platoon of popular forces. It doesn't seem like it at first, but you'll see you're on an island. We own the bottom half of the island and Charlie owns the top."

Hoyt said, "Yes sir. We'll get them out of there!"

"Good, captain. I appreciate your enthusiasm, but that is easier said than done. All of Kien Hoa Province has branches of the Mekong River running through it. It's a maze of waterways. It gives the Viet Cong easy boat transportation and makes our job tough. They are like a pack of varmints. As soon as we clear 'em out, they come back, like an infestation of rats. They hide in the surrounding land and use the waterways to move freely. We work with the brown water navy and do joint operations with their boats, but it just doesn't last. What we need is to win the hearts and minds of the local people. They have to want to keep the VC out. That's where MAT teams come in. You need to help them set up their own militia and show them how to protect themselves."

"Yes sir, that's a little different from the usual operation. I like the idea of village hamlet security. We'll give it our best sir."

"Captain Hoyt, it has to work. The traditional method hasn't been effective for this kind of war. We're dealing with insurgents and we have to help the locals keep the insurgents out. Otherwise they hide among the people and we can't get rid of them. The old methods were killing the people we were trying to help. Remember, one of Ho Chi Minh's fellow communists, Mao Tse-tung, said '…guerilla warriors must move among the people as fish swim in the sea.'

So, we have to get the people to move with us instead."

"Yes sir." Hoyt's thoughts were rushing in the back of his mind. *This isn't like running tank tactics. It's psychology and culture and too close for comfort. How do the infantry guys do it? Maybe I should try to get to a big base. Too late now.*

"Good luck to you Captain Hoyt," offered Colonel Cartwright as he stood up and stuck out his hand.

Hoyt shook the colonel's hand, then stepped back and saluted. "Thank you, sir."

HENRY HOYT LAID NEXT TO HER, A BEAUTIFUL young woman. She knew enough to smile and sigh to give the impression of pleasure while he pursued his fantasies. She also smiled inwardly as she recalled him entering the back-street bordello with an eager but cautious look on his face. He had almost immediately picked her out from the small group of suggestively clad working girls. She planned to extract her fee and a large tip from him, then send him on his way.

She moved over to her side and stroked his arm. "You are my sweet captain," she said. She thought, *this man does not look like a fighter. His arms and legs have little muscular definition and he is flabby around the middle. His belly button is in a sunken socket and his jaw is slack.*

Hoyt smiled at her sweet talk. He thought, *I almost*

can't believe that I am with her. She is slim and tight-limbed with a beautiful round face, wide eyes, a thin waist, and all the right womanly endowments. She's a lot different from my thick-limbed, indifferent wife back home. This is a pleasure that will embellish my plans for a successful tour in Vietnam. He said, "You are sweet yourself. What's your name?" He realized he had forgotten the small courtesy of asking her name in the rush of getting down to business.

She smiled and in a soft voice replied, "Chi. My name is Chi."

"Just Chi?"

"Oh, Nguyen Chi" she said.

"Ah. There are a lot of people here with that name. I mean Nguyen."

"Yes, captain, that is a common family name in this country. But I just call myself Chi because it is easier."

"Yeah. It's a pretty name."

"It means 'twig.' I am like a twig, thin and strong, but I can bend like a young twig when I have to."

Hoyt sat up and nodded slightly while looking straight at her. "That can be a good thing in this war. It's been hard on this country."

Chi sat up beside him and raised her eyebrows. "I don't hear that from many Americans. Most of them take my country for granted. The bombs and soldiers are destroying my country and killing my people."

"I am sorry," said Hoyt. "That is sad, but I enjoyed being with you today." He started putting on his fatigue blouse.

She smiled slightly. "Thank you, captain. The usual price is seven hundred piasters, but since you are so sweet I was extra nice to you."

He laughed slightly. "You are nice. I like you." He opened his wallet and pulled out one thousand piasters. "Here you are and something extra because you are so nice."

She looked at the money and glanced at his name on the fatigue shirt.

"Thank you, Captain Hoyt. Will I see you again?"

"Well, you just might. I am stationed not too far from here and hope to get back into Ben Tre a lot."

"Oh good. I hope to see you again."

"I like you, so you can be sure of it," he replied.

She stood on her tip toes and gave him a brief kiss on the cheek. "Good by sweet captain."

"Good bye, Chi."

As he entered the street Hoyt looked from side to side and then looked up to see the sun getting lower in the late afternoon sky. He thought, *I better not get caught on a back street after dark. Who knows where the enemy lurks? Chi was a great start to my time here. Now I hope they have good chow in that mess hall.*

EARLY ON THE MORNING OF THE NEXT DAY First Lieutenant Donald Van Howe slowly lifted the yellow and green plastic mat covering the back entrance of the hooch. His eyes scanned for trip wires and other signs of a sneaky VC incursion. Thoughts raced through the back of his mind: *there might not be enough of them around here to make a direct attack, but one could creep up in the dark and leave a nasty surprise. I hope the popular force troops here are watching.* Trung si Sang, the team's Vietnamese interpreter sergeant, followed the tall, lanky, lieutenant out the door.

Van Howe took his job as a military advisor seriously. Although he had no intention of making the military a career, he was in the Army because he believed in the citizen soldier idea, like heroes he admired in the American Revolution. After building scouting skills to become an Eagle Scout and developing a strong belief in the duty of citizens to serve their country, he signed up for the Reserve Officers Training Course, ROTC, in college. Being born in the shadow of World War II with a father who served as an officer in the Pacific Fleet, he never questioned whether he should serve in the military. It was doing his duty. It was protecting the United States. By the time he graduated from college in 1969 the Vietnam War had warped into something many did not expect. In his mind there were many troubling truths coming out about the war.

Van Howe, dressed in an U.S. Army issue olive t-shirt and fatigue pants bloused in jungle boots, close cut brown hair visible under a floppy, faded bush hat, ambled across the small dirt yard toward a tall, thin Vietnamese soldier wearing Popular Forces standard issue, olive colored fatigues with a corporal's badge of rank. The man had a high forehead and serious looking eyes. He looked directly at Lieutenant Van Howe with a ready smile and in a friendly tone said, "Chao Trung uy."

In keeping with the use of Vietnamese rank Van Howe responded, "Chao Ha si Tho. How are you this morning?" Van Howe thought, *I like Tho. He is a competent squad leader and shows promise to take over the platoon. He's a good second in command.*

Tho answered vaguely, "It is a good day, even in the monsoon season."

Seeing that Tho's smile had faded to reveal a worried look, Van Howe asked, "Any new reports?" *Information from popular force patrols and outposts often travels faster along Vietnamese channels than through our advisory network, especially since the Vietnamese are taking over responsibility for the war with President Nixon's drawdown of American troops,* he thought.

Tho said, "Sergeant Tang has a report from the middle hamlet. A People's Self Defense Force squad was patrolling a path into the hamlet. They were crossing a bamboo bridge. After the first man went over the stream, the second man spotted a trip wire on the left-hand rail. It was rigged so that any pressure on the bamboo rail would release a grenade pin and blow away anyone on the bridge. The first man got away because he used only the right-side rail of the bridge."

"Troi Oi. That's a surprise!" said Van Howe, looking at Tho with eyes wide. "Those VC from the top of the island keep pushing that hamlet." He recalled that the middle hamlet was almost halfway up the island, maybe three kilometers from where they were. The hamlet had a defense force of maybe 20 men of varying ages, too young or too old to be of regular draft age, and several young women. The men and women lived there and did a good job keeping the hamlet secure thanks to being armed with old U.S. Army weapons like M1 carbines, Thompson submachine guns, and Browning automatic rifles.

Tho continued, "It's hard to find VC. They come and go as they please on the water…mix in with the people."

Van Howe thought, *he knows what he's saying. His family lives in the middle hamlet. Tho's mother even claimed he has a cousin from west of Ben Tre who joined the Viet Cong.*

Tho added, "These VC are good at making traps with explosives, like the one on the bridge. Our people were just lucky they saw it before it killed them."

"Yeah," replied Van Howe nodding his head in agreement. "Those hamlet security people are good. They know how the VC work and who belongs in the area." He thought, *this is a good way to do counter insurgency. Better than two years ago when the American 9th Infantry Division swept through and shot everything and everyone up with all kinds of fire power, killing many civilians.*

Van Howe and Tho looked over as Sergeant First Class Tang walked up with a serious look on his face. "Chao Trung si nhat Tang," said Van Howe with a clear voice.

"Chao Trug uy," Tang replied. He was older and heavier than Tho with a wider waistline. But he had strong shoulders and a very visible scar on his cheek that gave him the look of a rugged, combat-experienced platoon leader, which he was.

Van Howe recalled the story behind the scar. *It was a souvenir from a VC attack on the ferry crossing during the TET offensive in 1968. There was an intense fire fight. Tang had cornered one VC dressed in black with a canvas satchel of explosives over his shoulder and an old Chinese bolt action rifle. Just a few feet away from Tang, the VC had raised his rifle and pulled the trigger, but the gun misfired. Keeping his cool, Tang yelled at the man to surrender, but the determined VC slashed with his bayonet. Tang parried the blow just as the blade ripped into his cheek. Filled with rage and pain, Tang smashed his rifle butt on the man's head and knocked him to the ground where he lay bleeding profusely. Tang had to dive for cover when a few rounds struck near him. Ignoring his wound and the vanquished VC he went on to help fight off the attackers. When he returned to the spot he found that the VC was done for, one of the fatalities of the day.*

"We had a close one in middle hamlet," said Tang.

"Yes, Tho told me."

Tho nodded his head in affirmation and looked squarely at Tang.

"We need to help patrol the area around the hamlet," said Tang. "Tho, I want you to take your squad and join with a squad from the PSDF in the hamlet. Go over the area. Check the trails. Look for more traps. See if there are any strangers. Talk to the people. Your family is from there. Find out what you can. Make it known that we will respond to any VC threats. Make sure the flag of the Republic of Vietnam is flying in the center of the hamlet."

Tho nodded and said, "It will be done."

Van Howe smiled and gave Tho a gentle clap of approval on the shoulder.

As Tho walked off to prepare his men, Tang remarked, "He will do a good job. He is a good soldier."

Van Howe nodded and said, "Yes, I think he is very good. Anything else on this incident?"

"Yes, we radioed the outpost at the head of the island. They will be on extra alert and check around their perimeter. Also, we have told our district chief what happened. He will send squads to check nearby villages."

"Tot. That is all good," said Van Howe. "You're number one, Truong si nhat Tang"

Tang smiled broadly. He thought, *it is helpful to have American allies who can speak well of me, especially with this command away from the district town. I am getting older and have little formal education. Maybe I can go to officer school with the right connections.*

Van Howe nodded when Tang smiled and said, "I want to let you know that we will have a new member of our team, a Captain Hoyt."

"Ah Trung uy, you have new boss. I hope he is good."

"Right."

THREE

The Secret Plan

Only halfway across the river, in the pale moonlight, the three women in the little wood plank sampan strained to paddle faster. They had left the concealment of the overgrown riverbank on the Ben Tre side of the river and strained every muscle to reach the protection of the profuse greenery on the other side. It was their return trip from a National Liberation Front meeting near Ben Tre city. Quick passage across the Song Ham Luong River might avoid detection by a government patrol boat with its heavy .50 caliber machine guns. Anyone suspected of ferrying supplies for the VC could be arrested, imprisoned or suffer a violent death, even innocent fishermen. Many victims had died in a loud cacophony of explosions, shouts, and splintering wood as bullets punched holes through fragile wood hulls and tore the flesh.

In calmer water one of them could row the small boat standing up at the oars. Tonight, they paddled in choppy water kicked up by a steady breeze, crouching on their knees to leverage more power and to present a lower silhouette on the horizon. All three wore black pajama-like aobabas to blend into the shade of night.

Tu had made crossings before during her years in the resistance. As the leader of the three-person cell, she was in the stern using her paddle to adjust the course and add powerful strokes to their efforts. The other two women were barely out of their teens but possessed strength and stamina built up by hard work on family rice paddies and fruit orchards. Either of them could run barefoot and bare-handed up a coconut tree and toss down the fruit in a matter of seconds.

The first paddler in the bow of the boat gasped, "We're making good time."

The second kept her head down and panted, "Uh. My muscles ache."

Tu's ears were pricked for the faint sound of a rumbling diesel patrol boat engine. Her senses went on full alert as her heartbeat spiked. Looking for a boat shape, she glanced sideways before down strokes of her paddle, expecting an interceptor would come from down river where the American Navy had anchored a destroyer escort by the ferry crossing.

Tu raised her head and whispered loudly, "Shh." *Was that an engine?*

The others paused briefly, heads going from side to side. There was no boat to be seen.

Tu said, "Keep paddling!" They were almost to the opposite shore, closing on the darker water shaded from the moonlight by vegetation. Then they heard the distinct clattering, clacking sound of the diesel. A boat emerged around the curve in the river. It was not moving fast but it was coming toward them.

"Into the weeds," ordered Tu in a loud whisper. "Pull it up on shore."

The sampan slid onto the soft mud and they jumped out, their bare feet sinking into the ooze. They pulled the boat over their footprints and nosed it into the weeds. Not a moment too soon, they crouched down among the weeds, fear stabbing at their hearts, panting for air as quietly as they could after their exertions.

The patrol boat stopped in the middle of the river. It shined a spotlight on the lone sampan settled in the mud. The light probed around them. The three women heard American voices with the unmistakable intonations of speculation and the higher pitched voices of their Vietnamese government allies. As the spotlight probed near them, a voice in Tu's head asked, *will they probe with rifle rounds or the deadly spray of machine gun bullets?* As she froze in place the spotlight was snapped off and only the throb of the engines could be heard. Seconds ticked by. Tu thought, *I can feel my sweat getting cold in the night air. How long will they stay there?* At last, the patrol boat's idling engines rose to a rumble and then a high-pitched roar as the lumbering beast took off up the river. After a short while only a quiet thrum could be heard from the engines. All three women emitted a sigh as they looked at each other, but they knew not to shout with relief because voices carry far in the night over water.

They walked a few kilometers to a safe house on the far outskirts of the middle hamlet. Though they were not far from the small government outpost on the upper end of the island, they did not worry that government troops would be patrolling at night. The popular forces seldom ventured out at night.

Inside the house, they sat on small stools with Tran Van Ban, a farmer and local VC fighter, and his wife. Three children were in the back of the house sleeping on a bed of boards smoothed by long wear, raised off the dirt floor, and covered with reed mats. The dim light of a tin can oil lamp cast faint shadows of the five adults on the thatched walls.

"Tell me comrade Tu, how was the meeting?" asked Ban.

"Ba Dinh was there."

"Yes, Nguyen Thi Dinh, our heroic general," said Ban's wife, shifting slightly on her stool, her eyes opening wide.

Tu smiled and remarked, "Yes, I admire her so much. She gave me hope after Diem's henchmen murdered my father back in 1959. At that time, she was getting ready to lead an uprising against the government and American imperialists. I joined in the concerted uprisings that year. We wanted to free our people from the violence, oppression, and suffering. We took over the outposts, kicked out the puppet officials, and brought justice to the most brutal of them. It was glorious. I suffered from their execution of my father but took out my grief in the revolt."

"Those were terrible times!" added Ban. "They were executing anyone suspected of being a revolutionary and uprooting families from their ancestral lands for their agrovilles. People were taken from their families and put in prison. They were beaten, tortured, and many were never heard from again."

"Yes, I was only fifteen, not even as old as my comrades here," replied Tu. She gestured with an open hand toward her younger companions. They sat leaning forward, intently listening to this bit of local lore.

Tu continued, "I was old enough to witness what was going on. It was horrifying. It burned a hole in my soul. I tasted revenge in the uprising but now I see it in a larger light. Ba Dinh helped me to see the meaning of the whole rebellion-why we must liberate all the people from the oppressors and how it fits into the whole history of our people fighting Chinese invaders and French imperialists. I was happy when Ba Dinh became one of the founders of the National Liberation Front in Ben Tre province in 1960."

"Yes," added Ban, speaking up after listening intently. "I have read the memoirs of Ba Dinh. The book was published in 1966. It is called 'No Other Road to Take.' It tells of Ba Dinh's early leadership in the August 1945 Revolution against the French. Then it tells about the early days of the American war and the concerted uprising in Mo Cay district in 1960. It shows the patriotism and determination of the people to fight the oppression that was ruining their lives, their families, their homes, and their ancestral lands."

Tu interjected, "Yes. I remember. Ba Dinh said we had no other choice but armed revolt to survive the brutality and persecution of Diem's cronies. I am glad she is now the Deputy Commander of our Liberation Armed forces."

Nodding his head approvingly with a smile on his face, Ban said, "Good, good. With your enthusiasm and personal memories of Ba Dinh you can tell others how she is a leader who inspires so many of us. I am glad that she has been recognized for her sacrifice and her work. But, now you must tell me what happened at the meeting."

"Oh," Tu responded. "The committee recounted the most damaging things that happened in Ben Tre Province. In 1967 the American 9th Infantry Division moved into the Delta and made things difficult for us. During Tet we almost held Ben Tre city against the enemy, but they dropped bombs and shells and killed many civilians to push us out."

When Tu paused, Ban said, "Yes. I was there. We found they would kill everybody just to take the city back."

Tu nodded with a frown. "The committee recalled how the American 9th Division expanded its campaign of death and destruction. There were massive killings of civilians by bombs, artillery, helicopter machine guns, and ruthless soldiers. Innocent farmers were gunned down in their paddies by helicopters. Jets dropped big bombs and napalm. Navy ships shelled villages. Soldiers shot women and children for nothing. It was a time of great fear and great sorrow in Ben Tre."

"Yes, yes," said Ban. "Why did they bring back those painful memories?"

"Because now we are going to get our chance to strike back," answered Tu. "We are going to hit them hard with a new campaign ordered by Hanoi."

"Oh, what?"

They all leaned in closer together. In a quiet voice Tu said, "The Lao Dong, that's the communist party, started planning an attack. It is called the Nguyen Hue Campaign and will be a widespread assault across all of South Vietnam early next year. They reminded us Nguyen Hue was the birth name of Emperor Quang Trung who defeated invading Chinese in the outskirts of Hanoi in 1789. Our province leaders said we will take part. It will be a small part, but important. The party has declared that the Delta is key to winning the south. Because we are near Ben Tre our job will be to spread the word, help organize other local forces, and motivate the population. We will also do small attacks."

"Good," said Ban. "What are the plans?"

"The plans will come. We will be given details when they are ready. There is a new senior cadre in Ben Tre named Phong. He will be our regular contact for operations. My brother will escort him here to see the area. For now, we should prepare, recruit fighters, encourage patriotism in the people. NVA soldiers will come from the north to help, down the Truong Son Trail, that Ho Chi Minh built."

"Ah, good," said Ban. "It will be a glorious time for the revolution!"

"Now comrades," said Tu, "we must rest. We have had a long day and tomorrow we must travel to our homes to see our families and organize fighters."

WHEN LE THAI TU WALKED THROUGH THE DOOR of the family house her mother, Kim, looked up from the cook pot with a visible relaxation of her entire body. Tu put her pack down on a rough, rectangular, wooden stool and embraced her mother.

Kim embraced her daughter warmly. Then she stood back and smiled broadly. "I am so glad to see you. When you are away for days at a time I worry that something bad will happen."

"Mother, I know that you worry. I am sorry that I must be away. I am sorry that we live in such bad times. There is no other way. We must fight for our freedom, for the future of our family."

"Yes Tu. I know. But I will always worry. When you father was executed it changed the world for me. It's not safe. I don't want anything to happen to you and your brother. You are all I have left. You are so brave, both of you, but this fighting is so frightening."

"I hate that we have to live like this, mother. But our work in the resistance is necessary. We can't just sit here and suffer from the cruelty of the government, their taxes, corruption, and arrests. If we don't do something to overthrow them, we will never be free."

"Yes, I know you are right, Tu, but it is still hard. With your brother in the resistance I worry more, but I know that if he did not join, the government would try to make him join the army or they would suspect him of being a resistance fighter anyway. He might as well join the VC. He wants to honor his father, to destroy those who murdered him with the guillotine in front of the village people. It is sad, though, because your father always wanted to be neutral. But now, even he would see that things are so bad we must be on one side or the other. There is no normal living."

Tu said, "That is true mother." She accepted a bowl of rice and greens from her mother and sat on a stool.

Kim sat on the other stool in the dim light of the oil lamp. She smiled as she watched Tu eat with a ceramic soup spoon, not saying much.

Tu thought, *I have secrets I don't dare tell my mother. I wish I could tell her about the latest plans for a new attack, but It would be too risky if she were forced to talk. I can't even tell her about our friend, Chi, now a spy in Ben Tre. These are big things.*

Tu said "Mother, remember when Chi and I were little, we played bamboo jacks together, or dragon and snake with other children. I still remember when we learned to row sampans and splashed the water all around.

"Yes. I remember very well," Kim replied, smiling

broadly. "Those are some of my fondest memories. But her family suffered so much. Her father was jailed and tortured. Her mother died of heartbreak and hard work trying to raise two children. Luckily, the children were taken in by their aunt, but they are bitter about the loss of their parents."

Tu said. "Yes. I am sorry for their misfortune." Yet, she reflected, *Chi has done well. She left to make her way in Ben Tre. She is making a good living from her work in a brothel and she is helping our cause. VC agents found it easy to persuade her to pass along useful information from her customers in the government and the army.*

Tu finished her rice and smiled at her mother. Then she washed the bowl, rinsed it with hot water from the kettle, and placed it on the shelf under the window.

"Thank you for the rice mother. I am tired and must rest. I hope you have a good rest too."

"I hope you have a good night, my daughter. With you home I will sleep better."

They slept on straw mats placed over wooden platforms in the corners of the house.

In the morning, before she departed, Tu said, "Mother, it is very important not to raise suspicion. If anyone asks, you must say that you hear nothing, see nothing, and know nothing."

Kim looked knowingly in her daughter's eyes. Tears ran down her cheeks. She hugged Tu closely and said, "Go my child, a grown woman. Be safe. Come back to me."

LE THAI NHA SAT NEXT TO DUONG THANH PHONG, the new cadre from Cu Chi who had arrived in Mo Cay District only a few days ago to help organize the next big assault. Nha had been assigned by the district cadre to show Phong the lay of the land.

They sat on stools beside a small table under the tin porch roof of a tea shop. The shop overlooked the ferry crossing on the Song Ham Luong and was located in a row of shops of various construction-thatch, tin, cement- that lined the road from the ferry. There, passengers and local villagers bought tea, cola, beer, drugstore items, local produce and clothing. Only a few meters away, the road led a short distance to the ferry ramp. They could see beyond to the swift muddy current of the river. Bits of tree limbs, palm fronds, and the occasional coconut were carried along in the flow, washed from the vegetation crowding the riverbank by the heavy monsoon rains.

Phong said "This is a good vantage point. We can see the comings and goings of ferry traffic and look across the road at the huts of the American advisors and popular force platoon. Those Americans have an odd-looking shack." He pointed across the road to an open area where the advisors' hut sat opposite a wooden shed sheltering a platoon of popular forces and some of their family members.

Nha replied, "Yes, they put that hut up in only a few days and had a cement floor poured too. If they only knew that members of my cell helped lay the cement they would be surprised."

The Americans' hut was a flimsy affair constructed of thin plywood half-walls nailed to steel stakes in the ground. Screen material was attached to the upper half of the walls. Two by fours strung between the walls supported a tin roof. Sand bags surrounded the lower walls to protect the occupants from bullets and explosions. The materials were a luxury by village standards.

As he gazed at the shack Nha thought, *I doubt it will survive a strong storm. Though, maybe its loose and flexible design may actually help it to stand up to strong winds. In any case,* mused Nha, *a few well-placed mortar or rocket rounds would cause considerable damage. How quickly could they scramble to the protection of their bunkers alongside their hut?*

"I can also see the American navy ship anchored in the river," remarked Phong. "It looks like a small destroyer type. No doubt, a command center for the enemy's river patrol boats. Yes, at this spot we can keep track of enemy forces on the road, and the water. We can see if the advisors go out on a mission too. With our other spies watching the district headquarters and the outposts we will have a great deal of intelligence. This will help us to move freely and attack when conditions are right."

After a pause Nha said, "Phong, you have much experience fighting the enemy. I hope to learn from you. Can you tell me about Cu Chi?"

"Oh, the Americans and the ARVN were always

pushing through our area. There is a big rubber plantation where they brought in their armored personnel carriers and many troops. But, we had the tunnels. They ran for many kilometers. We had good places to hide, storerooms, hospitals, sleeping rooms. They were all underground. They went down several levels. We hit the enemy hard and then went underground. They could only find us if they were lucky."

"Your reputation is known by many here," said Nha. "Is that why you were sent to help us?"

"That could be…but, there is more. One of my friends and best fighters was killed in Ben Tre Province. His name was Dang Vu Hiep. He was a very promising young leader."

"I am sorry."

"He was sent here from Cu Chi with a cadre from Hanoi to lead the fight for our cause. He was killed by American Advisors in the Huu Dinh Forest. His partner, Nguyen Tat Thanh, the cadre from the North, was taken prisoner. Then the government soldiers were able to sweep through the Huu Dinh and put down our resistance. Now we fire fewer rockets on Ben Tre."

"Are you here to avenge their honor?"

"That's part of it for me," answered Phong with an intense look in his eyes. "I am also here to help plan the Nguyen Hue Campaign. We must fight smart and defeat these puppet troops and the American aggressors. Ben Tre has a long history of successful revolution, of good fighting against great odds. I am here for all of that. We have much work to get ready."

"We will do it," said Nha with a respectful and encouraging tone in his voice.

"Now, look over there," Phong nodded toward a U.S. Army jeep moving off the ferry ramp. Two captains sat in the front seats. The jeep was not as beat up as the jeep sitting in front of the advisor's hut. Phong added "It must be from the headquarters compound in Ben Tre city."

The two insurgents watched intently, making sure to sip their tea as if they were just enjoying a break from their travels. The jeep came a short distance from the ferry and pulled in to an open area near the advisor's hut. A few of the popular force troops looked up from cleaning their rifles. One of the captains stepped out and walked around the jeep. The American lieutenant greeted him. The jeep pulled out and returned to the ferry for the return trip.

Phong looked at Nha with a slight smile. one eye squinting, and said, "That's our new enemy. They sent that captain to take over the advisory team."

FOUR

VC Island

The ferry crossing was quiet as the wet heat was building before the usual afternoon shower, slowing people down to a languid pace. Travelers stood in line on the road waiting for the next ferry, some with baskets of produce, others on bicycles or motor scooters laden with fabric, baskets of goods, or cages of ducks or chickens stacked up three or four high behind the driver.

While the MAT team waited for the arrival of their new leader, Van Howe decided to walk down to the small dock tucked away in the shallows beyond the ferry landing to check the team's Boston Whaler. Standing by the boat he considered, *the nice thing about the boat is, unlike the jeep or going on foot, it isn't going to hit any road mines or trip wires. In these rivers and canals it's more useful than our beat-up jeep. But there are hazards. The bow of the boat is riddled with five bullet holes. We never did get the story on how they got there. Was it an ambush? Was it a careless discharge of an automatic weapon by friendlies? It is one of the little mysteries of the Nam. Whatever their origin, the bullet holes are a reminder to be on guard.*

Before stepping onto the boat, he gazed out over the wide expanse of the river and saw the distant, low silhouette of palm trees on the far shore. He mused, *that's peaceful looking. If I were back in the world, Cathy and our baby daughter might be taking a boat ride with me for an afternoon. That would be nice.* His thoughtful reflection lasted only for a moment. The sound of motor scooter engines starting, getting ready to board the approaching ferry, snapped him back on task.

He checked the outboard motor, a forty horsepower Johnson in standard Army olive. It was securely fixed to the transom, and the fuel tank was full. The steering wheel and shift cables were all in good order leading from the little steering console on the starboard side aft to the engine. The deck was clear, except for a worn wooden paddle meant for engine breakdowns. He noted the absence of life preservers. *Oh well,* he thought, *this boat has a foam core between fiberglass skins, so it is supposed to be unsinkable. Maybe the Army reasons that life vests won't be needed in an emergency. Maybe it's better to be under water if someone is shooting at you.*

Being an old scout, he carefully checked the dock lines and adjusted the one off the stern by replacing the granny knot that had been carelessly tied by some previous hand, neatly tying two half hitches around the metal ring securing the line to the dock. Behind him, the ferry approached the landing with the usual roar of the engines and bow wash sloshing onto the landing ramp. Standing up to scan the deck for passengers, he saw a jeep with two men looking neatly dressed in their fatigues. He left the boat and walked briskly up the hill to the team hooch.

Captain Baker, the province Admin Officer, was in the driver's seat. He stuck out his hand in greeting and said, "Lieutenant Van Howe, how ya doin'?" Not waiting for a reply, he continued, "Brought your new team leader. This is Captain Hoyt."

Hoyt walked stiffly around the side of the jeep and shook hands with Van Howe. "Hello Lieutenant. So, this is MAT 23?"

"Yes sir," replied Van Howe, with the slightest bit of hesitancy upon feeling a note of condescension in Hoyt's tone. "Welcome, sir. It will be nice to have a full team."

Baker spoke up. "I'll leave you to get acquainted. Wanta catch the ferry on the return trip."

As Hoyt removed his duffle bag, rifle and field gear from the jeep Van Howe said, "Thanks Captain Baker. See ya around the compound sometime."

"Roger," replied Baker with a quick sideways glance as he put the jeep in gear. "Keep up the good work, Van."

With a smile, Van Howe waved as he watched Baker back up and pull out for the ferry.

Leading the way inside the hooch Van Howe raised

his voice to say, "Gents, Captain Hoyt has arrived. You all know he's our new team leader."

Three men were sitting around an army issue folding table cleaning weapons, monitoring the field radio and drinking coffee. They put down their weapons with a clatter and stood to greet the captain.

As he stepped in and gave a quick nod to the men, Hoyt quickly surveyed the room, darkened by screens filtering the sunlight. He saw three army issue steel bunk beds covered with jungle camouflage poncho liners, olive drab foot lockers for each man, a field radio hanging off the wall, basic gas operated kitchen appliances including a small stove and refrigerator, and military gear hanging off bunks and walls. There were M16 assault rifles, a .45 caliber automatic pistol, bandoliers of ammunition, TA 50 web belts with attached ammunition pouches, canteens, first aid pouches, fragmentation grenades, and smoke grenades. Hoyt could also see an extra field radio and batteries, a pile of C-ration boxes, an M60 machine gun with extra loops of ammunition, an M79 grenade launcher, and small crates of extra grenades. He gave himself credit with a touch of pride for recognizing all the gear and munitions. He thought, *these are well armed hombres.*

Van Howe pointed to a big, heavy set NCO with a ruddy complexion. "Captain Hoyt, this is Sergeant First Class Clarkson."

As they shook hands, Clarkson said, "Welcome, sir."

A man with a short-cropped afro and a tummy

protruding from his t-shirt stepped forward and said, "I'm Doc Jackson sir."

Hoyt shook Jackson's hand and said, "Good. Okay Doc."

Hoyt turned to the Vietnamese Sergeant with a round face and shock of black hair. He said, "You must be Sergeant Sang, or I should say Trung si Sang, our interpreter?"

"Yes sir. Welcome sir."

"Sergeant First Class Bradford isn't here right now because he's on R and R," interjected Van Howe.

"So, he's not here for his new commander?" asked Hoyt. "I am surprised you sent him on R and R when you knew I was coming, lieutenant."

"Ah, yes sir. That decision was actually made by our province command unless there's an objection from the team. Since things are stable here right now, I thought…."

"I see," interrupted Hoyt.

The three NCOs shuffled and hung their heads a little at the treatment given to their acting, but experienced, team leader by the new captain.

Hoyt said, "Have a seat, men. I've seen your files and know all about you. Let's get down to business. You can brief me on what's going on here. I understand there are a few VC running around we need to deal with."

The NCOs looked at each other and Van Howe and then sat down around the table.

Van Howe pulled a field map from the wide cargo

pocket on his trousers, unfolded it and placed it on the table. He began, "This will show the terrain. We're basically on an island formed by the Song Ham Luong and one of its tributaries, all part of the Mekong River."

"Yes. Yes. I already know that lieutenant. Move on!"

"Ah, yes sir. We pretty much own the territory around the ferry crossing with our popular force platoon. Up the island are rice paddies and coconut growers. It is fairly secure because it has a real good self-defense force. Beyond that, further up island are mostly scattered fruit farms and jungle, an area visited frequently by Mr. Charles, but there is a popular force outpost on the upper tip of the island. The outpost guys pretty much come out at day and hunker down at night."

"That's something. Why haven't you been able to fix that?" asked Hoyt.

"Well, sir, we work through the Vietnamese district chief. We advise and suggest, but our allies are calling the shots now. Vietnamization, sir. Major Crane says it's not like early in the war where advisors were practically leading operations, like when J. Paul Vann was the Senior Advisor in Me Tho. Even he had trouble getting the Vietnamese commanders to move. They serve at the will of the political system all the way up through province to Saigon."

"Yeah, I heard that," said Hoyt. "So, what can you tell me about why the middle hamlet is in better shape than the upper island?"

Van Howe cleared his throat, "It could be that

some of the families on the upper island are sympathetic to Victor Charles or they just don't support the government. On the other hand, the middle hamlet people like to be near the market and the ferry. It makes them prosperous. They are willing to fight for that, so they have a strong PSDF. The popular forces in the upper outpost are not very effective yet. They're pretty green. Many of them joined the popular force because it's near home and they don't want to be sent away in the ARVN. They're not keen on leaving the safety of their outpost to go out on patrol and they're not exactly eager to chase Charlie. The VC are more daring. Actually, they recently booby trapped one of the bridges near here and nearly took out one of our guys."

"Oh. What action has been taken?"

"The platoon leader, Sergeant First Class Tang sent out a patrol to clear the area and reassure the villagers," answered Van Howe.

Captain Hoyt drummed his fingers on the table and said, "OK." Then he looked over at Clarkson, and asked, "Sergeant, can you add anything to that?"

"Sir, I think Lieutenant Van Howe just about summed it up, so far. But, I can say that we have real good rapport with our popular force platoon here and they are good soldiers. They've been at it longer than most and have good leadership."

"Er, thank you Sergeant. I'll go to Mo Cay district tomorrow and see what else I can find out. Meanwhile, I know this team was up in the Huu Dinh Forest on a long-term search and clear operation. Had a coupl'a run ins with Charlie. Lost Captain Blake, my predecessor."

They answered at the same time. "Yeah," "Yes sir," "Yuh."

Hoyt nodded in recognition of their common experience, and said, "Tell me, Lieutenant Van Howe, what did you learn there, up in the Huu Dinh?

"Well sir, I learned that life is a temporary thing." He said this with a tone of finality that conveyed this was not a usual topic of conversation. The others nodded at the subtle push-back to the meddling of an outsider who would not yet grasp the meaning of the experience and the strong bond forged by team members who endured it.

Hoyt saw the hardened look in the eyes of the other men, as if he had overstepped an invisible line. He quietly lowered his head.

Doc Jackson spoke up. "Sir, the afternoon is winding down. Are you gettin' hungry by any chance?

Hoyt looked at his watch. "Yeah, it's going on 1600. What do you men eat, anyway?"

Doc replied, "Well sir, bein' we're close enough to province, we can run in and get some good canned food and maybe chicken or steak once on a while. It's better'n C-rats which, you see, we have stacked up in the corner." He gestured with a hand to the corner of the hooch behind him where several unopened cases of canned rations were piled up. "You know, we get kind of tired of them pork slices, spaghetti and meat balls, and all that stuff left over from WWII."

"Yes," said Hoyt. "I know what you mean, Sergeant."

Sergeant Sang nodded his head and added, "Yes, captain, we also go to the market here and get some fruit and vegetables and French bread. But we have to be careful to boil vegetables. I can eat them with no problems, but they can make you sick."

"OK," said Hoyt. "Well, what's on the menu tonight?"

Doc replied, "We're gonna fix hot dogs and beans."

"What happened to those steaks you were talking about?"

"Well, with Brad gone," answered Doc, "we just haven't been able to get to Ben Tre."

"Oh."

"But, sir, I fix beans up read good with brown sugar and mustard."

Clarkson added, "Yes sir, Doc makes 'em real good. You don't even mind the ants."

"Ants! What ants?" Asked Hoyt.

Doc stood and reached up to a shelf for a red cracker tin. He opened the lid to show Hoyt the brown sugar inside with a few ants crawling around on top. "Can't keep nuthin' safe from them ants around here, Captain. But they're OK once you cook 'em up."

When Hoyt wrinkled his nose, Clarkson spoke up, "It don't make no never mind, sir."

"It don't make no never mind? That means...that means, er, what?

"It means okay, sir," said Doc. "That's just Clarkee's Arkansan way of saying it's all right."

"Oh," Hoyt gave a weak smile and repeated, "It don't make no never mind."

They all laughed a little. It eased the tension brought by the new arrival.

IT WAS STILL LIGHT OUT AFTER THEIR MEAL. VAN Howe slipped out the backdoor flap and turned toward the sandbag lean-to on the side of the hooch. Its portals allowed a clear line of fire down a gradual slope toward a line of palm trees, a likely route of enemy attack from a stream bed. He pulled a five-pack of Panatelas out of his pocket and removed the cellophane wrapper. A flick of the flint wheel sparked a flame on his Zippo and, as he drew in the smoke, he told himself, *this'll keep the mosquitoes off.* After blowing a perfect smoke ring, he pushed the switch on his little cassette player.

As "In-A-Gadda-Da-Vida" played he leaned against the sandbags and took another drag on the panatela. A few minutes later, Doc Jackson came out of the hooch carrying the buckets they used to fill the makeshift shower from a barrel of river water. "Hey LT, you listenin' to the Iron Butterfly?"

"Yeah. Heavy stuff."

"I'll say," Doc agreed.

Van Howe turned down the volume. "You like it?"

"Oh, I like everything. Stones, Animals, some

Broadway tunes, and little Michael Jackson too. Also, Pop Staples. How come you like that heavy Rock, LT?"

"Well, I didn't say it was my favorite. I mean, I like Dylan and Motown and I do like Jimmy Hendrix, but on this 'In-A-Gadda-Da-Vida,' I'm jes' trying to figure it out. I was thinking it's something like being in the Nam."

"Woa, LT. How 'd you get that," asked Doc.

"Well, the hard rock is like Uncle Sam's raspy voice saying he loves you. It's a tough, consuming love. He wants to take your hand and lead you on a walk in the Nam. The steady beat of the drums and the grinding guitar are like falling from innocence. The keyboard flourishes and the electric guitar rips are beseeching voices begging you to come along, 'to walk this land.' The steady beat of the drums and relentless guitar are pulling and dragging you. It's a chaotic, raucous, fearful, burning experience. Rough and ragged. Ups and downs. It takes you to the drum solo. First, it's a steady beat nailing down your fate. Then the rising beat is like marching your butt in-country, one, two, one two. You hear the keyboard suggesting an eerie, quiet realization that you are in a different world. It takes a while. You might push back, but it keeps coming. After that, the guitar scratches out a few zings, like bullets flying. Then, the music builds to a crescendo of pounding artillery, machine guns, rifles, death and destruction. Maybe like TET in '68? You can almost see the flashes of artillery and the red and green tracers from automatic weapons. Finally, there's the pounding realization that the devil has taken your soul and the whole country is going down in crazy, riotous discord. Then, it abruptly ends. The future is untold. But you are hanging on the point of bewildering truth."

Doc chuckled "Holy cow, LT. You been taken meds from my bag? You got a mood on, man. But, ya know, it kinda rings true."

"Yeah, well, thanks, Doc."

"Yeah, you got the blues, man! Hey, ya know there's that song called 'Vietnam Blues' by Kris Kristofferson."

Van Howe smiled wanly. "Yeah, Doc, but that's different. That's about a soldier who lost his buddy and sees protestors who wouldn't appreciate 'im. Sure, that's part of it for me, but I got a deeper funk. It's news from the States that's disturbing. It's wanting to be an honest soldier and wondering if we're over here living a lie, playing somebody's game, not sure we're doin' the right thing or even doing the wrong thing right. It's the kind of blues that rob your soul, man. It's the deep blue Vietnam blues. I even think the people of this country have the blues too."

"Know what ya mean, Lt. Lota of guys don't wanna be the last man to die while we're goin' down a crooked road to hell."

"Yeah. Anyway, let me help you with the buckets, Doc."

FIVE

A New Leader

———————

Tu listened intently to Duong Thanh Phong, the cadre from Cu Chi. She was pleased he had selected her for squad leadership. Now, more than ever, she wanted to prove her abilities as a leader and a true patriot for the cause of her country's freedom.

Phong was seated in front of two squad leaders, Tu and Luong. Tu's brother Nha sat to the side. Phong spoke slowly, "In addition to naming Tu a squad leader, I am happy to announce that I have appointed Nha as my liaison for this area. This is an honor for your family."

Tu smiled and looked over at Nha who was beaming with pride. A momentary worry flashed in her mind. *Nha is my little brother and I want him safe. But, he's a fierce fighter. He survived the incredible fury and devastation of the American 9th Infantry Division less than two years ago.*

Phong continued quietly and deliberately, as if not

wanting to wake any sleeping villagers in the middle of the night. He did not need to worry because they were at the safe house of Tran Van Ban on the outskirts of the village. Yet, his tone conveyed the secrecy and urgency of their meeting.

"Your task," he said, looking in turn at the two squad leaders, "is to safeguard our travel and communication in your area of responsibility and inspire the spirit of the revolution in the people. Your area of responsibility is between the Song Ham Luong and the village Than Ngai. We want good access to the waterways and to the people in villages nearby. You will link with squads near the Song Co Chien." He paused for a few moments, giving them time to absorb his words.

Tu glanced at the other squad leader, Tran Luong. He was giving his full attention to Phong with a calm demeanor. She thought, *is he as nervous as I am? He has much grace and inner strength, such admirable qualities. He is handsome too, with his broad, kind face, soft eyes and strong arms. I remember him from childhood. His family was from the other side of the village. Now he is known as a quiet man of few words who acts decisively at the right time.*

Luong had joined the resistance when he was seventeen. He loved the village life, the prosperous feelings he had from the success of his family in working their rice paddies and orchards. After witnessing government brutality and oppression he was fired up with the spirit of revolution. Revolutionary cadre sent him away to be trained as a fighter in other areas of the Delta and he saw action on many occasions.

He had a reputation as a good fighter and reliable unit leader and was being considered for assignment as a platoon leader in the Ben Tre Province battalion. When he told his superiors he wanted to be closer to home they were disappointed to see him go but said he would be a strong asset as a local force squad leader.

Tu snapped back from her drifting thoughts as Phong continued, "We know that many of your fighters and innocent civilians were lost in the horrible attacks of the American soldiers and aircraft in the past few years, so you will need to reassure civilians and also recruit and train new fighters."

"I am pleased to be trusted with this, Phong," said Tu.

Luong added, "It is a big job for two squads, especially when there are Americans at the Ferry Crossing and in the District Town. And, there are good government forces in some villages and hamlets. Will we need to do this for a long time?"

"As you know, we have been directed by the La Dong in Hanoi to make ready for a big assault. It will be in the early months of 1972 during the dry season. Details on the date and time and the units involved will be planned over the next few months. More soldiers from the North Vietnamese Army, what the Americans call the NVA, are arriving to help rebuild the VC main force and guerilla units for the new attack. The NVA 1st Division is already west of here making preparations for the attack. More information will come as other units arrive around Ben Tre. All you have to do is keep things favorable for half a year or a little more."

Tu gulped and cleared her throat, "Yes. We will do that."

Tran Luong looked over at her and nodded approvingly.

Phong added, "We have a strong province VC main force battalion based in Ben Tre. They can help but will not always be available because they can be sent anywhere in the province. The main thing is to keep the government off guard. Harass them, but don't arouse them too much. Let them grow complacent while we prepare to conquer them."

Tu nodded.

In a gentle voice Phong said, "Tu, you and Luong need to work together and make plans for your area. You are both reliable and skilled leaders and I am sure the two of you will be able to coordinate your efforts and do a good job."

Luong spoke up. "We will work hard to justify your confidence in us."

Phong smiled and said "Remember the ancient teachings of Sun Tzu. You can outsmart the government troops. Know the enemy. Strike when the enemy is weak in leadership and discipline or when they are disadvantaged by the weather and terrain. Withdraw when the enemy has the advantage. Outwit them. Remember, we are strong because we know the way to our freedom. Many government soldiers are not inspired. That gives us the advantage of greater will."

Everyone nodded. Phong, smiled and said, "That's how we'ill do it!"

Phong took a breath and lifted his head slightly. "One important thing," he said in a firm tone,"is to deal with the American advisors. They motivate and help the government troops, so they are a problem, but they are hard to eliminate because they can call big guns and aircraft and there is always trouble when we kill one of them. The ones at the ferry are newly arrived so they are not too much of a problem yet, but the ones on the other side of the river, near Ben Tre near the secret river crossing have seen too much. If you can deal them a blow it will help."

Both squad leaders nodded slowly with a flat expression on their lips, as if considering the dangers of their assignments.

"Good," said Phong. "Nha and I will go alert fighters in other areas. They will have tasks like yours. We get stronger every day." He thought, *I dare not tell them one other thing now because what they don't know can't be given up to the enemy if they are captured. There is more to the plan to build strength in the Delta. By the time we attack we will have at least eleven thousand fighters and even more support troops making up six regiments or more. If the enemy knew that they would start building up more forces here.*

THE NEXT DAY TU MET WITH HER SQUAD IN A small clearing up-island. The other members of her cell arrived early.

"I am happy to see you, comrades," she said in a cheery voice with a smile.

"We've been worried that you are safe," said the taller one of them. "The popular forces sent a patrol out to chase us. They found the bridge where we set the explosive trap"

"They warned the villagers to watch out for us," added the shorter one. "The people's defense forces were out in force and patrolled a wide area. We had to lay low."

"I am glad you're safe," replied Tu. "You did a good job."

"Thank you, Tu, but there is one other thing," offered the tall one, giving a quick glance to her shorter cell mate. "The popular forces found our munitions cache near the stream. It took weeks of work to make those explosives."

Tu grimaced and made an audible, "Agh." Then she said, "That is bad news. Half our work gone to ruin! We have to do a better job of hiding them. They'll be looking for us there. You did well to find that out."

"We are lucky to have so many friends in this area," replied the tall one with one hand raised to emphasize her point.

In the next few minutes, other squad members arrived and greeted each other. Tu gestured toward a coconut tree and asked them to sit. They all squatted in the flat foot manner of Vietnamese villagers. There were twelve of them in all, three cells from the area, one of women and two of men, and one additional cell of NVA men. The NVA men were some of the first sent to fill in for Viet Cong who had been lost in American attacks in the past few years.

Tu swept her eyes over them, making momentary contact with each one. She thought, *I must let each of them know I see them for themselves.* Most of the squad members responded with a knowing return of attention in their gaze. But the leader of the NVA cell, Hoang Van Thiet, had a slightly amused look and a hunch in his shoulders that conveyed a touch of arrogance. Tu knew the NVA felt superior to the local fighters.

"Thiet," said Tu, "Have you had a chance to get familiar with the area?"

Thiet straightened a bit and with a serious look on his face said, "Yes, our cell has explored the trails and located the hamlets and forts as you suggested. We are getting to know your home area."

"Good," said Tu. "We must be ready to take on more aggressive work. We have instructions from senior cadre to safeguard this area for our people to use the waterways and trails for communication and supplies. We need to keep the government soldiers off balance but not arouse them too much. Also, we need to deal with the American advisors to weaken their influence."

Speaking with a slightly critical tone. Thiet said, "We'll need more food and supplies. We should collect taxes from the people and push more of them to help us fight."

Tu felt a flash of anger warm the back of her neck at the audacity of the outsider, but she kept a calm demeanor when she responded to Thiet. "Senior cadre in the province communist party have not called for more levies of any kind. We need the support of the people more than ever. They hate the government for its taxes and conscription of young men and we don't want to change that. The people already give us rice, pork, fruit and more. They make and mend our clothing. They make munitions and pungi spikes for us. They do much already. We can recruit some who are willing, but this is not the time to press them."

Changing his tone, Thiet replied, "Oh, I'm not familiar with the ways of the south. How can we convince more to help us?"

"We keep up our efforts to educate the people to our cause. We appeal to their desire to protect their homeland. We can make an example of some village officials loyal to the puppet government. We can appeal to their hatred of American imperialists. They have painful memories of the government devastation of our land."

"Yes," said Thiet. "I was not here then but we heard they butchered the people in the Mekong Delta. What happened?"

"They killed thousands every month. Our spies said they had an operation called 'Speedy Express.' Most of it was in the 1969 dry season and it hit this province heavily. They used helicopter gunships, B-52's, Phantom jets with napalm, gunfire from their navy ships and their river boats, special combat units, snipers, and infantry. They threw everything at us. They didn't care if they killed men, women or children. Many innocent people died. Thirteen thousand people were sent to the hospitals between January and June in 1969. It was horrible."

"That is bad," Thiet replied. "You had a very bad time. Very bad."

Sensing some sympathy for her cause, Tu said earnestly, "Thiet, we need your help. You are here at a good time. We can work together to fight back."

Nodding in agreement, Thiet looked at his two northern cell mates and said, "Yes."

Tu cleared her throat. "The other squad, the one Tran Luong leads, will cover the area toward Song Co Chien for now. We will work this area and the route toward Ben Tre. My cell will continue to gather information on the enemy forces in the area, talk to friendly villagers, and recruit volunteers. We will also set booby traps for enemy patrols. Cell two and Cell three, you are to rehearse for an ambush of enemy patrols when we have the opportunity. I think that may be soon because they will be searching for us near the stream where the munitions were found."

Then, Tu looked straight at Thiet, and said, "Cell four, you all have automatic rifles and an RPG 2 rocket propelled grenade launcher. The rest of our cells have only one automatic weapon each and these old Chinese bolt action rifles, except for the one American carbine we captured. So, I would like you to monitor the American advisors at the secret river crossing. If you can kill or wound any of them that will scare them off a bit, but, be careful. You must escape quickly and find a hiding spot because your strike will draw soldiers like a hoard of stinging wasps."

She paused and looked at them warmly. "Any questions?"

They all nodded in silent acknowledgement of the plan.

Tu smiled slightly and said, "Be strong, comrades. We have reason to be confident. Remember the battle of Ap Bac in 1963. It is not far north of us. 320 men of the 261st Main Force Battalion fought off the ARVN 7th Division. The fighters of the 261st were brave and disciplined. Their hearts beat passionately for freedom and they knew the weaknesses of their enemy. The ARVN showed cowardice, confusion, and incompetence, even with all the urging of their American advisors. If that is how the enemy fights, then we will win in the end."

The squad members listened eagerly. They nodded and smiled at the end of Tu's story.

Tu added, "That was not the only big victory. Remember, only a few months ago, in February 1971. It was the enemy invasion of our base areas, near Tchepone, in Laos, called Lan Son 719. We used tanks for the first time. Even with their iron birds we made them run. They lost men. They lost equipment. They lost fire support bases. We beat them badly."

The fighters gave rapt attention to her every word. They uttered words of encouragement: "Yes. We won. We can beat them."

Tu raised her fist. "Remember we fight for our people! We fight for our homelands! We fight for our freedom! Go now!"

They all stood and separated into their cells. With brief nods, smiles, and touches on the arm or elbow, they moved off in different directions. The clearing emptied. They left no sign they had ever been there. Clouds began to gather and darken for the afternoon monsoon showers.

SIX

New Developments

Captain Hoyt looked up from the field table where he was decoding a message. "They hit MAT 17!" he exclaimed.

Doc Jackson halted in mid-stride, about to exit the back door, and turned toward Hoyt. "Huh?" he said.

Sitting at the table, with his morning coffee, writing a letter home, Van Howe turned toward Hoyt with an inquiring look. Clarkson, sitting on his bunk, stopped lacing his jungle boots and looked up with an unmistakable expression of surprise on his face.

Hoyt quickly looked at them in turn and said, "That's what the message says. Two members of MAT 17 and some PFs were up river in a Patrol Boat. They got hit by an RPG at the upper end of the island. The rocket came out of the shoreline growth, hit them in the bow. They returned fire, but the boat was taking on water so they had to get out fast."

"Holy jeez!" uttered Doc, shaking his head.

"Anybody hurt?" asked Van Howe.

Hoyt leaned back and quietly said, "No. Luckily all the crew were in the stern and the boat still worked."

"Maybe they plugged the hole?" said Clarkson.

"Yeah," Hoyt replied. "They were lucky too. Only one round was fired. Charlie must've hit and run."

"Charlie must definitely be feeling bold," noted Van Howe. "First, they are stockpiling munitions near us and now they're taking pot shots at our boats. This is more active than just bothering farmers and harassing our outposts. Is somethin' up?"

"Could be," replied Hoyt. "Anyway, we're supposed to plan an operation to sweep 'em out. District is going to pull in the Regional Force RF's. We'll probably have a hundred of them plus our platoon to go after them."

"That oughta do something," remarked Clarkson, standing up from his bunk and tapping the heel of his freshly laced boot on the concrete floor.

Hoyt looked at Van Howe. In a definite and clear voice, he ordered, "Lieutenant Van Howe, you and the NCO's look at the map and plan our attack. If I approve it then we'll bring it to District. At this point we don't know what other resources will be available, like boats or choppers, so stick to the infantry maneuvers. The main thing is to catch or kill these VC and avoid getting our guys killed. Remember, there're lots of booby traps up there."

"Roger Dai uy," replied Van Howe. He used the Vietnamese term for Captain to reflect the distance he felt between them. He thought, *this guy is new in country and is way too formal for our little team. He thinks he's a big deal, but it just seems like he's trying too hard to prove himself, especially with second tour NCOS. He just doesn't seem to have it together, like Blake. Blake was a good team leader. Too bad good guys get zapped.*

Halfway out the front door Hoyt turned and said, "Right. Don't take all day. We need to get on it before Victor Charles does something else. I'm going over to give Trung si naht Tang the word on MAT 17."

"Roger," replied Van Howe.

Doc, Clarkson, and Van Howe huddled around the small table pointing at the map in a serious discussion of the terrain, the enemy, and the best tactical approach to find and clear Viet Cong. They covered details of the assault, communications, fire support and logistics.

"Basically, we can't work it all out now," said Van Howe, "because we need to know more about what resources district will provide. But we can give them a good run down on our best approach over the terrain if they insert us by boat."

"I agree" said Clarkson. "I like coming in from the top side of the island so we don't have to cross many big streams until we get where we found the explosives cache. They have a lot of activity in that area. If we sweep in with a large force they'll get pushed out and try to escape. Then we can bag them with a blocking force near the middle hamlet, like the jaws of a vice."

"Yep," replied Van Howe. "That kinda thing worked up in the Huu Dinh. Maybe we can use our PF platoon as the blocking force and get the RFs to do the attack. Be nice if we could move up there in patrol boats. They got enough of them around here."

"Yeah, the boats would be good for medevacs too," added Doc. "Also, we could move a medic team up to the middle hamlet with the Self Defense Force to handle wounded in the blocking force."

Van Howe nodded, looking over the table at the two NCOs. "Good thing we'll have plenty of troops since we won't use arty. Don't want to hit any civilians by accident. But, there's a problem. Charlie might try to blend in with the civilians or find a hiding place."

"We just have to catch them with their weapons and supplies," offered Doc.

"We have to catch 'em red-handed," Clarkson agreed. "Keep this under wraps."

As they all nodded in agreement they heard a familiar sounding, friendly shout outside. "Hey you grunts! Anybody home?"

Sergeant First Class Bradford came through the front door and dropped his bag. "Good to see you guys. Hope you have things under control."

Standing up and shaking hands, they all gathered around the arrival, ready to hear the news on his week off for rest and recuperation, which they all called R&R.

They all liked Bradford. He was a reliable team mate, an experienced soldier who had earned his stripes, and he had a sharp mind. Sometimes he seemed a little too intellectual, having earned his college degree in philosophy and history during his Army career, but he had a good sense of humor and always had something practical to contribute in any kind of situation, including combat. Although he had been offered Officer Candidate School he had decided not to attend because he had concerns about the war and thought he could do more good as a senior NCO rather than a second lieutenant.

"Hey Brad, how was Australia?" asked Van Howe.

"Just fine, LT. More sheilas than I could handle. They know how to party."

Doc looked at Bradford's tall, lean frame and thin face and said, "You must have had some relaxation. You're not too raggedy look'n."

"Yeah, I'm fresh as a daisy and ready to go. What you got cooked up?"

"Well, we got some action coming up," said Clarkson, "but, hey, is there anything new in the world?"

"Naw, same ol', same ol'. People in the U.S. are still riled up about the war and treating vets pretty bad. And…those Pentagon Papers are pretty big in the news. Everything is just stirred up. People talking about government lies. Protesters going wild."

The door opened briskly and in walked Captain Hoyt. Brad stiffened up a bit when he saw the double captain's bars on Hoyt's collar.

Van Howe raised his hand in an introductory gesture and said, "Captain Hoyt, meet Sergeant First Class Bradford, just back from R&R."

"Good to meet you sir," said Bradford offering his hand in greeting.

Hoyt squared back his shoulders and took a quick breath, then shook Bradford's hand saying, "Well, you're back. It's a good thing because we have work to do. I hope you're ready to go."

"Uh, yes sir. Always ready to go."

"Alright. Let's get down to business," said Hoyt. "What plans have you come up with lieutenant? Let's be quick 'cause I'm taking the jeep to province to find out more about MAT 17. Probably be there overnight." In the back of his mind he thought, *maybe I'll have a little fun too.* He could picture himself getting away from the compound and following the back street to the bordello. The pleasant image of Chi floated in his mind. His heart beat more quickly with the rush of passion.

That night, Bradford and Van Howe sat at the table under the glow of a kerosene lamp. Bradford was reading a book he had brought back from R&R. Van Howe was writing a letter home. Doc and Clarkson were laying in their bunks reading Louis L'amour novels. Sang was over at the PF shed listening to one of the soldiers singing Vietnamese ballads. The high-pitched melody floated through the night air.

A chuckle emerged from the back of the hooch. Looking at Clarkson's bunk, Van Howe saw a gauzy, fuzzy image through the mosquito net. A glow emanated from the jerry-rigged reading light strapped to a steel cross-piece on the bunk. They all used the lights for reading, a luxury for men living in a primitive hut. The power source was a used 15-volt field radio battery, which, even when run down, still yielded twelve or so volts, enough to power an automobile bulb purchased in the Vietnamese market or "souvenired" by the supply sergeant in the province compound. The bulb was placed in packaging of an M79 grenade launcher round, like half an egg shell, stuck on a wire coat hanger taped to the brick-like battery. The whole thing was a flimsy contraption, a masterpiece of GI ingenuity. Anything was possible when it came to creating comfort in the field.

"Hey, these Louis L'amour books are great," declared Clarkson in a voice loud enough for all to hear.

"Yeah, which one do you have?" asked doc.

"The Lonely Man, one of the Sackett series."

"Oh yeah, I read some of them. Good series!"

"Yeah, I read a bunch of them." replied Clarkson. "I think there's more'n a half dozen. What you read'n?"

Doc replied, "It's called Radigan, 'bout a guy fighting for his ranch."

Van Howe added, "Yeah, I'm readin' Flint right now. It's 'bout a guy with cancer saving a woman in a New Mexico range war."

"Yeah," said Clarkson. "In the Sacket series you really get to know the characters, like Jubal Sacket. He's a rough, tough guy."

"Yeah," agreed Van Howe.

Doc interjected, "Ya know, Louis L'amour has

written a lot of books. I think he's written a couple books a year going back into the fifties."

"Your right Doc," Bradford replied. "He actually sees the places he writes about, they say. Ya know, he's traveled all over the west and, really, all over the world as a merchant seaman. He even hoboed across the country, did all kinds of odd jobs sawing lumber, ballin' hay, skinnin' cattle, even boxing. He actually coached some good boxers. All that travel'n and all the different people he met, gives him a lot to write about. His books are sellers too. Not bad for a self- educated man who never went past tenth grade!"

"That's somethin'," intoned Van Howe quietly.

"Yeah," added Bradford. "There's a lot of smart people out there without formal schooling. Some of 'em were figuring things out long before their know-how went into the school books. It's best not to underesti-mate 'em, especially with so many fancy pants posers around."

"Yeah, Yeah, You're right, Brad," agreed Van Howe. "Ya know, I like those pocket books that fit into your fatigue pants. If you have to go to Can Tho or Saigon you always have entertainment while you're waiting for rides."

"Yuh," agreed Doc.

The conversation dwindled down. Clarkson flipped to the next page in his book. Doc adjusted his reading light. Brad Ford turned his attention to the book on the table. Van Howe looked over at him and asked, "Is that the book you brought back from Australia?"

"Yeah. It was given to me by this woman I met."

"Looks like a serious book."

"That was one thing I liked about her. She liked to party, but she had a mind that took me places. I spent the whole week with her. Donna Benton. It was hard to leave her back there."

"So, you went to Australia to drink and chase women, but you got hooked on Donna?"

"Yeah, I started out in party mode. Was at a bar in Sydney. Loud music. Lots of girls in mini-skirts. Lots of GIs spending their money like there was no tomorrow. It was a hot scene. Everybody was wild. But there was this one girl sitting at the bar, kind'a detached looking, a little sadness in her eyes. She was a looker. Dirty blond, curly hair, pretty face, nice lips, good figure."

"Yeah. You were doing party reconnaissance?"

"Well…I had a couple drinks and was talking with the guys at the bar. All of us were looking the girls over. Some were sitting at tables in groups. Some were dancing with GIs. It was a mixed crowd. There were girls out with their friends and some just looking for a pickup too. I was getting tired of the usual scene, but I wanted to meet a woman. She just looked different. After three scotch and sodas I got my courage up and walked over near her."

"This is a good story," said Van Howe

Bradford nodded with a slight grin. "She was talking to the bartender, saying she had just returned from New York City. But her voice told me she was an Aussie. I heard her say she loved New York for all the things to do and see as long as you were careful walking on the right streets. That was my opening. I just said, 'Hey you like New York too?' She spun around on her bar stool and looked at me, had a surprised, curious look on her face. I couldn't tell if she was annoyed or interested. She looked at me for what seemed like a long time, at least three seconds, like she was trying to read me. I must have had the right expression on my face because she nodded and said 'yes.' I picture that moment clearly."

"You got my interest. What happened?" As he said this, Van Howe thought, *I remember when I met Cathy in the Boston University Hiking Club.* He pictured her light, honey blond hair and easy smile.

"Well it went moment by moment. We talked about New York City, Chinatown, Broadway, the art shops, the Met, the Guggenheim, SoHo, Bob Dylan, Janice Joplin, The Stones, Mayor John Lindsay, the gritty streets, the Bowery, the cabs, the great little food shops, the pizza, you know, all of that, even the JFK Airport. I mean, we just clicked. It wasn't just what we were talking about. I really liked the way she talked. Not just the cute little Aussie accent, but how she would tilt her head a little sideways and consider something I said, how the pace of the conversation changed and we were on the same wavelength. It was exciting. I was falling in love right there."

"That's somethin' Brad," Van Howe remarked with a slight tone of awe.

"After the bar, we walked on the waterfront in

Sidney harbor. We were talking all the time. It got late, but it felt like we didn't want to end the magic. So, we went to dinner in a nice restaurant. Told me she's a lawyer working is a law firm there. She said I sounded like I had an education or read a lot of books. Told 'er I had a BA and an RVN."

"RVN, yeah, Republic of Vietnam," interpreted Van Howe listening intently to Brad's tale, leaning forward, elbows on the table.

"After dinner, we both seemed tired out by the intensity of it all. I said I hated to part but maybe it was getting too late. She leaned back in her chair and said, 'maybe it is but I really like you.' I said 'you're the kind of woman I want to treat decently so maybe we should call it a night and you can give me your phone number. She leaned forward and wrote her phone number on a napkin. I said thanks and we got up to go. As we were walking out the door, she put her arm in mine and leaned a little on me. She said, 'I want to go with you now.'"

Bradford leaned back in his seat and stretched his arms over the table.

Van Howe looked directly at him and said, "So… good. She went with you. Hope you had a nice hotel."

"It was nice. I wanted a nice one, after the dust and mud of this place," replied Bradford. "She didn't seem to think it was a problem. After that, we met several times that week and parted with an understanding that we would meet again."

"Well okay, man. You lucked out!" Pointing at the

book on the table, Van Howe asked, "So, did you read this book she gave you? Let's see, it's called The Arrogance of Power by Senator Fulbright."

"Didn't do much reading yet but she told me about it. She said Fulbright made a solid argument against this war and people should've listened. After all he was the head of the Senate Foreign Relations Committee when he wrote it."

"She was pretty impressed by it then?" asked Van Howe.

"Yeah, it's Fulbright's point of view. She wondered why people didn't pay attention to the Chairman of the Senate Foreign Relations Committee. She said it's hard to believe we could be that dumb. I said maybe she didn't know just how much arrogance there is in D. C."

"Well, maybe she's an idealist 'n still doesn't believe our collective IQ can be moronic. Too many know-it-alls."

Bradford nodded and said, "She may be a little idealistic, but, as a lawyer she's seen the troubles people get into. She said our politicians have a talent for digging a hole too deep. Maybe she sees us more objectively that we see ourselves, being from a different country and all that. She wishes we would live up to our own ideals. But, with all the stuff coming out about these Pentagon Papers in the New York Times, the Washington Post and all it looks like we're a little crazy."

"Yeah, it doesn't look too good," Van Howe replied. "They say four presidents lied while we were gettin' into this war. That's like the four horsemen of the apocalypse!"

Bradford laughed, "That's an interesting way to put it. Anyway, I told her I would read the book and write to her."

"That's nice. Looks like you met your match with a woman who thinks deep and gets on your wavelength. No doubt she was impressed with your studies in philosophy and history."

"Maybe," replied Bradford. "We were in sync. She's well rounded, good looking and we had fun together. I wanna get back to her."

"Great, man," Van Howe said with an encouraging tone. "So, let me know what you think'a that book when you get done."

CHI LAID IN HIS ARMS ON THE BED WHERE THEY relaxed after moments of passion. Hoyt had been full of ardor. She played her part with consummate professionalism. He had arrived and been so eager in his embrace that she barely had time to greet him and exchange pleasantries.

"Oh, my sweet captain," said Chi. "I'm happy you come to see me."

"Yes," he replied almost in a whisper. "I've longed to see you."

"Was it difficult to get away from your American friends?"

"Oh, not too bad. I check in with headquarters and looked into some supplies for my troops. Said hello to a few people. It can all be done quickly when you are on my mind."

"Oh," she blushed. "You are romantic. You are my romantic man."

"Yes. I think of your beautiful black hair, your pretty round face and sweet lips. Then I imagine your delightful figure under a nicely fitted au dai. You definitely are on my mind. You are my China doll."

"Ah, sweet man, but I am not Chinese."

"Yes, oh yes, I know. You are Vietnamese. It is just a term that comes to mind."

She turned onto her side and looked at him with a practiced, sweet smile. She thought, *he sees all Asians in one way. He doesn't see individuals. He doesn't care. How ignorant!*

With a mildly taunting tone she said, "My eyes are different than your American women, the round eyes, but not all slant eyes are the same."

"Yeah," he said with a rising blush in his face.

She thought, *I have him on the hook. Now I will set it deeper. He is not a complete oaf. He has some human qualities.*

"Do you see me as your Asian conquest?" she said in a toying tone.

"I, I … think you are a beautiful Vietnamese woman… very beautiful, not just any girl."

"Oh," with a big smile she lied, "I am just kidding you because I like you."

He responded, "Oh," in a tone of relief. He thought, *I can't get along with my wife, but it would be pretty bad if I couldn't get along with a call girl. I pay her to get along with me! I can't be totally alien to the opposite sex.*

She put her hand on his chest and said in a sweet, soft voice, "It's fun to talk with you. Tell me how things are going for you."

"Oh fine. I am the boss of this mobile advisory team at the ferry crossing. They are good men, but I need to let them know who's boss."

"Ah yes. Are they experienced?"

"Yeah. The NCOs are all senior. Some have been over here before. Even the lieutenant has been into some action up in the Huu Dinh."

"Hmmm," she intoned. In the back of her mind she recalled hearing about the Huu Dinh from others in her network. *The Huu Dinh was a disaster for our side,* she thought. *These men must be the ones who caused all the trouble and ran our forces out of there.*

"So, how will you show them you are the boss?"

"When I get back I will lead them on a new operation."

"Oh, will it be in your area?"

"Yuh," he said and then cleared his throat. "We're going to sweep the island from top to bottom to clear out some VC who've been causing trouble."

"Oh, that's brave. Are there many of them?"

"Well, we think there are a couple squads. Just in case, we'll get them with a whole company of RFs."

Seeing a chance to appear innocent, Chi asked, "Tell me what is a squad, and a company?"

Hoyt chuckled "Heh, heh, you are a city girl. They are military terms. A squad is about ten or twelve men and a company is one hundred or two hundred men."

"Oooh. I understand now," she said with a nod and a smile.

Hoyt's chest puffed up a bit and he raised his chin. He smiled and looked into her soft eyes. He said, "Now my sweet Chi, I am doing these things to protect you and your people. We will rid you of these insurgent VC and free your country."

"That's so brave," she said in a soft voice. She thought, *we will never be free until these American imperialists leave here. The Viet Cong are the true liberators of our country. My ancestors want me to help rid us of these invaders.* She added, "I worry for you. When will you do this brave mission?"

"In another week if our district can organize a few things."

"Good. I hope you will be okay when you do this and then I won't worry."

"Thank you my dear. I will see you after it is done."

Hoyt looked at his watch and said, "Oh, I am sorry. The time goes quickly when I am with you. I have to go."

He leaned over to kiss her. She gave him a warm hug and a quick kiss. "I will miss you until next time," she purred in a warm tone.

He put on his fatigues as she pulled on a silk robe.

He gave her another hug and said sweetly, "Good bye until then."

Chi nodded and made a sad look on her face. She thought, *I must quickly send a message.* After he left she realized, with a soft spoken, "Ahh," *tomorrow is my friend Tu's regular visit to the market in Ben Tre.*

SEVEN

Laying Traps

———————————

Nha watched for the start of the soldier's planned attack, the one Chi reported. He stood ready to warn the others.

Disguised as a coconut seller, his bicycle burdened with baskets of coconuts, he was dressed in well-worn black aobaba work clothes, a conical straw hat, and the usual tire tread sandals. He looked like a regular part of the market scene, standing by a vegetable stall in the row of shops stretching along the road to the ferry. He could see down the road for approaching troops from the district town and across the road to the popular force platoon's barracks and the hut where the American advisors lived.

As disembarking ferry passengers walked by, he said, "Buy a coconut," or, "Have a sweet drink. I will open it for you." He gestured toward a small machete on a wooden block behind him.

Passengers stopped, took nuts in two hands and

shook them to feel the weight and the movement of the liquid inside. Nha cut off the tops of the nuts for them. They tilted their heads back and took long draughts. Then they said, "Cam on," in thanks and smiled while handing Nha a few coins. This ritual had started hours ago. The ferries came and went. Passengers went about the tasks of their day. Nha kept his vigil thinking, *it won't be long now, if it is happening today.*

His senses quickened when he heard the rumble of heavy trucks and their churning engines in the distance. They pulled up near the market, raising dust, belching diesel fumes, brakes squealing. He counted five two-and-a-half ton trucks the Americans called a deuce-and-a-half, full of soldiers, more than one hundred men. Their uniforms had the regional force insignia. They carried M16 assault rifles, M79 grenade launchers and M60 machine guns with long, gleaming bandoliers of 7.62 NATO rounds.

Nha thought, *they are loaded for the hunt.* He gulped quietly as the soldiers jumped off the truck beds. Sergeants pulled them together in little groups on the sides of the road. They smoked and joked as all soldiers did and casually looked around at the buildings, the people and the dock.

Nha noticed movement of men at the popular force barracks. A platoon formed in front of their shed and a sergeant inspected their rifles, canteens, extra ammunition, radios, and rations. He noted, *they too are armed like the regional forces.*

Thoughts rushed through Nha's mind. *I can drop*

these coconut baskets at my cousin's vegetable stand and race with the bicycle down the trail with the news. No, I must stand fast and see where these soldiers are going. Is this the attack Chi told us to expect? His heart beat faster. He could feel the wet sweat on his back. He tried to force a calm look on his face and stay in the role of coconut vender.

The ferry started to load for its trip back across the river. An approaching man stopped in front of Nha and pointed at the baskets of coconuts. Wiping perspiration from his face with his sleeve he said, "Hot day! I want to buy one of those." Wielding his machete Nha skillfully chopped an opening in a tough, green nut. He handed it to the thirsty man and said, "Cam on," as he pocketed the coins. As the man walked toward the ferry holding his drink, Nha slowly loosened some of the lashings holding the baskets of coconuts to the bicycle. He looked over at his cousin's vegetable stand to see just where he would drop the baskets.

In the distance Nha saw a half- dozen river patrol boats heading for the landing. Regional force sergeants bellowed orders and soldiers lined up, ready to move onto the boats. Nha *thought, only two patrol boats can pull in at one time. The ferry won't be ready to leave for a while, so the patrol boats will be delayed. That gives us time!*

With a quick glance, he saw that the Popular force platoon was preparing to move up the trail toward middle hamlet. He thought, *it looks like the Popular Forces are marching up island and the Regional Forces are landing up river to sweep down the island. They want to catch us in a vise. It's time to alert my comrades!*

Moments passed quickly. The PF platoon soldiers had assembled at the start of the trail, standing casually, smoking cigarettes, rifles slung over their shoulders, chatting and joking. Taking only one empty basket with him, Nha pushed his bicycle up the trail away from the ferry crossing. He gripped the handlebars and looked ahead, toward the place where the trail entered into a canopy of trees and faded into the shadows. His arms were tense. He could feel the sweat dripping down his back. He sensed the eyes of the nearest soldiers on him, their voices more hushed, a pause in their talking. Nha forced a half smile and looked up at them. He nodded to acknowledge them. Several of them nodded back. He forced himself to walk the bicycle steadily toward the trees.

As he moved into the shadows of the trees Nha mounted the bicycle, determined to quickly reach his contact outside the middle hamlet. To avoid the risk of being recognized as strangers they had selected a clearing beyond the hamlet as a rendezvous point. He thought, *we are well prepared for this after the warning from Chi.*

Phong and the two squad leaders had selected evacuation routes for their fighters and planned to leave only one cell to finish laying booby traps for the attacking troops. The fighters had spent days preparing improvised munitions. Sympathetic villagers had prepared dozens of pungi stakes made of bamboo sharpened to a fine, hard point capable of penetrating a soldier's jungle boot. These had been placed along likely approaches for the government forces. The locals were warned not to use those trails. VC leaders knew the local people could easily turn against them if any of them were harmed. The final set of booby traps would be placed by the cell members taking advantage of this latest intelligence about the government's attack.

The munitions were all improvised from available materials. They were made mostly by stuffing empty red mackerel cans or glass jars with explosive powder, metal fragments, stones, or nails, all to be ignited by a percussion detonator on a trigger mechanism, like a grenade. Some of the devices were made of unexploded artillery or mortar shells fired by the government into the area. Some of the parts came from the black market where corrupt government soldiers sold their own supplies or bartered for a bottle of cognac or some other luxury stolen by sources in Ben Tre. When the black market couldn't supply enough gun powder the guerrillas improvised by mixing their own. They got Ammonium Nitrate from fertilizer and aluminum powder from paint shops. When the two were mixed together in the right proportions they yielded an effective explosive. Boom. Boom.

As Nha rushed down the trail, he remembered these plans and thought, *the government has done a good job of supplying the means to blow itself up. But, I must hurry. Haste is critical to our success and the escape of the last cell members.*

He entered the clearing and saw no one. He paused and stood on the edge of the clearing, dropping his bicycle to the ground, and catching his breath. Then, he caught a movement in the corner of his eye, on the left, and heard a voice.

"Nha. Nha," the voice whispered loudly.

Nha smiled as he saw the thin figure emerge from the bushes, an M1 carbine with a thirty-round banana clip in his hand. He recognized the man with the narrow face and only one ear. His left ear had been torn off by a bullet in a fire fight last year with the local PF platoon. He had been lucky to lose only an ear. It was actually a running firefight. A three-man cell of Viet Cong was being pursued by a squad three times larger, all armed with automatic weapons. The three cell members carried only one -semi-automatic carbine and some old Chinese rifles, yet their discipline under fire was good and their marksmanship gave them an edge to escape.

Nha spoke to the man with one ear, "Thi. I have news."

"Good. This hiding and waiting is making me nervous."

"Yes. The soldiers are coming. The ferry crossing platoon is coming this way on the trail. The ones from district are on boats going up river. There are one hundred of them. I think they will attack from the upper end of the island. We must move quickly."

"I see. They are trying to trap us," said Thi. "We will give them a surprise. The boats are going against the current and will take time to maneuver. We will be ready."

"Good," said Nha. "I will go alert our spies to watch what the soldiers do." Old men and children would not go far from their homes for fear of being targets, but they would keep their eyes and ears open while doing their usual work gathering fruit, fishing, and picking coconuts.

Anticipating the attack, Thi and his two cell mates had already started to prepare the day before. They had placed several traps near landing spots on the upper island but limited their work to avoid risk to the local population. Now they would add the finishing touches. Along with pungi stakes, their knapsacks carried three captured 60- millimeter mortar rounds and one refurbished 105 howitzer shell along with a dozen red mackerel can grenades and enough trip wire to rig up multiple booby traps.

They guessed the government troops would come through a network of small trails and pass over several small bamboo bridges. Otherwise, it would be slow, hard work for those troops to cut through thick undergrowth and they would lose the momentum of their attack. They would want to take the easy route. The trails and bridges provided the best ways to channel them to their doom. The three cell members split up, each working on assigned pathways.

Thi pictured a trap he had placed yesterday. He had dug a hole in the ground about a half-meter deep. Then he pushed bamboo pungi stakes into the soft, damp bottom with the sharpened ends upright. He had been careful not to lean in too far. A fall would be fatal. If impaled on the stakes he would die a painful death, or worse, be found half-alive by the attacking troops. They would laugh, and gesture. They would say, "VC chet. VC dien cai dou." He thought, *I don't like the idea of being called a dead, crazy VC by callous, laughing troops.*

Shaking that thought from his mind he remembered ensuring that the bamboo points were all standing upright in neat rows, menacingly threatening pain and suffering for any invader who fell upon them. With satisfaction he remembered placing vegetation over the hole and carefully smoothing his own footsteps. He thought, *if one of them is impaled or even if they discover the trap first, the thought of falling onto more pungi stakes will put fear, or at least caution, into their hearts and slow them down. They will know it will not be easy to take this island.*

Thi found a spot for another trap. He attached a thin wire to the base of an innocent-looking, long, narrow branch that grew over the trail at the height of a man's face. It was the kind of branch someone might brush aside to avoid getting poked in the eyes. The sweeping motion of the branch would pull the concealed trigger wire just enough to detonate a 60-millimeter mortar round. The explosion and subsequent shrapnel spray might hit several unwary soldiers, especially if they were bunched together.

Near a cross trail, Thi quickly constructed a savage device. He lashed a sharpened bamboo stake to a whip-like sapling and then pulled this natural spring back into the bushes restraining its forward plunge with a thin trip wire. The spear would whip into the chest of a surprised soldier with enough force to penetrate deeply. Thi mused, *this horrible device will sow terror into the minds of my enemies. Their guts will churn, their knees will wobble, and sweat will pour out of them while they listen to the screams of their pierced comrade.*

As Thi brushed forest debris over his tracks he heard the rumble and roar of loud diesel engines in the distance. *That sound carries even over a kilometer. It will take them a while to get here.* In his mind's eye he could picture the boats circling in the river, one or two of them at a time breaking out of formation to go to the shoreline. The boats approached quickly and then reversed engines with a loud roar to ease up to the muddy riverbank. A squad of soldiers slid or jumped off each boat and sloshed through the sucking mud to gain firmer ground. They fanned out to secure the area, their weapons pointed into the thick undergrowth, their eyes searching for Viet Cong defenders.

Further down the same trail Thi dug a small hole in the ground. In it he placed a cartridge trap. It was a short pipe, open on one end, with a firing pin in the bottom. A standard 7.62 machine gun round, discarded by an unwary enemy soldier, was placed into the pipe to rest on top of the firing pin. The tip of the round protruded up through the earth and vegetation so that a careless footstep would trigger the cartridge and fire a bullet straight up to rip, tear and maim. This foot buster would be a nasty, and maybe lethal, surprise for the attacking troops.

Just a few meters further down the trail, Thi emplaced three more similar foot traps. These were made with bamboo tubes since the metal ones were in short supply. He thought, *as I place these traps I can almost feel the pain of my victims.* He shuddered. *The attacking soldiers are Vietnamese, just like me. It is too bad that men of the same blood and heritage must kill each other because of their beliefs, their alliances, and their unlucky circumstances. But it is too late to think of such things.* With a shrug, he placed his last trap.

Thi quickly finished his work, brushing the ground clean of his footsteps, and spreading more branches, fronds, and other forest debris over the trail to make it look undisturbed. He pictured his cell mates doing the same thing with urgency after hearing the sounds of troops landing. He remembered, *my assignment is the furthest from our rendezvous point. My friends are rushing there now, and I want to see their faces again. We can crouch in the storage cellar of the safe house.*

As he started down the trail a sharp scream, muted by the distance, penetrated the undergrowth. It was the piercing, anguished scream of a man falling onto pungi stakes. Thi grimaced as he rushed further along. Sooner that he expected he heard a loud explosion in the jungle behind him. He shuddered at the thought of his handi-work – the shrapnel tearing into a bunch of soldiers and everything around, spraying bits of flesh and blood onto tree trunks and leaves. He quickened his pace with the knowledge that the shocked soldiers would be pumping their fear into a horrible, angry desire for merciless revenge, like a hoard of angry insects.

LATER THAT DAY, AFTER THE GOVERNMENT TROOPS had swept through the area, village spies rallied outside a stick-walled, thatched roof farm house to report how the action went. The sun was low in the sky, its light filtering through clear patches in the canopy and into the clearing around the house. Nha and two of Thi's cell members stood outside the doorway, waiting for the others.

Spies had stationed themselves at safe points throughout the area, at remote houses away from middle hamlet and out in well-established fruit and coconut orchards. Fortunately, the government forces, trying to win people over, no longer damaged and destroyed these places with shells or killed innocent civilians.

A picture of the day's events emerged from the reports. As many as one hundred government troops stormed the top end of the island while the PF platoon and some regional troops set up blocking forces on the end near the ferry crossing. Apparently, they hoped to push escaping VC into these ambushes and snare or kill them. The attacking troops that landed from boats came down the many trails at a surprisingly quick pace with a wide, but uneven front. They ran into the traps that had been prepared by Thi's cell. Several of the troops were wounded and at least two were killed. The government troops in the middle were slowed down by the booby traps, but the ones on the flanks moved more aggressively, undeterred by reports that troops in the middle of the assault were delayed.

As the spies pieced together the day's events, one more arrived from her distant post. The others looked expectantly at her. They could see the grim, sorrowful expression on her face. Something looked wrong!

As the others gathered around her, she croaked, "Thi Chet! He's dead! I'm sorry. I'm sorry!"

A palpable groan emerged from the group. Some shook their heads. Nha's mouth hung open as he moaned, "Agh."

"What happened?" asked Nha, almost in a whisper.

"The soldiers carried him to the road in a poncho. They laid him down on the side of the road for all to see. I do not know him that well, but I stood in the middle of the crowd and saw it was the man with one ear. I heard the soldiers talking. He was running away from soldiers chasing him and came right into others hiding in the bushes across his path. He saw them and started firing his carbine, but it was too late. He was outnumbered by so many."

Everyone hung their heads. Nha said, "He was hounded by the attacking troops and could not get to the safe house."

The other two cell members nodded their heads and grunted, "Uh huh."

"He went down fighting! He died in glory for the revolution," Nha proclaimed.

As he said these words Nha thought, *Thi is a hero. I hope the others will see that too. But, my gut is churning, and my heart is howling. I've seen too much screaming in Mo Cay.*

EIGHT

After Action Report

V an Howe and Bradford maneuvered from the top of the island with the main attack force. Their fatigues were wet to their knees with river water and mud and wet on their backs with sweat brought on by their exertions in the high heat and humidity. They kept an interval of 10 paces to avoid being easy targets and to back each other up. They had to watch their footing to avoid tripping on rough terrain and grasping vegetation as they looked intently for signs of trip wires and pungi pits. With all of that, their senses were ramped up to peak level as they searched for snipers or any movement in the undergrowth. They each had their weapons at the ready, locked and loaded, fingers on the trigger and thumbs on the safety lever, ready to flip into single shot or full-automatic firing.

They had to halt several times when men ran into pungi pits. Then there was a big explosion when a man tripped a booby trap. Van Howe could feel the blast even from a distance behind. The used their radio to report these incidents in parallel with the Vietnamese officers and make sure of medical evacuation. When they passed the bloody spot near the explosion, Van Howe said in a low voice, "Brad, I think our guys are doing well. They keep moving even with the casualties."

Moving steadily with their Regional Force troops they hooked up with Hoyt, Clarkson and Tang's Popular Force platoon in the blocking position. Field radios from all units and district headquarters hissed and chattered with the report of one VC KIA and friendly casualties.

Tang was holding the handset of his radio when Hoyt walked up to him. Hoyt said, "I call this a success."

"Yes, Captain, but at what price? We lost more men than the enemy."

"Well, check with your headquarters and let me know what you find out," replied Hoyt.

By mid-afternoon, the advisors made it back to their hooch, all sweaty and tired. Dried mud was caked on the fatigue pants of Bradford and Van Howe from jumping off the patrol boats into river muck up to their knees.

"A cold beer is gonna taste real good," proclaimed Clarkson as he reached into their propane refrigerator for a handful of cans.

Van Howe smiled and replied, "Thanks Clarkee," as he grabbed a cold can and popped it open. He took a swallow and said, "Aah! I like that cool tingle on my parched throat! It's a relief!"

The others followed suit, drinking down the cold beers and exclaiming, "Aah. Mm. That's the way to end an operation."

Clarkson said, "Ya know, you can drink all the canteen water you want but it ain't nothing like a cold beer on a hot day."

"I believe you're right, Sergeant Clarkson," Hoyt offered. "Especially after a good operation."

They stood there, looking at each other, seeing they had all made it back, having a few moments to pause and relax after their exertions.

Van Howe thought, *why was there only one enemy KIA? Intelligence reports had indicated several dozen VC on the upper island. Men had been lost or wounded.* Then, he heard a knock on their bamboo front door. He turned to see Popular Force platoon sergeant Trung si nhat Tang and his first squad leader Ha Si Tho.

With an expectant tone in his voice Captain Hoyt said, "Come in. We want to hear your report."

Tang and Tho entered the hooch still carrying their M16s, slung upside down over their shoulders. They nodded and smiled at the Americans and said, "We have more to report." They each said, "Cam on," as they accepted cold beers from Clarkson. Tang cleared his throat after taking a swig of beer. "Tastes good."

Captain Hoyt gestured toward the table and chairs and said, "So. What else did you find out?"

Taking a seat, Tang said, "There are no other KIA or

prisoners. Only the one. He has only one ear. When we put all the information together we figured there were only a few VC setting traps and shooting a little. There were not dozens of them, as we expected. With the size of our force we would have flushed out more if they were there."

"Yeah, something don't add up," offered Clarkson. "Maybe some of them slipped through our fingers or went to hidey-holes."

Tang nodded and added, "The one we caught just ran into our blocking ambush. He was a fighter, though. The district captain said he must have set some of the traps that got our men. Then he outran more than one hundred men. When he ran into our blocking force we shot at him. He was wounded and fell, but he got back up and attacked, firing rounds on semi-auto-matic. He would shoot and run and then duck for cover. He kept doing it. He had our men hugging the ground. He winged a few of ours. But he slowed down and then we hit him again. If he could have kept up his ferocious attack he might have broken through. He was a warrior."

"He was tough," added Tho.

"You gotta admire the fight in a guy like that," Clarkson remarked.

"Yeah," affirmed Van Howe quietly, nodding his head.

The others grunted in acknowledgement.

Tho spoke up, "He was not from here. No one recognized him."

"Too bad we couldn't capture 'im," stated Bradford. "If we can find out where they come from, we might know how to stop 'em or how many we havta deal with."

"That would be good," added Hoyt. *I'd be in good with the colonel if we could bring in a prisoner. It would definitely help my career. The intelligence information would be useful.*

"The district captain," said Tang, "made a point of saying that these VC must have a good information network. Somehow, they knew we were attacking, and they were ready for us. Those traps were planned. Preparations were made. They only left a few to counter us and the others escaped. They will come back and we'll have to do this all over again."

"So, is there a leak somewhere?" asked Van Howe.

"The captain is going to investigate," Tang replied. "He will ask the district intelligence officers to review all communications and contacts in Mo Cay and Ben Tre to see if there are any radio messages that were not encoded or find out if someone told a relative or friend what was happening. No one will admit to that, but they can be watched. Very few know about an operation before it begins. That keeps it quiet, but some are needed to plan and prepare, so they know about it. Maybe it was an innocent mistake, but men were hurt, enemy escaped. It's not good."

"You're right," proclaimed Hoyt. "This should be given top priority."

LATER THAT DAY, AS THE SUN FELL ALONG ITS downward arc toward the horizon, the team settled in for the night. Bradford stood by the stove, stirring a pot and sniffing the aroma wafting up.

"What'sha got there, Brad?" Asked Clarkson.

"Oh, you know, some of my GI Jambalaya."

"Oh yeah. That was good last time."

"Yeah," added Van Howe. "What's in that recipe anyway?"

"Well. That's just it. There is no exact recipe, just a few basic ingredients and a little experimentation."

"So, we're part of an experiment?" teased Van Howe with a grin.

"It's a little more definite than that," replied Bradford with an amused smile. "I mean, this one has that mac and cheese that Clarkee brought back from Ben Tre. Then I mixed in some pork slices from the C-rats. Also, some canned peas we had up on the shelf."

"Don't forget the Tabasco sauce," added Doc. "That last batch you made was kind of mild. Needs lots of Tabasco sauce."

"Woa. Hold down there, Doc," implored Van Howe. "You can always add that stuff later. Maybe a little pepper in there would help the flavor?"

The radio interrupted. Hoyt picked up the handset and responded. "This is Roughneck 6."

"Roughneck 6, this is Tiger 6. Standby for a coded message."

Van Howe pulled his code book out of the cargo pocket on the side of his pants. Clarkson grabbed a pencil and paper from a pouch hanging on the wall near the radio. They all heard the message over the speaker. After Clarkson and Van Howe decoded it they handed it to Hoyt.

He held it in both hands and slowly nodded his head as he read to himself. "So, the district troops are going to build a fort up island. It'll be on that stream where Tho's squad found the VC munitions."

Clarkson offered, "That was a real good spot for Charlie. He could make bombs and move 'em by boat."

"Yeah," agreed Van Howe. "They could bring their sampans right up that stream."

Clarkson added, "A fort up there will put a crimp in their plans!"

Bradford finished his beer and tapped the can lightly on the table. He said, "They'll want us to send a squad up there while they build. Our PFs can patrol the area and keep Charlie off their backs. Tang and Tho would probably like bragging rights for protecting the district troops."

"No doubt," remarked Hoyt. "I gather they plan to have it all done in a week. It's just mud, sticks and sandbags so with all the district manpower they can do it."

"The faster the better to stop Mr. Charles," added Bradford.

"Yeaaaah," said Hoyt in a slow drawl. "Van," he said nodding toward Van Howe, "After they get done next week you and the guys can go up there with the Whaler and show Charlie we've taken over the waterway. It'll also show the troops in the fort they have an important job denying Charlie one of his favorite travel routes."

"Yes, sir." Responded Van Howe. At first, he pictured numerous sampans going down the stream carrying VC and their deadly bombs. Then he imagined himself and the team in their Boston Whaler pushing upstream, as the new owners of the ancient route. After these mental images he wondered, *why isn't Hoyt going? He seems to be going to Ben Tre a lot. We're being sent up a dangerous waterway to show the flag and Hoyt isn't going to claim that dubious glory? There's something funny about this guy.*

As if Hoyt could read Van Howe's quizzical thoughts, he quickly added, "Yep, I'll be heading up to Ben Tre to coordinate plans with the operations officer. After this last sweep operation, and with plans to build the outpost, no doubt there will be new missions in store for us."

"Roger," replied Van Howe. He looked over at the others as Bradford was taking his GI Jambalaya off the stove and Sang was setting plastic plates on the table. "One of us can stay here to monitor the radio and coordinate support if needed. Doc, maybe that should be you, so we know where you are in case we need to be patched up."

"Sure thing, LT."

"There will be four of us in the boat. We can put two men on the bow with 16's. I'll steer. And maybe Brad you can get behind me with the blooper. Those

M79 shotgun rounds will be like an old-time blunderbuss blowin' up pirates."

"Yeah," said Bradford. "With Clarkee and Sang pointing their 16's up front they can pinpoint an ambush 'n I can hit 'em with a big round before I get into their sights. I'll load it with shotgun rounds. Wouldn't want to use a high explosive round. Might bounce off a tree right back on us."

"That's a plan," said Clarkee. "On the other hand, if we don't see 'em first, they're gonna get you and LT, but we can swing around and fire 'em up on full automatic, that is, if they don't get us too."

"I hope you'll be quick," said Van Howe, "because if they knock me off the steering wheel the boat is gonna spin into the bank and stick in the mud. Probably go way up the bank and be hard to get off. Good target for Charlie."

Bradford chimed in, "On second thought, maybe speed will be our best bet. If we move quick up that stream, even if Charlie hears us coming, we'll go by the ambush so fast they won't have a target for long. They won't be able to get us all. We might even be able to shoot back and get some of them."

Van Howe leaned back on his stool, his face set in a smile that seemed more like a grimace. "Well, gentlemen, say your prayers and oil your weapons. We'll just have 'ta see what happens."

THAT NIGHT, THEY WERE ALL IN THEIR BUNKS covered over with mosquito nets. It was only nine o'clock, 21 hundred hours military time. Bradford and Doc Jackson were reading books. Clarkson was looking at a letter from home. Sang listened to a tape recorder with earphones. Hoyt was snoring lightly. Van Howe lay with his arm behind his head and stared into the dark underside of the bunk above him.

He thought, *it was a busy day. It was a Delta day doing the Nam thing, doing what grunts do.* His visual recall was vivid, so vivid he could feel his heart beating faster as he reviewed the day's events. There was the excitement of going up the brown river, Song Ham Luong. They went up the middle of the wide water because the distance to the edges offered some protection from a nasty surprise. Sure, they were easily within RPG range, but those rocket propelled grenades would need a good aim to hit them the first time. After that, they could turn the boat's machine guns on the attackers. Van Howe recalled the muddy river banks, with vegetation growing right down to the edge, good concealment for Mr. Charles. He could see the muddy water carrying branches, bits of wood, coconut husks and other bits of vegetation down-stream, the current swirling against the banks and licking the mud.

He recalled the boats rounding the top of the island and turning in toward the overgrown riverbank. There was a muddy ledge where the swift river carved away the land as it rushed toward the sea. The boats went in by twos to drop off the infantrymen. The district forces were well disciplined. They readied themselves on the bow, M16s pointed toward the jungle. As soon as the boats touched the muddy bank the first wave jumped down and struggled through the mud. The next wave covered their advance until the first gained secure ground. When Van Howe and Bradford jumped in they sank further than the lighter Vietnamese. Their boots plunged down into the thick, wet mud and disappeared. They were up to their knees. They had to lean forward to break the suction and pull their legs up. It was work. They were sitting ducks. He remembered thinking, *how I envy the lighter Vietnamese for their ability to seemingly dance through the mud. Of course, they are local men, guys who grew up doing this all their lives.*

In his mind's eye he recalled how the troops took it slow in the first hundred yards. They hunkered down, looked around, and moved ahead with caution. They knew a sniper could be waiting or they could run into a booby trap. They expected a squad or two of the enemy. They knew that even a squad could inflict a lot of damage on a larger attacking force. Probably every man was thinking the same thing. Who would be the first to get zapped? Would it be a dead kill, or could they survive a wound?

They could hear a few rifle shots pop off to their right flank. Automatic fire from M16s replied. It was probably a VC taking shots at the troops followed by the overwhelming firepower of their response. He recalled tightening his grip on his M16. He put his thumb over the safety lever. He had told himself: *better keep the safety on. I don't want to shoot any of our guys with a twitch on the trigger.* He remembered feeling the comforting weight of the .357 magnum at his hip, a reassuring back-up in case the M16 jammed. Before jumping off the boat, he had made sure the snap tab on the holster was securely over the pistol. He had also checked to see if the two fragmentation grenades were secured to the heavy web of the pistol belt. He recalled the weight of the two bandoliers of magazines crossed over his chest. He had been ready.

His stomach tightened as he remembered the piercing scream of the man who fell in the pungi pit. Then the explosion came, he recalled with a slight shudder. The platoon point man was caught in a loud blast of fragmentation that peppered his body all over. Body parts were blown all over the trail. Leaves were covered with blood. His crumpled, distorted form was tossed onto the mud. He had stumbled into something big. So big that the following man took shrapnel in the arm and screamed as the hot metal burned and lacerated his skin. Charlie had done his handiwork. Medics ran to help. After a pause, the column moved on.

The troops moved forward more cautiously than before. The platoon leader called in the casualties on the radio as Van Howe walked past and gave him a grim nod. Bradford used their radio to call in to Doc and district. No doubt they were glued to the speakers tracking every move.

Laying in his bunk that night Van Howe felt his pulse quicken, his back tighten-up, and the sweat on his neck, even in the cool of the night. He recalled, after the explosion and the loss of the rifleman, he was intensely and soberly focused on every move, his own moves and every move around him. Every nerve in his body was on high alert. His guts twisted into a knot and he sensed the blood rising from his neck to his head. He strained his eyes looking for trip wires, grenades or anything that signaled a trap. He knew that just because men were in front of him he was still not safe from being blown away. The first men down a trail could walk right past a trip wire only to have the second or third man step into an ear blasting, limb shattering, gut splattering oblivion. Laying in his bunk he remembered the feeling that every step could be his last. He remembered looking at his boots and wondering if his legs would be blown off today. Would he be able to walk on two feet tomorrow? Would he even want to live with only half a body?

Van Howe relived the feeling of sweat pouring off his neck and back in the heat of the day. He saw himself tightening his grip on the rifle while he realized that he needed to hold it more loosely, balanced in his hands, so he could move it quickly and respond in the instant of an attack. He felt confident yet fearful simultaneously with the realization that his legs kept moving forward, one step in front of the other in spite of every impulse telling him that this was crazy and that he should stop. But he moved forward because it was his duty. This was his training. This was a moment of truth. He was showing these Vietnamese soldiers that American fighting men are with them every step of the way. And, he took comfort in knowing that Brad was right behind him, ten paces away, keeping a good interval in case one of them hit a mine, there to look out for each other.

A FEW DAYS LATER, VAN HOWE AND BRADFORD were down at the dock getting the Boston Whaler ready for their trip up the creek. They bailed out rainwater from the night before, filled the gas tank for the outboard engine, checked the steering cables and shift levers on the console and put some paddles on board in case the engine failed.

"Are you ready for tomorrow?" asked Van Howe.

"Yeah. As ready as I can be," said Bradford. "I feel a little like we're going up the creek to a weird, spooky place, like in the book by Conrad, The Heart of Darkness."

"That was the Congo. Maybe not much different from Vietnam. Do you think the soldiers in the new outpost are going crazy like Kurtz in the book?"

With a distant look on his face, Bradford replied, "Maybe not yet, but could be. Why wouldn't they go crazy being stuck up a creek in a remote outpost in the middle of a nasty war with their own countrymen, spurred on by larger nations? They would be like Kurtz confronting the dark side of human existence and thinking about the 'horror' of it."

"You're such an intellectual, Brad and you're

depressing, man. Look at the positive side of this stuff. We might get blown away going up that creek. Then we won't have to worry about this war anymore."

"Yeah, the worrying is bad. But, you sound kind of morose?"

"Having this conversation with you kinda reminds me of a bad dream I had the other night after Hoyt blessed us with this mission. Now I wonder if I am losing it, if I'm up to it."

"Oh man. You gotta be more up to it than Hoyt. Clarkee told me he almost pissed himself when that one-eared VC started shooting. It was like he didn't know whether to point his rifle up, down or sideways."

"Thanks for the vote of confidence, but you haven't heard my dream. Anyway, anyone can get unstrung around here and Hoyt's really just a new guy."

"Yeah, well, what's your dream?"

Van Howe sat up in his seat and cleared his throat. "Well, we're heading up the stream in this boat. Everyone's in their position just like we planned." He pointed to the bow of the boat. "Clarkee and Sang are up front there and I'm steering with you behind me."

Bradford leaned forward and said, "Uh huh."

"We go up stream for a while. The engine is humming. The boat is moving pretty fast through the water. The stream gets narrower, only four or five times wider that the boat. The jungle comes down to the edge. You can't see much back in the bushes. The turns are hard to get around, but we try to keep the speed up. Everybody is concentrating, trying to peer back into the overgrown banks." Van Howe paused and looked straight at Bradford.

"Yeah, Yeah, go on. What happens?"

"Then, we're going around a turn and, all of a sudden, a hail of rifle fire comes from behind the bushes. Sang is hit and slumps down. Clarkee starts shooting full automatic. You fire off a blast with the M79 but at the same time a big, fat RPG round streaks out at us and hits the middle of the boat, blowing it in two. Clarkee is floating in the bow section shooting back at the Charlies and we go zig zagging past him. Then the water gushes in over the broken section and we slam into the opposite bank just past Clarkee." Van Howe paused to take a breath.

"Don't stop now. What happens?" urged Bradford leaning forward.

"Okay. You jump out and start pouring rounds into Charlie. I'm standing in the back of the Whaler firing my pistol at 'em. Enemy fire strikes the back of the boat, shredding the fiberglass and putting holes in the engine. I jump overboard to escape. The last thing I remember is being down deep in the stream, maybe under six feet of water thinking I am safe for a few seconds. The revolver is still in my hand with maybe one round left in it. I have to surface but fear coming up into a load of bullets. The only thing I can think of is to swim underwater to the same bank where the ambushers are, only upstream. There I can reload and come in behind them. I swim for the bank and my lungs are bursting for air." Van Howe paused again. He sucked in air as if he were surfacing from underwater. He looked away for a few seconds, aware that Bradford was looking right at him, waiting.

"Then what happens?" asked Bradford urgently.

"I dunno. That's the end of the dream. I woke up in a sweat."

"Jeeze, LT. You got me going on that one. I can see it got to ya. Maybe we should walk up there instead to that fort?"

"Not hardly, Brad. Too many booby-traps up that way."

"Yeah. That's true. That's true."

Van Howe sat up straight and looked straight at Brad's face. "Ya know, Brad. I had my bad dream, but I'm worried 'bout you. Seems like you been tossing in the rack and mumblin' a lot. Somethin' botherin' you?"

Bradford turned a bit and looked up at the sky. He took a deep breath before responding. "Yeah. Could be some bad memories."

"Uh huh," replied Van Howe quietly. "If you want to talk about it, it's okay with me."

"Okay, well. Maybe a little humor would be good," said Bradford. "Let me show you how I got my lighter engraved on R and R. But we have to go up the hill so we don't blow up this gas can."

They walked up the hill toward their hooch. Brad tapped his pack of Lucky Strikes, urging one tobacco soldier up for a smoke. Sticking it between his lips he pulled out his Zippo, opened the lid with a metallic click, and flicked the flint wheel, making the usual zip sound. He sucked up the blue and yellow flame and exhaled a cloud of blue smoke. Then he closed the lid with a distinct snap. Van Howe said, "Brad I can see that engraving on your lighter. How does it go?"

Brad squinted at the lighter in his palm and announced, "FOR THOSE WHO FOUGHT FOR IT FREEDOM HAS A FLAVOR THE PROTECTED WILL NEVER KNOW."

"Yeah. I thought you said it was humorous. Where'd ya get that?"

"Oh, I read it somewhere, but the humorous story is the one I didn't use. I heard it from a squad leader on my last tour. But I got a question for you. How come you have nothing on your lighter?"

"Don't wanna give nothing to the enemy."

"Yeah, well, can't hold back my feelings. Besides, if I get captured Charlie may like this saying."

"Yu. I suppose it's universal. Maybe the NLF will adopt it."

"Yeah, anyway, the one I think would give them the state of U.S. morale is the one I didn't use. It's a cynical kind of humor. Let's see, how does it go? Oh yeah, WE THE UNWILLING LED BY THE UNQUALIFIED TO KILL THE UNFORTUNATE DIE FOR THE UNGRATEFUL."

"You're right," responded Van Howe. "If Charlie finds Zippos like that he's gonna get more confident about winning."

"Yeah, sure, but Charlie already knows we have low morale. He gets it off the TV, the papers and his spies all around us. Not to mention all the lighters GIs drop all over the country."

Later that day, after nightfall, it was quiet in the advisor's hooch. Van Howe was trying to sleep but his mind raced with thoughts. *Tomorrow, we take the boat up that narrow stream into Brad's "Heart of Darkness." It's freaky. Tomorrow will be a day of reckoning.*

NINE

What Now?

Within a few days after the government attack the two Viet Cong squads returned to the island. Tu and Luong were eager to meet Nha at a safe house on the upper end of the island.

When Nha entered the doorway Luong stood up and said, "Nha, good to see you." As Tu gave her brother a welcoming embrace, she said, "I am glad you are safe!"

Nha looked at them with sadness in his eyes. With a choked-up, raspy voice he said, "Thi chet. He was killed defending the island. He couldn't reach the hideout. He was ambushed by government troops."

"What happened?" asked Tu, echoed by Luong, almost in unison.

Nha spoke slowly, "The cell fighters did everything we planned. They set explosives and pungi traps. We killed and wounded the soldiers. But, our spies had bad news. They saw the soldiers bring Thi's body to the road at the ferry crossing. The soldiers said he fought very bravely against big odds. He just kept charging at them, firing his weapon very fast, making them kiss the ground and dodge his bullets. Then, Thi had to stop and reload. That's when they got him. He showed them courage and the spirit of the revolution."

Luong scowled. After a few moments of dreadful silence, he said somberly, "He was a brave fighter."

With tears welling up in her eyes, Tu added, "He grew up in my village. His father was taken away and imprisoned on Con Son Island by Diem's cronies. Thi worked hard in the paddies and the orchards to support his mother, little brothers and sisters. I admired his strength of character and devotion to his family."

"I knew him when we were training to be fighters," added Luong. "He told me he resisted when the government came to recruit young men for the ARVN. They accused him of being loyal to the Viet Cong and threatened his family. The last thing he wanted was to join the government. He took part in the concerted rebellion with Nguyen Thi Dinh in 1960. He told me he was greatly inspired by the battle of Ap Bac in 1962. When his younger brother was old enough to take care of the family he joined up as a regular. We fought together around Ben Tre. I heard many stories about his life."

Tu lifted her head and sighed. "He was kind to our family. He said it was because others had helped him, but I think he had a good nature. VC cadres sympathized with him after his father was taken. During that first year, some of the cadre even came to help his family harvest their rice. They told him to take care of his family but someday he could join them and fight against the oppressors. After the government guillotined my father in front of the whole village my family was devastated. We were so numbed with pain that we could hardly carry on. Thi had great sympathy for us. He and his mother came to our house and shared in our grief. He helped to harvest our rice and fruit. Thi always had a kind word of encouragement for me and it helped me get through that horrible time."

Tu paused, pensively. "He did even more," she recalled. "Thi helped us avenge our father's murder. It was several years later. He was an experienced fighter by then because he had joined up with Nguyen Van Tra, father's old friend from the Viet Minh. Tra was a frequent visitor. He was an influential cadre, but he made time to look after our family and Thi's."

"Yes," interjected Nha. "Tra was like an uncle. He told us stories about father. How he was a brave fighter. How he always looked out for his fellow fighters. How he was respected for his steadiness and his thoughtfulness."

Tu smiled and continued, "A few years after father's death, Tra and Thi came to us and said there was a chance to deal a blow to the government soldiers. Those soldiers always propped up corrupt officials, stole our chickens, took prisoners, and treated people harshly. We were ready to get even."

"We waited years and years to get even," added Nha.

"Tra told us how it could happen." said Tu. "Spies had reported Captain Huong, the executioner, and Lieutenant Tach, would be vulnerable. Tach was the one who made unwanted advances toward me every time he came to our village. They had plans to officiate at a ceremony to install unelected village officials. It was something they liked to do. Their superiors would send them out on these minor affairs and they could be the big men. They would strut about the village and show off. They usually brought only about twenty soldiers for these events."

Luong listened intently, shifting his gaze between Tu and Nha as they spoke. When he looked at Tu he could see her eyes look upward as if she was seeing into the past to recall details of the incident. He remarked, "Ahh, this was a big chance for you."

'Yes," Tu responded, slowly nodding her head. "We assembled two squads of fighters and set up an ambush on the trail leading from the village. We waited until after the ceremony and the customary eating and drinking. Usually, the new officials would provide liquor, Biere Larue and Ba Muoi Ba. Captain Huong always liked free drinks from fawning officials."

Tu gazed at Luong and cleared her throat. "They came down the trail carelessly, boisterously. Seeing that their officers were lax, the troops failed to be attentive. It was dusk. There was an open spot in the trail. Thi set up explosives to greet the men on point. Our fighters had good fields of fire and many had automatic weapons. We shocked our prey. They were confused by the explosion. It killed two men outright and threw the others back. Before they could react, we cut them down with a blaze of bullets."

Tu lowered her voice as her body trembled slightly with the intensity of the recollection. "After the hellfire noise of so many weapons, when our bleeding victims lay motionless on the trail, there was an eerie, arresting silence. No one moved. It was the silence the dead can't hear. The world had turned. Seconds ticked by. I was consumed with the overwhelming awareness that we had succeeded. Captain Huong would no longer terrorize innocent villagers, and Lieutenant Tach would not try again to force himself on me. They were dead."

Luong looked at Tu. In the moments after speaking her whole body relaxed. She was suspended in a distant gaze. He quietly said, "It was done. Justice was done."

Tu sighed and looked at him. "But, it can never make up for the great loss of our father in such an unfair and ruthless way."

Nha added, "Thi helped us many times. He is in my heart forever."

LATER, THEY SAT AROUND A COOKING FIRE IN AN open-hearth eating rice and bits of fish from white, ceramic bowls. As Nha sprinkled nuoc mam over his rice he said, "We were lucky to get a warning from your friend Chi about the government attack. If it weren't for the loss of Thi we could claim a big win over the puppet soldiers."

"And you did well too Nha," offered Luong.

"We used our time well," added Tu. "My squad went to Phuoc Me Trung and Vinh Thanh and over to the Song Co Chien to tell people the revolution is alive. Some young men and women promised to join us soon. They will be needed for the big push next year."

"Yes," added Luong. "My squad went around Thanh Ngai and Luong Thoi. We met many who support us, and some will start training soon or help with supplies and munitions."

"Good, good," Nha replied. "Now I can tell you the latest word from Phong. He is going to an important meeting near Tay Ninh along the Vam Co River. When he comes back he wants me to meet with him for a report on our progress."

Tu and Luong both nodded. After a brief discussion about the report for Phong, Nha yawned and said, "I wish you a good night. I must sleep."

As the cooking fire slowly turned into glowing embers Tu and Luong talked late into the night.

She said, "I like the night. It is easier to hide from our enemies. It is easier to attack our enemies. Sometimes all is still and we can rest."

"You are a true fighter, Tu."

She looked at his face in the faint glow of the fire. "What inspires you, Luong?"

He said, "I like the wisdom of Uncle Ho. At one training camp I read a copy of his <u>Prison Diary</u>. They only had a few of them. It was a worn and water stained little book that could fit in your pocket. The editor, Phan Nhuan, wrote that it would help us to understand Ho. It made me feel that he was an indomitable spirit, a great patriot and very wise. He could look beyond adversity with good humor. One of his lines said, 'The authorities, having pity on my loneliness, invited me to live temporarily in the prison.' I loved that his spirit could soar even when they were holding him down."

Tu smiled. "Oh, I like that. I have heard of that book. I'd like to read it one day."

"I hope so," he said. "It also showed me Uncle Ho knew the wisdom of Sun Tzu. Some of his verses said, 'Attack, retreat, with unerring strategy: Then you will merit the title of great commander.' Who wouldn't follow a leader like that? His words lifted my spirit."

Tu smiled and looked at Luong. A feeling of quiet joy rose in her. She thought, *Luong and I grew up in separate hamlets of the same village and we hardly knew each other. It is strange and fortunate that, in the midst of this war, we are now together and I want to know him more.*

As Luong returned Tu's gaze she demurely averted her eyes after lingering momentarily.

His pulse quickened with her brief hint of something more between them, but his sense of mission controlled his emotions. He held Tu's hand and said, "Good night. Let's hope we have a peaceful rest."

The next morning, the three VC rose to the sounds of an awakening forest. Birds called out and monkeys chattered as the warmth of the sun raised the humidity along with a pleasant, earthy smell from the damp ground and dewy leaves. It was peaceful and quiet. They knew soldiers were not likely to come this far up island. Even if they did messengers would come and give warning.

They walked outside holding oranges and grape-fruits in their hands. Tu and Luong sat on a coconut log and Nha sat on a rough-hewn stool.

"Luong, you and Thi fought together?" asked Nha.

"Yes. We had both been at a training camp in the Plain of Reeds, west of My Tho, near the Cambodian Border. We were with the 504th Main Force there. That was a few years before the big Tet offensive. We had months of training and then became provincial fighters for a year afterwards. The cadres gave us many classes on Marxism, the teachings of the Communist Party, and the crimes of the American imperialists and bandit puppet soldiers. They even taught us some English language to know what the enemy says."

"Yes, that is like the training I had," said Nha, "but I was with the 514th in Dinh Tuong Province near My Tho."

"Me too," added Tu as she pulled back the skin off a grapefruit to reveal a succulent section of the plump fruit.

Luong nodded. "Thi was always interested in learning more about the early fighting from the August Revolution in 1945, and how Nguyen Thi Dinh traveled down the coast to sneak weapons into Thanh Phu, or how we fought the French after the big war with the Japanese. He was very inspired by the courage and patriotic dedication of Nuyen Thi Dinh and the other leaders of the concerted uprising in 1960. He was proud that he had taken part by attacking government outposts and helping to make roadblocks to harass government troops. He told me that in those days his revolutionary passion was fueled by hate for Diem's tyranny and the loss of his father, but he had grown to realize we must go beyond emotions and learn to emulate our great leaders if we are to liberate our country."

"He was like so many of us," said Tu. "Nha and I felt the same things after the loss of our father. During the uprising, I helped supply our fighters with food and wrote slogans on tree trunks to encourage the population. I also attended the big rally of ten thousand people for the Ben Tre Province Liberation Front Committee. That was on December 26, 1960. It was in My Chanh, near district town. It was a big affair with electric lights, and microphones and flags. Representatives of many groups spoke to the people."

"I heard about that rally," replied Luong. "I had participated in raids on the government outposts during the uprising, but I was caring for wounded fighters and could not attend."

Tu looked at Luong and said, "We all did what we could." She touched his sleeve gently and smiled.

Turning to Nha, Luong said, "I know the 514th Battalion too."

"How is that?" asked Nha.

"Well, when Thi and I were apprentice fighters we were sent to the demolition platoon of the 514th for practical training in tactics and weapons. They were one of the best platoons in the 514th and led many successful attacks. We learned how to use the Bangalore Torpedoes to breach the enemy wire and get inside their defenses. They were not just brave fighters. Their morale was strong, and many unit members belonged to the People's Revolutionary Party or youth group. They would say 'our hearts and minds are our nuclear weapons.' Thieu and I felt we were fortunate to be part of them for a while."

"What happened to you after that?" asked Tu.

"After Tet, we were given separate assignments. Our paths crossed many times as we fought against the government and the terrible American 9th Infantry Division."

"Oh yes," said Nha. "We all know how hard those times were. They came at us with helicopters, B52's, Phantom Jets, Napalm, patrol boats, special forces and a huge infantry force. They shot at everyone. They wounded more than 13,000 civilians. We all breathed easier after they left in 1969. Between that and our losses during Tet of 68 we have been weakened a great deal. But now, we are building strength and soon we will beat our enemies."

They sat silently for a moment reflecting upon all they had said.

A gentle breeze swept in from the river and rustled

the branches of the coconut palms. Then they heard a loud *thud*. It came out of nowhere. They turned toward the sound and saw no one.

Tu laughed, 'A coconut. It fell from a tree. That's all."

"No," said Nha "That other sound."

They all sat up and listened intently.

"It's an iron bird," exclaimed Tu.

Nha stood facing the sound and cupped his hands behind his ears. "It's getting louder," he announced.

"The trees are tall here," said Tu. "They won't see us." She thought, *if they see us we will look suspicious and they will shoot at us. Maybe rockets. Maybe machine guns. The iron bird soldiers have often shot without warning from the sky. They even shoot innocent farmers.* "We should hide in the house," she added.

The helicopter came much closer. The whup, whup sound of its blades filled the space between the trees as they stood near the door of the house. Putting his hands behind his ears again, Nha said, "It's turning! It's turning toward the stream. That's where the puppet soldiers are building a new outpost. Near the creek. Near our old munitions cache."

"Maybe the government officials are visiting to see how well they are building the outpost," suggested Tu.

"They can't land there," said Nha. "No clearing. But they can get a good look at how they have cut down trees and how they are making the mud walls. Our spies say they are making good progress. The officials in the iron bird will be happy."

They could hear the helicopter make several passes over the area of the new outpost. Then it turned away from the island and flew toward district town.

Luong said, "They have worked quickly to build that outpost. It won't be easy to use that creek to move ammunition and supplies."

"Yes, but it will be a good way to ambush the soldiers who bring supplies to the outpost," replied Nha.

"Ha," said Tu. "We can turn their little plan against them. We should plan an attack on that new outpost and the one at the head of the island too."

Luong replied, "I agree. We will baffle them. They think they have cleared the area, but it will not be safe for them. We will make them hide in their forts. But, we should not attack too strongly so they will not be provoked. I think we just want to keep them off balance so we can do more important work recruiting and preparing for the big push."

"Good," said Nha. "I will leave you to it. I will go to Ben Tre and prepare to meet Phong. Good luck to you both." He hugged his sister and clasped Luong's arm. "Farewell."

"Be safe little brother," said Tu. Her eyes followed him as he disappeared down a trail heading toward Ben Tre.

After a lingering pause, she turned toward Luong. She looked briefly into his brown eyes. He returned a momentary look of affection. She dropped her eyes and thought, *I hope he can't see the blush I feel rising up my neck. This is no way for comrades in arms to behave. But I do like his round handsome face. His intelligent expressions are so interesting. I missed him when we were away on our separate missions.*

With a flutter in his heart, Luong thought, *I think she likes me. She is a good woman. If times were different I would want to spend more time with her. No! I want to spend more time with her now, but we both have responsibilities. Life is too dangerous. Life is not normal. We are fighting for our liberty, for our country.*

Luong said, "We should sit down and make plans." In the back of his mind he thought, *I did not say what kind of plans, but she will think I mean plans to fight the enemy. I would like to make plans to spend more time with her.* He sat down on the log.

Tu thought *I do not want to encourage him in the wrong way.* She did not sit next to him on the log and, instead, sat on the stool opposite him. She pulled a map out of her pocket and opened it up on her lap. She hesitated. Her feelings for him lingered. Her inner voice said, you must talk of military things.

He did not start talking either. He stared off into the surrounding jungle for a moment. He could feel that she was waiting for him to say something. He turned half way toward her, not wanting to meet her eyes again, and said, "It is peaceful in this little spot right now. I remember peaceful days when I was growing up."

"Yes, me too." replied Tu in a soft voice. "Like when

my family would rest in the house at night and my father would tell us the story of Luc Van Tien."

"Oh yes, Luc Van Tien," he replied. "I loved to hear that story too. I remember it was written by Nguyen Dinh, an anti-French writer who lived in this area. It had 2,000 verses, a love story about the adventures of Luc Van Tien, a young scholar, and Nguyet Nga, a beautiful and virtuous girl."

Tu smiled and said, "My father would say that the story taught all the important virtues: humility, kindness, filial piety, courage, determination, and loyalty. He said people loved it because it reminded them of our traditional virtues at a time when the French were putting pressure on our way of life."

"Your father was wise," said Luong, "I like that Nguyen Dinh, the author, built the story on the Buddhist doctrine of nhan qua, that good and virtuous people will always be rewarded in the end and the wicked will be punished."

"The story reminds our people that we have the virtues to resist the wickedness of a corrupt government and invaders like the French and the Americans," Tu added.

"Our culture is strong and our people will endure," said Luong. "I enjoy this conversation, but it reminds me that we must look at our duties now. Let's look at your map and see how to fight our enemies."

One day later, the squads were on the move. Luong had assigned a cell to find hiding places for a stockpile of munitions. Another cell observed the activities of the soldiers building the new outpost to find out their habits, and the strong and weak points of their construction. All of this information would be needed for the plan to harass the outpost and frighten the puppet troops. Another cell placed small booby traps where the soldiers worked cutting trees or patrolled around the outpost.

Similarly, Tu had instructed Hoang Van Thiet, the NVA cell leader, to determine the best way to harass the outpost at the head of the island. She knew he was eager to prove that he could make a good plan. Another cell searched good spots to ambush any government sampans moving along the creek. Meanwhile, she arranged for the evacuation of both squads in the event things got overheated and the government countered with another attack.

Tu mentally reviewed her plan. She wanted to get in touch with her old friend Chi to see if she had any new intelligence. She planned to provide Chi with a secret radio so any new information could be sent quickly with code words. There was so much radio traffic going back and forth between the ARVN units or the American Units that one more transmission should not stand out too much. She chuckled to herself about how fortunate they were to easily get the radios. Her contacts in Ben Tre had picked up several good US military radios that a corrupt Vietnamese supply officer had sold on the black market.

Tu was a little worried about her discussion with Hoang Van Thiet. She had said to him, "Thiet, you have had good training and experience in the NVA. I would like to put that to good use. Your job will be to observe the top outpost and determine the best ways to worry them and the best routes for escape after attacking them."

He had replied, "I can do that. My cell has had good training. We are all eager to prove that men from the north have the true revolutionary spirit."

Sensing a little cockiness and over confidence Tu asked, "How much actual action did your cell see?"

"Oh well, we were rushed down here so fast that we only took part in one action. It was an attack on a police station near Cu Chi. Our platoon seized the police station and before the ARVN counter attacked we escaped to the tunnels to hide and wait it out."

Tu had replied, "That is useful. Remember that it is different here. We do not have tunnels like Cu Chi, only a few hidey holes and cellars where it is dry enough. You will have to find more flexible escape routes and find ways to delay and fool the enemy. Right now, don't start anything until I give the order. We can't risk an action until we are ready. Just observe for now."

"Yes, Miss."

She reflected on it, *I can't tell if he was being sarcastic and belittling my gender or if he was being obedient. It is an assignment that he should be able to handle so I'll give him the benefit of the doubt. I may be winning him over. He seems friendly now.*

TEN

Up the Creek

____

They walked down to the boat, ready to go up the creek to the new outpost. Van Howe, Bradford, Clarkson, and Sang were loaded with gear – web belts with ammo pouches, grenades, and small packs, along with hands full of a field radio, an ammo box of grenade launcher rounds, rifles, extra bandoliers of M16 ammo, net hammocks, and a can of boat fuel. The Boston Whaler was bobbing lightly on the tidal swells.

"It's how we have fun, right?" asked Bradford, a playful grin on his face. At the same time, he thought, *this could be our last boat trip.*

Van Howe smiled faintly, *what dangers lurk up that narrow creek?* He cleared his throat. "Alright, we gotta plan. Like we went over yesterday, Clarkee and Sang you get the front of the boat, one shooting off the right, the other on the left. I'll drive, and Brad, you get behind with the blooper and those shotgun rounds We'll have fire power all around."

With a short chortle and raised eyebrows Sang pointed to the five bullet holes in the bow that they inherited from another MAT team. "But Trung uy, do you really think this is a good idea?" The others looked expectantly at Van Howe for his response. Anything to lighten the mood for their mission.

Van Howe stood behind the mid-ship steering wheel and looked at Sang. "If I had my choice I'd want a big patrol boat and some steel armor, but that boat don't fit in the creek." They all chuckled nervously.

Van Howe added, "But seriously gents, do we still think it's a good idea to forget the flak jackets?"

"I think so LT," said Clarkson. "Those things weigh eight pounds and they don't really stop bullets, just frags. On top of the ammo belts and grenades we're carrying they would just sink us if we have to go in the water. If we had life vests that'd be another thing, but it would still be too much junk in the way."

"Yeah, better go light," added Bradford. Sang nodded and smiled faintly.

"Roger that," Replied Van Howe. "Okay. The plan is for us to go around the bottom of the island and up the river on the other side to the creek entrance. Ha si Tho will meet us on the other side with his squad in a couple of motor sampans. They will go in front and behind us at an interval of ten yards. That way Charlie can't get us all at once. With fourteen men, we'll have enough fire-power to scare Charley off. That is, if our intelligence is good and there aren't that many of 'em." They all nodded. He cranked the engine. The olive drab, forty horsepower Johnson outboard chugged and emitted dark smoke, a smelly mixture of gas and oil fumes. As it warmed, the engine settled to a reassuring thrum.

As he eased the boat off the dock Van Howe recalled the latest intelligence from their district headquarters. Village chiefs had reported increased VC activity. Farmers had seen armed VC passing through the area. People had been visited by VC trying to recruit them to join the National Liberation Front or supply food and labor. He thought, *something's up!*

Moving down the river Van Howe thought, *Hoyt seemed excited about sending us to check the area and take prisoners. If he's so hot for us to get out there why didn't he go too? He just gave orders and went to Ben Tre. He'll probably make a big deal with the colonel if we actually do get a prisoner.*

After they motored to the other side of the island, Ha si Tho met them as planned with two sampans off the entrance to the creek. The popular force men in the boats nodded or raised their weapons halfway in recognition. Tho signaled for one boat to take position in front of the Whaler and his boat fell in behind. The sampans churned the brown water with long shaft props powered by little gas engines, like lawnmower engines, attached to the stern.

As they entered the opening to the creek the men straightened up or leaned forward, every eye trained on the overhanging vegetation, every rifle at the ready. Moving as swiftly as they could through the bends in the creek, being funneled into the dark inner reaches of the island, Van Howe recalled his dream. *It was a nightmare, but it could become real in an instant.* Looking around, he saw his fears were well placed. Vines and greenery overhung the water. The thick growth prevented seeing much beyond the muddy banks. *It's spooky.* He wondered, *was the dream a defensive vision born out of my gut and primordial instincts? But now, as the three boats move on, every second ticking away without incident, maybe the next few seconds will be the same. Would instant follow instant without interruption?*

Going around one last bend they could see ahead to the muddy bank in front of the outpost. A few coconut logs lay half way into the water to form a crude dock. As he eased the Whaler onto the mud bank, Van Howe saw the fort sitting in a wide, open area of cut down trees, maybe as wide as a football field. The tension drained from his body. He reflected, *that wasn't so bad!*

A coconut log-corduroy walkway led from the stream bank through three rings of circular concertina wire and placements of claymore mines up to the entrance of the fort. It was a triangular construction of sandbags and mud-covered logs in the usual French design. Thick mud had been scooped from the stream and dried almost as hard as cement. A watch tower in each angle of the fort gave sentries a view of the surrounding area. Gunners could fire at cross angles with the other towers to create a barrier of bullets against an attack.

Trung si Khiem, the fort commander, a regional force platoon sergeant stood at the entrance with a big smile on his round face. "Chao. Pleased you are here," he said, sweeping his eyes across all the visitors. "We are making good progress on our outpost. Come and see. Let me offer drinks." He signaled to three soldiers with machetes. They grabbed coconuts from a pile and sliced off the tops to make drinking holes. The soldiers proudly offered the water-filled nuts to their visitors. Khiem motioned toward log seats placed under a thatched lean-to and said, "Come, we talk."

After tilting his head back to drink from the coconut Van Howe exclaimed, "Ahh, that is good! It is so good on a hot day!" He held the coconut up and smiled broadly. He thought, *It's important to show appreciation for the hospitality. I like having friendly allies in this remote post, right in VC territory.* Sang was there to interpret but he just watched. It was unnecessary to speak because Van Howe's body language reflected his pleasure.

Trung si Khiem smiled as the others followed Van Howe's example. Then his smile faded. A more serious expression emerged on his face. With Sang interpreting, he said, "We finished building the fort. We put up our defenses. We have claymore mines, barbed wire, and our mortar is sighted on likely targets." He pointed to a single 81mm mortar tube set up in the center of the fort, surrounded by a protective ring of empty wooded ammunition boxes and sand bags. Clarkson, a heavy weapons expert, stood up to get a better look and nodded his head in approval.

"When we were building the fort," continued

Khiem, "we had a full company of regional forces protecting the area. The VC did not bother us too much then – only a few rifle shots and some grenades tossed at us. We had only one soldier wounded slightly in the leg. Now we are on our own with one platoon, three machine guns and our mortar. With all the trees cut down the VC can't get too close, but at night they shoot automatic weapons and rockets."

Nodding his head slowly, Van Howe said, "You have done well, Trung si Khiem. What do you need to make a better defense?"

"We hope to have more soldiers to relieve some of our people so they can get rest. Also, we need to keep the waterway free from attack so we can get supplies. The helicopter pilots don't want to land here because the jungle is thick, and the VC could attack at any time. They say it's not worth the risk when we have a water route."

Van Howe nodded slowly and thought, *that's easy for the pilots to say. They can leave it to the ground pounders to take their chances on the creek.*

"I wonder if they have been patrolling the creek banks?" asked Bradford looking at Van Howe. Sang interpreted the question.

Khiem responded, "We sent out a squad today because we knew you were arriving. One of our men saw fresh footprints. They were in a good place for VC to ambush your boats."

They might have ambushed us, thought Van Howe. *My fears and premonitions have reasons.*

"Thank you, Khiem," replied Van Howe. "Your efforts are useful. You may have prevented an ambush. It will be good to keep up the patrols on a regular basis." After Sang interpreted, Van Howe reached out with two hands to grip Khiem's hands. They shook hands deliberately. Khiem smiled broadly and bobbed his head with the tribute to his good work.

"Amazing grace!" said Clarkson sotto voce, thinking how lucky they were.

Bradford gave him a knowing look and a nod.

Khiem asked, "I hear that you will stay a few days?"

"Yes. We plan to visit the middle hamlet and maybe set up patrols to help you," replied Van Howe.

As they stood, Khiem gestured to a large lean-to against the opposite wall and said, "You are welcome to shelter there. We have plenty of rice and dried shrimp. Please look around to see how we are ready to defend our fort."

All of the visitors nodded and said, "cam on."

As the visitors walked their gear over to the shelter, Van Howe quietly said, "Be sure to look over their rifles and the mortar and their routine. Don't be too obvious, like it's an inspection. Khiem might get offended if he thinks we don't think he's on top of things."

"No problem, LT," said Clarkson.

"Roger that," added Bradford.

"Ya know, though," said Van Howe. "Just because we had a lucky break today doesn't mean they like patrolling regularly. A lot of these outposts are known for hunkering down and letting Charlie run wild all around them. We gotta get 'em out there to subdue Mr. Charles."

"Yuh," replied Clarkson.

Bradford added, "Never know, we might catch us a Charlie too!"

EARLY THAT NIGHT, AFTER A GOOD MEAL OF RICE, dried shrimp and some kind of leafy green stuff, the Americans sat in their hammocks. Van Howe made notes on a small pad he kept in the plastic wrapper for his map. Clarkson cleaned his M16 and Bradford sorted through the few items in his small canvass pack. Sang was up in one of the towers with a soldier on lookout duty. Van Howe had asked him to talk with the fort defenders to get their views on how things were going and hear how confident they were with the security of the area.

Bradford cleared his throat. He jerked his thumb over his shoulder toward the sandbagged roofs over the inner walls of the fort. "I guess if Charlie sends any rockets our way we can duck in with the RFs," he said.

"Yeah, that sounds like a plan," replied Van Howe. "It's either that or run outside to ask Charlie to please stop shelling us,"

Clarkson looked up with a wry smile, "You looking for volunteers, LT?"

"Well, on second thought, maybe we should just

huddle in there with our buddies when we're getting shelled."

"Got my vote," said Bradford

"Affirmative on that," added Clarkson.

They all drifted away from the conversation. Bradford laid back with one leg on the ground to push his hammock in a gentle swinging motion. Clarkson sat up in his hammock, swinging and wiping oil on his rifle barrel. Van Howe pulled out a pen and started working on a letter to Cathy. He wondered, *what was she doing? I hope she is safe at home with the baby.* His mind drifted to the picture of them he had back in the hooch. Two smiling faces, mother and daughter, wide-eyed with blonde curls. *Beautiful! Will I ever see the baby's face as a child, as a woman? What will the future be?*

Bradford sat up and quietly asked, "Lt, you writing home again?"

"Yeah. Letter to my wife."

"You work on those letters a lot."

"Yeah, it's like an ongoing conversation, thousands of miles apart, a little disjointed from reality."

"Disjointed?"

"Yeah," Van Howe replied in a low voice. "I can picture her in the world back home. The world with houses, cars, streets, supermarkets, people going to work. She hasn't even seen our world." He emphasized the word "even." "Yeah, she can only imagine our jungle and paddies, different people, different ways of doing things. I can't even tell her what we're really doing. Don't want to worry her. So, I write about the family, buying stuff from PACEX, the weather, and easy stuff. Sometimes she tells me things that are going on with the news, like anti-war protests, stories about people running to Canada, The Pentagon Papers, what Nixon is saying, and, you know, like that."

"Yeah, sure."

"Talk'n 'bout writing letters, are you keeping up with your Australian sheila, Miss Benton?"

"Oh yeah, man. Not as much as you do, but I write her. Had to. She kept bugging me about that Fulbright book."

"Oh yeah. Wadya tell her?"

Bradford reached into his breast pocket and pulled out a crumpled pack of Lucky Strikes. He tapped it on the bottom and pulled a cigarette up with his lips. He flicked a flame out of his beat-up old Zippo and pulled a drag of smoke. Then he responded, "Told her I agree with Fulbright. We tend to think that might makes right. Because we have great power we think it's a virtue to get involved like this. When it isn't so easy we apply even more force to prove we are superior. We ignore opposing ideas and the realities of culture and history. That's where the arrogance comes in. We are strong enough to do it, and if we do it then it must be right."

"Yeah, it sounds like a juvenile personality disorder, like ego or vanity over wisdom," reflected Van Howe in a low voice. He pulled a panatela from a cardboard five-pack and, after carefully removing the plastic wrapper, sniffed the fresh tobacco.

Bradford nodded with a mild grimace, "Yeah, using

force is not always the best approach, like old Sun Tzu taught. The wise general knows what he's gettin' into and sometimes wins without fighting." He flicked his lighter and held the flame under Van Howe's cigar.

"Thanks for the light." Puffing out rings of blue-grey cigar smoke, Van Howe answered, "Seems to me that wisdom works in the grey areas. But then, it's hard to see everything. So, what does Fulbright say about this situation?"

"He says South Vietnam can't win now. Not enough political stability, not enough will to fight for themselves, too much corruption, not ready for democracy. He says we're like boy scouts trying to drag an old lady across a street she doesn't even want to cross."

Clarkson gave a final wipe to his gun barrel, tucked the oil cloth away in his pack, and piped up, "Hey, I know I can count on you guys when it gets tough, even if you think too much, so I'll just say this. Ya know, I actually wonder if you might make sense on some of this. I'm not sure we really know what we've got ourselves into over here or if it makes sense how we're doing it. They say the Pentagon Papers show we can't trust the big boys in D.C. and Cronkite, Mister Trustworthy, said we can't win. I used to think Cronkite just didn't know. Now I see he's right. Besides, we all know that the place is too corrupt to stand on its own. Maybe we backed a loser. I just wanna know if there's a better way to stop Communism!"

Bradford looked over at Clarkson with a smile, "Old buddy, I think you put your finger on it. Maybe we should've asked that question before we rushed in. Did we really consider our options? For one, we should've realized that the Vietnamese haven't wanted the Chinese in here for thousands of years, so if we had left them alone they would've been a barrier to Chinese aggression. Who knows? But it sure enough doesn't make sense to bomb and kill off millions of Vietnamese civilians to win their hearts and minds. Communism looks pretty tolerable compared to losing your family to a napalm strike!"

Looking at each of them in turn, Van Howe said, "Well gents, 'round and 'round we go. We're knee deep in the big muddy, as they say in Mississippi. Only it's the big Mekong. But, before we get back to reality, I wanna know, Brad, if your Australian lady asked what you're doing here if you don't think it's too smart?"

"Well, I had to explain that it's not all cut and dried when you grew up in the shadow of nuclear communism. You're busy with a career, going to college and not really getting an honest picture from politicians. I mean, we kind of slipped into this war by supporting the French, and thinking we were supporting democracy. Plus, we mistakenly thought it would be easy to hold down a third-rate power like North Vietnam. I mean, the picture wasn't clear, I had a career in the big green machine, and the American public mostly supported it all in the early stages. I didn't question it. I relied on our leaders to make the right decisions. I mean, it's easy to get caught up in it when it's your country, your army, and you're not sitting back objectively with good information.

"So, you told her that? Wha'd she say?"

"I wrote her just the other day. It'll take a while to hear from her."

"Seems like you're getting serious with her. How'd you get so deep so fast?"

Looking at the cigarette in his hand Bradford contemplated a response, "Yeah, well I guess I'm just working through the seven veils of the feminine mystique. She's worth it."

Both Clarkson and Van Howe gave him curious looks. Almost simultaneously they exclaimed, "What? What's that?"

A smile broke out on Bradford's face as he saw their surprised expressions. "Yeah, that's the seven veils of the feminine mystique. It's something I've been thinking about since I met her and decided I wanted to know her better. It brought back all my old flames and what went right or wrong in those relationships. So now, I kinda have a better approach for a special woman."

"So, what are the seven veils of…"

Just then a loud explosion hit the jungle side of the fort wall. Immediately after the blast, there was rifle fire. Soldiers fired their M16s over the walls. A mix of automatic fire and single shots answered from the tree line.

"Sounds like an RPG!" yelled Clarkson. They grabbed their weapons and bolted out of the hammocks. Clarkson and Bradford held their M16s at port arms as they ran. Van Howe had the M79 Blooper in his left hand and a bandolier of high explosive shells in the right. His .357 magnum flapped on his hip as he pounded over the ground.

They were breathing heavily by the time they hit the wall, more from the adrenaline rush than the short dash. The rifle fire slowed. Then it was quiet. Everything in the jungle held the silence, waiting for the next eruption. The defenders looked cautiously over at the tree line for muzzle flashes or signs of movement. Nothing happened. Then, with the relief of uninterrupted quiet, the creatures of the night started chirping and clattering again.

"Hit and run," pronounced Clarkson with a tone of certainty.

Van Howe opined, "Mr. Charles knows our guys don't like going out at night. So, they're free to come up and hit us, maybe get a lucky shot, probably makes our guys more scared of the dark."

"Yeah, they attack when they have the advantage, and stay low when they don't," added Clarkson.

"Well, they know how to put Sun Tzu into practice!" Bradford retorted.

"Well, tomorrow's another day." said Van Howe. "Clarkee, Brad and I will go over to Middle Hamlet to check out the PSDF. Maybe you, Sang and Tho can get some of these guys out for more patrols. A team from Tho's squad can set a good example. Maybe you can get Khiem to feel like it's good for his reputation with the district honchos."

Clarkson replied, "Sure thing LT. I ain't no sweet

talker, but between me and Sang we can get old Khiem to eat it up, or maybe like it better anyhow."

"That'll be good," replied Van Howe. "Time for me to jump in the hammock."

Both NCOs chimed in with, "Roger that."

"Chao Trung uy, Trung si nhat," said the short PSDF platoon leader, wearing a black aobaba, his head bobbing with a huge smile as he shook hands with Van Howe and Bradford. They had just arrived in Middle Hamlet, escorted by a team of Ha si Tho's troops, with arrangements to be picked up early the next day.

Van Howe thought, *we don't have Sang with us, but a few words of Vietnamese and a lot of gestures should work. Our visit is a big deal for the platoon leader here because they don't get a lot of attention. They want to show they're ready. It will be the talk of the hamlet for a while.*

The platoon leader took them to the center of the hamlet and gestured to a few log benches under a coconut palm. A young girl in a blue au dai brought a tray with bowls of rice and tea. They all used chop sticks to pull clumps of sticky rice from their bowls. Van Howe and Bradford smiled broadly and said, "Tot. Tot! It's good."

As they finished the meal, a man in a white shirt, carrying an M2 carbine came up and nodded deferentially to the platoon leader who smiled and nodded in return. When they exchanged a few words, Van Howe thought, *The platoon must be ready for inspection.*

As they approached the heavily armed assembly of men and women, Van Howe could see a quiet call to attention. When they were about ten yards away the platoon leader gave a palms-down signal with his hands and the militia immediately moved to a line of prone positions on the ground, conveniently strewn with palm fronds. Weapons were at the ready as if alert for an attack. The platoon leader gestured to the Americans inviting them to inspect the line.

Van Howe started at one end and Bradford at the other. As they passed each man or woman they looked directly at them and paused to nod or say "tot." The men were older, beyond draft age, and the women were younger, perhaps without children. They all had a look of serious determination on their faces. Their weapons were clean and well-oiled, a hodgepodge of old US World War II carbines, Thompson Sub Machine Guns, Browning Automatic Rifles, and a few M1 Garand and M14 rifles.

After completing the inspection Van Howe walked over to the platoon leader and said, "Tot. Tot lam. Very good." He said it loud enough for everyone to hear. The platoon leader smiled effusively, and they shook hands. After a brief pause Van Howe pointed to the platoon leader's ammunition belt holding short magazines of bullets. He asked, "beaucoup, beaucoup?" He then half turned and swept his hand along the line of combat poised militia.

The platoon leader nodded several times to show he understood the question: Do they have enough ammunition? He pointed at his ammunition belt and enthusiastically said, "Tot. Beaucoup."

"OK. Number one." replied Van Howe.

After dismissing the platoon, the leader escorted the two Americans around the hamlet center, occasionally nodding to a man, woman or child. He seemed to know everyone. Van Howe and Bradford followed suit, smiled and said, "Chao, Chao."

Van Howe glanced at Bradford and said, "Brad, I can still picture a talk by J.P. Vann in Can Tho. He said we should 'put a man with a rifle behind every tree.' He would like this."

Bradford replied, "Yeah, these people are ready, and they can tell what strangers might be VC."

As the sun moved lower and shadows darkened the open ground in the center of the hamlet the platoon leader paused outside a house built of thatch and wooden poles. He gestured to the Americans that they should enter and stay the night. Then he smiled and gave them a reassuring look, saying, "Cam on."

Van Howe and Bradford both replied, "Cam on lam." and entered the house.

"When we stay the night," remarked Bradford, "it shows we have confidence in their defensive capabilities."

"Yuh," replied Van Howe. "I think we can be pretty sure they will be on the alert tonight. If we went out on ambush with them it would just show we're worried. This way we honor them."

Bradford remarked, "Oh good, we can string our hammocks between these poles."

"Yeah, pretty nice place for the night. Just the same, I'm gonna keep this hunk of iron ready." He held up the .357 magnum and hefted it in his hand. Then he placed it in the top of his boot under the hammock.

After a few minutes of swinging in his hammock, Bradford said, "I hope that platoon is as good as they look."

Van Howe replied, "Yeah. I'm just gonna take a look outside for a minute."

He went to the door. It was dark outside. The night had gathered around them like a heavy cloak. A lone sentry in a black aobaba stood outside the door. A Thompson submachine gun was slung over his shoulder. Further out, in the center of the hamlet three men sat on logs with rifles cradled in their laps. He could hear the intermittent, low murmur of their voices. He figured that others were standing guard on the perimeter of the hamlet. He thought, *the militia is taking care of us. It might be a good night.*

WHEN THEY ARRIVED BACK AT THE NEW OUTPOST in late morning of the next day Clarkson and Sang greeted them with smiles and firm handshakes. They proudly reported they had persuaded Khiem to send out patrols twice a day.

Clarkson said, "Me and Sang went out with the first patrol yesterday afternoon. We got delayed with all the map reading and discussion about the direction of travel. They just weren't used to it and they weren't eager to go."

Sang chimed in, "They got more motivated once Ha si Tho volunteered to lead a combined squad of one team of his own men and one team from the outpost. He did the same today with another squad.

Clarkson added, "Oh yeah, to calm Khiem's fears about risks we agreed that the patrols would be short-two hours, and only two kilometers. That won't cover much of the territory between the new outpost and the one at the head of the island, but that might change when they get experience.

Sang chuckled a little, "The troops were happy because they didn't run into any VC. They did discover VC booby traps and were able to blow them in place by tripping the wires from a safe distance."

Bradford replied, "Maybe they'll be ready to do ambushes in a few days."

"We'll know more about their readiness when Tho returns with the afternoon patrol," supposed Van Howe. "Good work, Clarkee. Good work Sang,"

"Roger LT."

"Thanks LT."

"Ok. Brad and Clarkee, how about following up

with the outpost troops to see how well they cleaned up their gear after a patrol?

"Roger," said Bradford

The two NCOs walked off. Van Howe turned to Sang. "Hey, Sang, maybe you could tell me what you learned from talking to the troops?"

Sang's round face brightened and his eyes widened. "Yes, Trung uy. There are a few things. Most of the men are new recruits but are willing because they have been promised a regular break from outpost duty. A few have their wives with them and others want to go see their families or girlfriends. They have been trained in basic infantry tactics but need more experience. A very interesting thing is that Khiem was promoted because of his family connections to the district chief. He was an average soldier and a fairly good corporal, but he is new to being a sergeant, and commander of an outpost."

"Good job, Sang," said Van Howe. "That's good information. We'll be here for a few more days so keep talking to the soldiers. Tell them that we'll show how to make it safer for them."

Sang nodded and said, "OK."

* * *

TWO DAYS LATER VAN HOWE AND SANG WERE IN one of the corner towers talking to Khiem. They looked out at the surrounding jungle and the space cleared for the triple concertina wire surrounding the fort.

Van Howe pointed to a place where the ground

dipped, a natural avenue of attack for the Viet Cong. He said, "That would be a good place to put a few more claymore mines, Trung Si Khiem. You have already put one there, but it is a good route for the enemy to attack. Two more would protect against waves of attackers and give you a back-up."

Khiem nodded with a slight tilt of his head. "Ahh yes, Trung uy, I was planning to do that, but we had so many other tasks in building this new fort."

Van Howe simply smiled and said, "Yes, there is much to do. Our district intelligence reports more VC in this area. It would be good if you could show them a nice surprise."

Khiem laughed. "I would like to give them a good welcome! We will do it this afternoon."

Van Howe studied a thick sheet of paper in his hands, a sketch by Khiem and his mortar crew showing pre-planned targets. It showed where mortars would be fired on likely attack points. "This looks good. You have good use of your mortar, Trung si Khiem."

Just then, a shout came from the tree line. The morning patrol was returning. Ha si Tho lead the squad, followed by Clarkson and Bradford. Behind them a soldier pulled on a rope with one end attached to a prisoner's neck. A stout stick was thrust horizontally under the prisoner's armpits and his hands were tied behind his back. He struggled to keep up, half stumbling. The men in the squad walked with their chests out and gestured triumphantly to their friends on the wall of the fort. Some of them waved their rifles over their heads to signal they were returning victoriously from their mission.

Van Howe looked at Khiem, "Troi oi! What a surprise!"

Khiem smiled broadly and nodded. "Beaucoup troi oi!"

They hurried down from the tower to greet the returning squad at the gate.

"Hey LT look what we got!" exclaimed Clarkson.

"Yeah. Definitely looking good!"

Ha si Tho walked up to Van Howe with a big smile. He said in English, "Truong uy, our patrol good. We capture VC."

"Good work, Ha si Tho. You number one," said Van Howe as he shook Tho's hand vigorously. Khiem was already congratulating the returning troops.

The prisoner was on his knees facing down. Sweat stains showed on the back of his black, mud stained aobaba. Van Howe noticed he was a young man, fit-looking but tired.

All of the advisors, Khiem and Tho took seats on logs under one of the thatched lean-tos. The noonday sun was baking the mud fort and heat rose from the ground. Tho spoke in animated Vietnamese and Sang interpreted. "We patrolled between this fort and the up-island fort. Halfway along we made radio contact with a team from the other outpost. They had a patrol coming toward us. The map showed a trail leading from their position to ours. We decided to wait on the trail in ambush to see if the other team would flush out VC. It worked!"

Bradford added, "Tho reminded everybody that we needed to take prisoners, to wait for the command to fire before shooting unless we took fire."

"Yeah," said Clarkson. "These guys were great. Nobody jumped the gun. It wasn't long before this one Charlie came down the trail. He was hurryin'. Had an M2 carbine. He was looking over his shoulder like he was running from the other team. He walked right into us. Old Tho just stepped out on the trail and pointed his M16 at 'im. Charlie just stopped frozen with a shocked look on his face as our guys popped out of the bushes and surround 'im with weapons pointed at his middle. There was nowhere he could go. A couple of our guys even went to block the upper trail to make sure he didn't have any friends. He was all alone trying to outfox the other patrol. Well, we got 'im."

"This is a big deal, gents," remarked Van Howe. "You done good! District is going to like this. You guys can have the honor of calling this in. Tho, you call your people first. Looks like the district chief will have juris-diction, but our intel will be all excited. That is one of our best patrols. Tho, you number one!" Then, holding his arm out to the group, he said, "You all beaucoup number one!"

Tho beamed from ear to ear as Clarkson gave him a friendly slap on the back. The others looked at each other with big smiles as they happily shrugged off web gear and moved off to relax.

ELEVEN

The Prisoner

The prisoner squatted flat-footed in a corner of the fort, arms bound behind his back. His skin chafed where the thick hemp rope was tied to his ankle, tethering him to a post. He moved his arms and twisted his back as much as his bindings would allow. He thought, *it feels good to move a little.* His eyes faced the earth, but he could see a soldier sitting nearby on a crude wooden stool, rifle across his lap, eye burning with contempt. He thought, *my fellow countryman hates me even while I fight for his liberation.*

One of the American sergeants came over with a bowl of water. With his hands tied, the prisoner drank from the bowl like a dog, splashing water on the ground. He thought, *I must drink to survive and escape.* He raised his head from the bowl and uttered, "cam on."

The sergeant said, "Okay."

They must want to keep me alive. They won't torture me right now.

He watched them talk on their radios. The Americans gathered their packs. The Vietnamese corporal gestured with his arms and quietly gave a few orders. Some of the Vietnamese soldiers assembled. One came over and untied the rope from the pole. The prisoner was pushed through the gate. A soldier held the rope tied around his leg. With his arms still bound behind his back he stumbled along the narrow path toward the boats.

The sun had fallen halfway toward the horizon by the time the boats reached a muddy landing. Other soldiers were there with trucks and jeeps. A Vietnamese captain stood on the edge of the road and looked at him, bound and crouching in the back of the wooden sampan. As the boat was pulled up onto the muddy bank two soldiers yanked him up and pulled him over the side. He could barely keep his footing in the thick mud as he was shoved forward. He glanced at the crowd of curious bystanders. He recognized one, a sympathetic farmer and supporter of the cause. The old farmer stood still, except one of his eyes half closed in a distinct squint. The captain gestured toward a truck. The prisoner was heaved up and thrown in like a sack of coconuts.

It only took an hour to get to district town but the roads were rain washed with deep ruts and bumps. The truck jolted, lurched, and bounced most of the way. Bound as he was and unable to anticipate the next jolt as the truck bumped along, he banged again and again on the steel sides and bed of the truck. His backside and arms were sore from the punishing impacts by the time they arrived.

This truck has stopped at last, he thought. Soldiers dragged him roughly off the truck and pushed him toward a low cement building. He could see they were in a large compound. *This must be the district headquarters. It's like the descriptions of our spies.* They pushed him toward a block of cement cells with iron doors. Standing at an open cell door, they finally untied his hands and released him from the cross pole that had twisted his arms behind his back. He was hardly able to move his stretched and leaden arms.

The low sun cast a dull light through the single, high cell window as he stood rubbing and stretching his arms. A bare, unlit bulb hung from the cement ceiling on a wire. A straw mat lay on the floor at the edge of the cell, taking up half the cell's width but allowing space for a bucket and small, plastic jug of water. He thought, *I am trapped, no escape. They have me and the information from Phong carried in my head. I can't let them weaken me. I can't give them anything.*

As he squatted beside the mat, he thought, *just yesterday Phong entrusted me to carry more information to the squads. I can't let them have it!* He held both hands over his head as he swayed back and forth. He thought, *what do I know? What can I make up to fool interrogators? I know they beat information from us.*

His mind raced through the plans. *I know the*

January 1971 Plenum of the Lao Dong Party ordered an all-out attack of the south in the dry season next year. It will take place around the time the Catholic minorities celebrate Easter. Our job in the Delta is to keep the ARVN, mostly the 7th Division, occupied to prevent them from helping ARVN forces in Saigon. The NVA 1st Division, now in Cambodia, and VC regiments will be the main attack forces here. Smaller VC units will have other targets. Right now, there are regimental forces in the provinces just north and south of Ben Tre. But they might already know that. How can I fool them? They might not know about the VC base camp on the eastern edge of Ben Tre province near the South China Sea and the other local forces we have contacted to get organized and ready. How can I keep them from getting inside my head?

He pressed his hand up to his forehead, as if to keep secrets locked inside. Eventually he fell into a fitful sleep on the mat. The prison was quiet except for an occasional cough or frightened moan from the other cells and the sounds of the guards' boots on the concrete floor of the hallway.

The first sounds of early morning were the clinking and jangling of keys, footsteps, and then a clanging of bars as the cell door was thrown open. Two soldiers rushed in and pulled him up from the mat, half asleep, arms flailing. They held his hands behind his back and shoved him along the hall to a small room. There, they tied him to a chair. He sat there all alone. Time ticked on. Second followed second, minute followed minute. He thought, *I'm hungry.* His stomach growled.

Abruptly, the door opened. In walked an American captain and a Vietnamese sergeant, with the insignia of an interpreter. They sat in metal folding chairs opposite him.

The sergeant said, "I'm Sergeant Dai and this is Captain Caputo."

The prisoner looked at them with alert eyes. He squirmed in his chair and stretched his neck from side to side. Large circles of sweat had spread under his arms. The back of his black shirt was sweat-soaked in the center.

The captain asked, "Chieu Hoi?"

The prisoner recalled, *Chieu Hoi, is where the government welcomes a defector with "open arms." Some defectors are now scouts for the ARVN. Some of those defectors were captured by the VC and punished. I will not betray the cause. The government murdered my father. I will die first!* The prisoner said nothing.

The captain repeated his question more loudly, "Chieu Hoi?" After waiting a full ten seconds and getting no response he slowly and deliberately asked, "What is your name?" Again, no response. "Where are you from?" No response. "Are you VC?" The prisoner's face was like a mask without expression. He did not blink. His body remained motionless except for the slight rise and fall of shallow breathing.

The captain stood up and looked at the Vietnamese sergeant. "You try. Tell him what will happen if he doesn't cooperate." The sergeant nodded.

The prisoner thought, *this is a well-practiced routine.*

The captain frowned while shaking his head and left the room.

The sergeant leaned back in his chair and briefly stared at the prisoner. He fished under the flap of his breast pocket and pulled out a pack of Salem cigarettes. After tapping one up he offered it to the prisoner. Getting a shake of the head he put it in his own mouth and lit it with the flick of a scratched-up Zippo, one with a MACV medallion, the insignia of American advisors, on its side. The sergeant looked at it and said, "The advisors will treat you fairly." He paused, letting silence emphasize his words. The prisoner closed his eyes. Sergeant Dai scowled and leaned back in his chair.

For the next fifteen minutes Dai repeated the questions the captain had asked, but there was no response. Dai threw up his hands and emitted an exasperated "Argh." He stood up, lit another cigarette and paced the small room. After a few seconds, he stopped and looked hard at the prisoner. Then, he sat back down and said, "If you don't answer we will have to turn you over to the ARVN. If you help us we can keep you in a good place. We need some information."

The prisoner looked up and said, "I'm hungry."

Dai sat up, more alert. "We'll feed you. Then we'll talk." He stood up and rapped on the door. Two soldiers came in and removed the prisoner.

Back in the cell, the prisoner gulped water. Guards came with a bowl of rice and greens. He used the ceramic spoon to quickly shovel the rice into his mouth. After emptying the bowl, he scraped the spoon on the bottom several times but there was nothing left. He held the bowl up so sunlight from the window shined inside it. After examining the bowl, he sat down on the mat.

Within an hour he was back in the room with the captain and the sergeant sitting across the table. Dai said, "We hope you enjoyed your meal. Now tell us your name."

"Le Thai Nha." As he spoke, he thought *it is better to use my real name. There might be people here who can identify me. I will fool them with other information.*

"Where are you from?"

"Thanh Ngai."

"Are you VC?"

He thought, *I want them to work for this one. If I tell them too soon, they won't be satisfied with slow answers. I need time to think. I need to deceive them with small bits of truth and then feed them something else.* He paused. He cleared his throat. He looked down at the cement floor. He squirmed in his seat. He thought, *they already suspect I am VC because I was carrying a carbine.* He said nothing.

After repeating the question several times with no response, the captain stood and leaned forward, his face only two feet from Nha. "Tell us now. Are you VC?"

Nha nodded his head slowly looking directly at the captain. "Toi VC," he answered.

The captain stood back. He looked at Dai and said, "Good. Now we're getting somewhere!"

The captain sat down. He cleared his throat. "What were you doing when you were captured?"

"I was going to see my family. I was up west of Saigon getting training from cadre."

"Where was your training?"

"Not sure. It was in a jungle clearing where the cadre took us on a night march. It was dark. I had trouble with my footing on the rough trails. No time to see much."

"Okay," said the captain. "What is your unit?"

"I don't have a unit. I was just recruited by VC. I was a farmer. They came to my village and encouraged us to join them. Then the government soldiers came to enlist young men. I don't want the government to send me far away to fight. I had to do something. The VC said I could stay near home, so I joined them."

After hearing the interpretation, the captain leaned back in his chair. "Whoa. we've heard that before." He looked at Sergeant Dai and said, "A lot of the chieu hois say that. Villagers are caught between VC and ARVN. They just want to stay home."

Sergeant Dai nodded slowly several times. The captain smiled. Dai said, "If he is only a poor farmer why did they give him a weapon so soon? Usually they make them lookouts first until they prove themselves."

Captain Caputo sat up straight in his chair. "Well Dai, they are short of fighters. Tet knocked them back. The 9th Infantry hit them hard. They need to build up their forces. They don't have time to put recruits through long training. That might explain it."

Dai frowned slightly, "If you say so, Captain, but that was a good weapon. It was an automatic carbine with a big clip. New recruits might only get an old Chicom bolt action rifle."

Captain Caputo looked at Tang and said, "Hmm. You may have a point there, Tang."

Nha listened to them talking. He thought, *I know a little English from my training. They don't believe me. But I will keep to my story.*

Captain Caputo turned deliberately and faced the prisoner. "Where are the VC who came to your home? Where will you join them?"

Nha nodded his head. He thought, *nodding my head doesn't mean anything for those questions but it looks like I am being agreeable.* He paused. Then he answered, "The VC who came to my home are from other villages. They hide in the jungle somewhere. They told me to go home after my training and they would contact me."

"Okay," said the captain. He knocked on the door for the guards. "Take him back to his cell."

After Nha was taken away Captain Caputo turned to Sergeant Dai and asked, "What do you think?"

"Hmmm. It's possible he's a poor farmer who was pushed to join the VC. I have interrogated many VC chieu hoi who say that. It is also true that in the outlying hamlets of Ben Tre many people have bad opinions of the government because they are influenced by VC and it would be normal for him to join them. That all rings true…but."

"Go on," said Captain Caputo, with an eager tone.

"Yes. The prisoner said he was sent somewhere he does not know for training and was returning home to meet people from somewhere he does not know at some time he does not know. His story does not tell us much."

"That's true," agreed Captain Caputo. "Anything else?"

"Yes. The biggest thing is a big contradiction!" Dai said, emphasizing the word contradiction by holding out his open hand. "Look at the weapon he was carrying when captured."

"Yes, I see your point," acknowledged Caputo. "That is the part that doesn't fit."

"Yes," Dai said with conviction. "He was carrying an M2 carbine. For the VC that's a pretty good weapon when they don't have AK-47s. They wouldn't give one of those to just a new recruit. That would go to a good fighter or a leader. A new recruit would not usually be that lucky."

"Yes. Yes," said Caputo. "If he was a new recruit, he would be better off not carrying a weapon. He would not be expected to fight, and he would blend in better with other travelers."

Dai added, "There is one other thing. He is slightly older than most new recruits. Now they are getting younger people. Many of his age were wiped out by TET, or the 9th Infantry in the Speedy Express Operation. I think he's an experienced fighter or cadre and that weapon fits the picture."

Captain Caputo nodded slowly. "Right. Right. You

know a lot about how things are, Dai. You've convinced me. This guy is full of it! He's not some homesick farmer who wants to work in his paddies. He's some clever Charlie who's lying through his teeth and probably has a lot to hide! The big question is, how to get it out of 'im? He's not gonna cooperate with us so we can't hold 'im. We're gonna hav'ta give 'im to the district chief."

Dai grimaced, "Too bad for him."

Early the next morning two guards barged in to Nha's cell. They yanked him off the mat, tied his hands behind his back again, and shoved him down the hall. This time he was put into a different room. He was forced down hard on a low, wooden bench in the center of the cell. The guards took up positions on either side of the door.

Nha thought, *the American won't come today. They didn't believe me. They turned me over to the Regional Forces or the ARVN. That's bad. They abuse their prisoners. I have seen what they do. I have heard many reports too. I must be strong. I will die for the cause. Many others died to free our homeland from imperialist oppressors. Now I will too. I must bear the pain.*

The sunlight filtering through the high window grew brighter as Nha crouched on the stool breathing in the close, sticky, warm air. The soldiers stood motionless. He wondered, *how is Tu? Do my people know where I am?* His inner voice declared, *it doesn't matter if they know where I am. I am alone. My body aches to be free of these bonds. My arms are sore from being stretched and tied backwards day after day. I can feel my stomach tighten into a knot. My head throbs. They make me wait so my fear builds. Terror is the way they do things.*

Nha heard footsteps echo down the hall. They were heavy, slow, steady. A big Vietnamese sergeant came through the door. His downturned, tight lipped face was screwed into a frown. His right hand loosely held a rubber hose about half a meter long. He positioned himself in front of Nha, gripped the hose with both hands. and glared down at his victim. The seconds ticked on. With a hard, deliberate, but quiet voice he demanded, "What is your name?"

"Nha."

"Your full name."

"Le Thai Nha."

"What were you doing when you were caught?"

"I already told the American captain."

The big sergeant stepped closer and raised the hose. He placed it on the top of Nha's head. He waited. Then he tapped the hose lightly on Nha's head.

"Hold your head up," the sergeant commanded.

Nha lifted his head slightly.

The sergeant used the hose to trace a path down Nha's face, starting at his forehead, down his nose, and to his chin. "You answer to me now," said the big sergeant as he lightly tapped one end of the hose in the palm of his hand. "Now, tell me what you were doing when captured?"

"Going home."

Smack went the hose. It struck Nha across the side of his head leaving a purple whelt. He grunted.

"What were you doing, Nha?"

"I was walking on the trail to meet someone."

"Ahhh," said the big sergeant. "Who were you meeting?"

"VC fighters."

"Where were they?"

"I don't know."

Whap, went the hose. This time it struck Nha across the ear, opening the flesh, drawing blood. Nha gasped.

"Why were you meeting them?"

"I was told to join them, to go with them."

The sergeant stepped back, nodding his head slowly. He demanded, "Who told you to meet them?"

"A message was left for me."

"Hmmm," intoned the big sergeant, hefting the hose in his hands. "The American captain told me you claimed to be a newly trained VC. Are you a communist?"

"I'm not a communist."

"Then, why did you join the VC?"

"To fight the oppressive imperialists for the freedom of the south."

The sergeant tapped the hose in his hand and looked at Nha with raised eyebrows and a wry smile. He said, "That's what the communists say. You sound like a communist."

"No, no," said Nha. "We are not all communists.

Many just want to free the south no matter what Hanoi says."

"That sounds too high minded," said the sergeant. "I see the peasants around here. They want to farm their crops, or fish, and stay in their villages. They have no allegiance to communism or even the government. The only thing they like about the Americans is their money, their goods. They only want to live like their ancestors. You could live like that, but you carry a gun, a very nice gun too. So, tell me again, if you're not a communist, why did you join the VC?"

"I told you the truth."

"Tell me more," demanded the sergeant, slapping the hose in his hand.

"Alright, alright. I first joined for revenge. Diem's henchmen murdered my father. He was not a communist. He was a teacher. He spoke his mind about Diem's tyranny and they cut off his head."

"That sounds more believable," said the sergeant. "It's hard to get the truth out of you."

Nha glanced up momentarily, but then dropped his gaze to the cement floor.

The sergeant stepped forward, still holding the hose. "You were carrying an M2 carbine, a very good weapon for a new recruit. Who gave you that weapon?"

"My training cadre gave it to me after I completed their course."

"You are lying, Le Thai Nha! Around here the new recruits get old bolt action rifles, not good American carbines."

Nha said nothing and kept his head down. He hunched his shoulders as if expecting a blow from the hose.

The sergeant gestured to the two guards at the door. With a piece of rope as long as a man is tall they tied a loop around Nha's arms behind his back. Then they inserted a police baton in the loop and twisted the rope to take up the slack. With a nod from the sergeant, they made a few turns of the baton. The rope twisted and tightened around Nha's back-stretched arms and began to pull them sharply inward.

Nha gasped, "Agh!"

"Now," said the sergeant, "tell me how you had that weapon."

"I told you," said Nha, "It was given to me after training."

The sergeant nodded. One of the soldiers held Nha upright on the stool. The other twisted the baton.

Nha gasped. *I can take this pain*, he told himself, not so much from a clear thought, but from a gritty determination bursting through the pain. "Are you a VC leader?" asked the sergeant. The soldiers twisted again. The sergeant demanded, "Do you want your arms pulled out of their sockets?" He waited, but there was no response from Nha other than a grimace.

Another twist. Nha moaned loudly. "Agh!" He panted. His chest heaved.

The sergeant picked up a bucket of water and held it over Nha's face. "Tell me, VC. What unit are you with?

Where are they? Where are other units hiding?" He shouted. "Tell me!"

He tipped the bucket slowly. The soldiers jerked Nha's head back. Water poured and splashed over his face. It went up his nose. He swallowed water. He jerked against his bindings. He shook his head, sputtering. When the torrent stopped, he blinked his eyes and gasped for air.

The sergeant put the bucket on the floor. "Tell me now!" He struck with the hose. Another lump rose on the side of Nha's head. A line of blood oozed from his split ear.

Seconds passed. The sergeant stepped back. He shook his head vigorously and yelled, "Stubborn VC. Beaucoup dien cai dau!" The soldiers held Nha up on the stool. "I have another idea for you, Le Thai Nha. We'll get information from you. We will take you on a helicopter ride. You'll see how far it is to fall if you don't speak." With that he turned on his heels and left the room.

Back in his cell, Nha tried to rub his untied arms. He could barely move them. He feebly gathered thoughts from his numbed mind. *My arms hurt. My elbows are twisted. My shoulder sockets are throbbing. I know about the helicopter rides for prisoners.* He pictured himself sitting on the edge of the back seat, his arms tied behind him. *The big sergeant yells questions over the whirling sound of the long blades and the roar of the bird's engine. He slaps my face with the back of his hand. Then the soldiers shove me to the floor near the open door. The doorway looks very wide. I am help-less. They hold my head down. I can see the paddies, trees, tangled vegetation and rivers five hundred meters below. The height is dizzying. The sergeant strikes me again and again with the hose. He hollers questions. I don't answer. They shove me half way out, but they hold on to my feet. Then they pull me back. The big sergeant yells, "If you don't answer you'll go all the way!" Will they push me out?*

LE THAI TU LOOKED AT THE THIN, HUNCHED OVER farmer in disbelief. She asked, "Are you sure it was my brother?".

The farmer said, "Yes, I am sure it was your brother. I got a close look at his face. He passed close by me as I stood in the crowd. They put him in a truck with his arms tied behind his back. One of them said they would go to the district town."

"Thank you for coming quickly," she replied in a calm voice. Her inner voice said, *keep the calm mask of a squad commander on your face even when you are screaming inside. They have my brother. My little brother. He is good and kind. I have always worried about him. Now my fears have come true. What will our mother say?*

Tran Luong, who had been standing nearby, came over and stood close by Tu.

She looked in his questioning eyes and barely whispered, "They have my brother."

As his sad eyes searched her face he replied empathically, "I am sorry. It is terrible news."

She reached out to hold his open hand. "Thank you," she replied softly.

"We have people at the district town," he said. "We will find out what is happening to Nha. There must be a way to rescue him," he said, emphasizing the word must.

"He won't talk," said Tu. "He is brave and dedicated. He would rather die for the cause."

"Yes." Luong replied in a low voice, lowering his head. "He is carrying important information from Phong. No doubt it is all in his head. No paper for the enemy to see. We must find a way to help Nga. We also need to get the message again from Phong to continue Nha's mission."

Three days later Tu met Luong and two cell leaders at a safe house. They sat on low benches in a tight circle. Hoang Van Thiet, the NVA team leader, reported what he found about Nha through their spies. "Our people in the district compound say Nha is there." He paused and looked at Tu. "But, they have been interrogating him. Some torture, but he is alive. He is tired and worn down. The government soldiers talk of taking him to Ben Tre town for higher level interrogation. They suspect him of being a cadre who knows a lot. The soldiers are talking about the helicopter treatment."

Tu's facial expression stiffened and her body tensed. She placed a hand over her heart then rubbed her temples with both hands. She pictured a helicopter flying over the paddies, 500 meters high. It circled around while men inside threatened her brother. They slapped his face and demanded that he talk, pointing to the ground far below. They threatened to throw him out if he wouldn't talk. He held himself up, stared back at them, and kept his mouth shut. They slapped him again and dragged him to the open door where they forced his head out and made him look down. These images raced thru Tu's mind. She told herself, *don't imagine what would happen next.* Then, Luong's voice interrupted her thoughts.

"Maybe there's a way to save Nha," offered Luong. "We have a radio message from Chi. The fat captain from the MAT team was bragging to her about Nha's capture. He told her he had given special orders to his men to find a VC spy and they have scored a great blow to the VC. The truth is we know that they were just plain lucky to capture Nha. That captain is a sneaky, blabbering, blubber boy who will tell any story about himself to look good. I wonder what his superiors think?"

Tu's eyes widened as she looked at Luong almost with a smile. "You're getting carried away with disdain for our enemies. There must be another reason Chi sent us the message. How can we save Nha?"

"Sorry. Yes, she said the captain also bragged he had been given the honor of picking up the prisoner at district town and bringing him back in his jeep to Ben Tre for interrogation."

"Oh, that gives us a chance. They will be vulnerable," exclaimed Tu in a hopeful tone.

As Hoang Van Thiet watched Tu's face he was enthralled by every expression from sorrow and pain to inspiration and joy. He told himself, *I really like this woman. She is beautiful and has deep feelings. She likes Luong, but maybe I can impress her now. Maybe deeds can win her over.* His thoughts jumped out in words: "I will free him."

"What?" asked Luong.

Tu turned to Thiet with a surprised look on her face.

Thiet, a little surprised with his own words, stammered, "Ah, yes. I will go with my cell to ambush the captain in his jeep and free Nha."

"That is bold and dangerous," said Luong.

"There are risks," replied Thiet, "But it is direct and quick. It is worse if Nha gets to Ben Tre. We NVA soldiers are good!" he said with a glance to Luong, knowing he had upstaged Tu's other admirer. "And more than that, we accept the risks." With that he rolled up his sleeve to show a tattoo on his forearm. It said: 'Born in the north to die in the south.' "We are here to win at all costs."

"You are a brave comrade," Tu acknowledged. "If you can save Nha I will be relieved. I will be very happy. Thank you for stepping forward."

Thiet nodded saying nothing, His inner voice asked, *is it bravery or reckless courage?*

Luong cleared his throat. "We still need a plan to

get back to Phong and carry his message. It must be in person. The radio might not be enough to get all the details and a long message is vulnerable to interception by the enemy. It must be in person."

The VC talked while their host brought them a pot of tea and glass cups. After some discussion, they decided that Tu would go on the ferry to Ben Tre and meet Phong. There would be some danger if she were seen as a suspicious traveler by soldiers checking papers. To distract the soldiers, Luong's squad would harass the outpost at the head of the island. The soldiers at the ferry crossing might consider scrambling into boats to rush up there and find them. Meanwhile Thiet and his cell would stage an ambush to rescue Nha.

TWELVE

Turnabout

Captain Hoyt drove the jeep off the ferry ramp, threaded through a throng of foot passengers and pulled in front of the mobile advisory team hooch. Doc was standing by the sandbag bunker at the front with a long fork in hand, poking at some steaks sizzling on a makeshift barbeque. Hoyt smiled and remembered when the guys put that contraption together. Clarkson had a buddy at the Ben Tre compound who had used a welding torch to cut a fifty-five-gallon oil drum in half longwise and also "donated" a piece of wire mesh steel grate purloined from some motor pool equipment. Bradford and Van Howe had fashioned a cradle for the drum from metal barbed wire stakes. Doc punched some air holes in the base with a hammer and a bayonet. The whole thing made a pretty good grill. Good and smoky.

Doc stiffened up a bit, a half effort of attention, barbeque fork in hand, one eye on the steaks. "Good morning Captain Hoyt. Already back from your mission in Ben Tre?" He thought, *I better not laugh knowing what that mission might be. We all know Hoyt is attracted there on a regular basis while we're left to tend to more basic military matters.*

"Right Doc. Everything is squared away. Any trouble here?"

"All is secure and in accordance with the highest military standards." Doc chuckled and noticed that Hoyt smiled at the note of sarcasm in his voice. "Well sir, maybe not exactly according to regulations. You're just in time for a steak and eggs breakfast, Captain. How do you like 'em?"

"You go ahead, Doc. I just had a good breakfast at the mess hall – real fine sausage, bacon, muffins and fruit. I even had ice cream for breakfast. My favorite flavor, strawberry."

"It's your lucky day, boss."

"Thanks Doc," said Hoyt. "Got the mail bag too." He half raised a red nylon bag as he opened the bamboo front door. It slammed shut behind him.

Bradford was sitting at the table reading a book. Clarkson was at the stove looking under the cover of a boiling pot of potatoes and Van Howe sat opposite Bradford writing a letter.

The men looked up as Hoyt said, "What kind of crap are you reading now, Bradford?

"Sir?"

"You were reading that Fulbright peace book before. That man's an egghead and wants to go easy on the

Cong. Thinks he's smarter than the President and all the generals. You need to be reading about how we're gonna kick Charlie's butt!"

Bradford put the book down and looked at Hoyt as the others stiffened at the insult. "Well Captain, I was studyin' real hard how to whip Charlie on my last tour here with the 9th Infantry Division. Studying hard reality in the field. We did it all – patrols, ambushes, chopper assaults, large unit combat operations, out in the paddies, humping through the mud, down the jungle trails. We had one of the toughest generals in the war and there was a lot of bloodshed, a big body count. Got a Combat Infantryman Badge to prove it. But Charlie is still here, the war goes on, and the people back home are protestin' in the streets."

"Ah, okay," replied Hoyt, thinking *Bradford's got more combat experience than I'll ever get.* "I didn't mean any criticism. I respect your experience. So, what're you reading?"

As Hoyt stood looking at Bradford, the others loosened up a bit. Bradford replied, "It's The Practical Cogitator."

"The what? Cogi-who?" Everybody turned toward Bradford with curious looks.

"The Practical Cogitator. It's a was published back in 1945 as a collection of the best thoughts by important writers. One of the authors was a destroyer commander in World War II. He wanted an anthology that would fit in a soldier's tunic."

"Oh," said Hoyt with his jaw slack and mouth half

open. "Never heard of it. For an NCO, Sergeant Brad-ford, you read a lot of deep stuff."

Van Howe rolled his eyes. He was not afraid to express his awareness that Hoyt was so obtuse that he could simultaneously express his ignorance and be condescending to the very man who was providing some enlightenment. He interjected, "So Brad, how do ya like the book?"

"Well it helps to take my mind off things. It's a little more high-minded than combat and killin'. It's like a thoughtful friend for down-times."

Hoyt leaned against one of the double bunks and said, "Yeah, well I've got some good news for you men. First off, the colonel is real pleased that we captured that VC. You did a good job on that. So now the colonel wants me to go down to district town and bring the prisoner back to Ben Tre for some expert interrogation before the ARVN gets 'im. So, I'll just take the jeep down there with a couple of PFs and bring 'im back. Meanwhile, you can get ready for another operation. I want you to work with the PFs to increase surveillance around all avenues for insurgents. The intelligence guys at province think our prisoner was some kind of cadre or courier and things might be gettin' hotter. Get the self-defense force from middle hamlet and the outpost troops to step up patrols too."

Van Howe looked at the serious, unsmiling, straight faces of the NCOs. He thought, *I'll bet right now they're thinking what I 'm thinking — that Hoyt wants to do the glory job while we do all the hard work. Well, that's the*

Army for ya! We're doing the "grunt" work and that's just what we are — a couple of grunts — infantrymen in the boonies. He replied to Hoyt, "Yes sir. Have a nice trip with the prisoner."

That afternoon, after Captain Hoyt departed for district, the team was in their hooch cleaning weapons, checking ammo, changing radio batteries, reading letters and preparing for the next day's operation.

Suddenly, Clarkson's voice erupted from his bunk. He exclaimed, "Holy crap! Those lousy bums!"

The others jerked their heads around and looked at Clarkson. "What's wrong, Clarkee?" asked Doc.

"I'm reading this letter from my buddy Randall. He had a nasty run in with Army haters back home, couple 'a times. Don't people know that we're dying for 'em?"

Bradford's face was drawn into a deep frown. In a quiet, respectful tone he asked, "Wadda ya mean Clarkee?"

"Okay!" replied Clarkson. "Listen to this." He flipped the first page open and started: "This is from my long-time buddy Sergeant First Class Randall."

The benches scraped on the concrete floor as the others pulled closer to listen. Their heads leaned in toward Clarkson sitting on his bunk.

He cleared his throat, "I'll just read this part: 'I was shipped back home about two months ago. While I was at Oakland they said I had to wait a few days because the Army needed a senior NCO for temporary duty and they would get me new orders. At that point, I was just happy to be back in the U.S.A., so I didn't complain.

When I called my wife and two daughters they weren't happy about the delay, but they were relieved that I was back in the U.S.A. They said they could wait a few more days as long as they knew I was safe.'"

Clarkson looked up briefly. He continued, "'To celebrate our arrival I went to this bar in L.A. with another E7, Johnny Hill. You might know him. He's a big guy, did amateur boxing when he was younger. Well, we walked into this bar and there was a whole bunch of long-hairs with torn jeans, and sandals. We were in our uniforms because we didn't have any civvies. They were older than hippies, dressed like anti-war protestors. When we walked in they quieted down as we sat on stools across the bar. We tried to order a couple beers and this one loudmouth said 'We got a couple killers here. You lifers are murderers, baby killers.' Then the rest of them got courage and started in with 'you dirty killer, you're animals, you're crazy to go to Vietnam.' The bar tender shook his head as if to say we should leave. Johnny Hill was off his seat. His fists were clenched. There were four men and a couple of women, but I think Johnny could have beat them all to a pulp. I knew if there was any fighting we would be in trouble with the brass, so I told Johnny to 'cool it. All bad for us. We got to get out of here.' He let me pull him out of there but could have just as easily gone back and knocked them all down. It's a good thing he wanted to keep his stripes. He worked hard for them.'"

"Oh man, that hurts." exclaimed Van Howe.

"Wait," replied Clarkson. "That's not the worst of

it," He lifted the letter and started to read again: "'I had another bad experience. The special temporary duty they gave me was a burial detail. A young soldier's body had to be returned to his family in Ohio and I had orders to be the escort since I was on my way home to Pennsylvania. I was to attend the burial and comfort the family."

"After that experience in LA, I put a lot of emotion into thanking that family and showing I cared deeply. I was proud to be there for them when they got that folded flag. The next day I was in line to get on a flight back home. I was still feeling down about the young man I had escorted and his family at the funeral. This guy walks up to me. He was in a suit, about 25 years old. Seeing my uniform, he asked what kind of duty I was on. I told him I had just escorted a soldier who died in Vietnam. The guy said, 'Serves him right for being dumb enough to go to Vietnam.'"

"I felt like slugging him right there. He must have known I would be busted for that. I just stared him down like I was taking him apart with my looks. He looked hard at me. I snarled, 'You coward, bastard!' Then he flinched and hurried away. I guess he figured I was getting ready to sacrifice my stripes and beat the crap out of 'im.'"

"Makes me sick," Doc blurted. Everyone else murmured agreement.

"Yeah," interjected Bradford. "I heard some things like that. Thankfully, most of the guys I know say it didn't happen to them. Oh, there are bad things like people looking at you unfriendly-like in the airports, home town people asking how many you killed, or a lot of college kids spouting nonsense and treating you like a loser, pariah, persona non-grata. One guy who lost an arm, a stranger came up to him on the street and asked if he lost it in Vietnam. When he said 'yes' the guy says, 'serves you right for going over there.' But the worst thing is when you are out of uniform and you won't say you're a vet because too many will come down on you. We signed up to serve in good faith. People confuse that with the evils of this war. Things aren't right."

After a dark silence Van Howe spoke, "A soldier goes to lay it on the line for his country. He follows the example of his father, his grandfather and all the others who were willing to sacrifice for those at home. But now, because this is war is unpopular, people take out their hostility and frustration on vets. The politicians sent us. We're only doing our duty, but we're paying the price right here and we'll pay it again at home."

"Yeah," added Bradford. "Some of the haters feel justified morally, but I'll bet some of them feel guilty for dodging the draft and letting others go die in their place. They work that guilt into anger and blame GIs. And, there are some mindless monkeys who will join a cause to get attention and excitement when they don't even know what they're doing. It's pathetic."

"Amen to that," intoned Doc.

"Beats all," added Clarkson.

THE NEXT DAY CLARKSON AND A PF SOLDIER TOOK Van Howe, Bradford and Sang in the Boston Whaler up the Song Ham Luong to the outpost at the top of the island. They were dropped off in VC territory.

When Van Howe jumped out of the boat he said, "Thanks for the ride Clarkee. Better get back before dark." He thought, *leaving this boat here would be too big an invitation for Mr. Charles to set up a trip wire. Not nice! Boom! Sin loi Americans.*

They arrived inside the small fort and went through the usual greetings with the outpost commander. Van Howe showed a written operational order. They sat down while Sang read through the entire page.

The order said the overall mission for local and district forces was to stop VC infiltrators moving across the island and to eliminate any enemy activity in the area.

A Squad from the upper outpost was to patrol down along the Song Ham Luong and link up with a squad from the ferry crossing moving up river under the command of Ha Si Tho. The PSDF from middle hamlet were to help secure the lower part of the island and prevent infiltration toward the ferry crossing.

A squad from the new outpost on the creek was assigned to set up listening posts on the other side of the island. A platoon of Regional Forces would be deployed on river patrol boats to monitor activity on the river and to provide a reaction force if any of the listening posts detected enemy activity.

With a worried look on his face the outpost

commander said, "I understand this order. My higher ups called on the radio and said you would bring the order. We are to do everything necessary to comply."

"Thank you, Trung si," Van Howe replied. "Don't worry about us taking half your men going on patrol. We have forces standing by to help."

The commander smiled glumly and said, "Cam on, Trung uy."

While Van Howe made radio contact with Doc Jackson and Tho back at the ferry base, Bradford observed the men in the outpost preparing themselves for the operation. He knew they were not accustomed to venturing much beyond a kilometer from the relative safety of their base. He thought, *this will be an exciting departure from their routine. No doubt they feel more confident having American advisors with them. They know we can use our radio to bring all kinds of support when things get bad.*

The messages between Van Howe and Tho took a while with all the coding and decoding required. They called back and forth several times, but finally the picture was clear. Tho reported that delays with the Regional Forces would prevent his departure until the next morning.

Van Howe walked over to Bradford who was scooping sliced peaches from an olive drab colored C-ration can with the standard issue brown, plastic spoon. "Hey Brad, Good thing we brought our hammocks 'cause we're gonna be staying here tonight."

Bradford paused, plastic spoon in mid-air, "Same ol', same ol'. Just another delay in my long career."

"Roger that."

The quarter moon filtered dimly through the overcast sky. The advisors swung on their hammocks between poles holding up the thatched lean-to roof on the inside of the fort wall. Their fatigues reeked of standard Army issue bug lotion and permeated the moist night air around them.

Van Howe awoke to the muffled noise of Bradford muttering and fighting the web of his hammock. He knew from the agitated movements the nightmare was worse than usual. He thought, *Brad might toss himself to the ground? Better wake him up.*

"Brad. Brad," he whispered as he shook Bradford's shoulder.

"Agh," uttered Bradford as he opened his eyes and twisted in the netting.

"Bad one, Brad?"

"Yuh," He swung his feet to the ground and held his head between his hands.

Van Howe waited quietly as Bradford regained his composure. He reflected, *I've never asked before in all our time together, especially the long nights out in the boonies. I've seen enough, so now I'm going to ask.* "Wanna tell me?"

Bradford looked up and scrunched his face. He

pulled the crumpled pack of Luckies out of his pocket and fished one out while Van Howe flicked the flint on his Zippo.

"Well…it's about my first tour in Nam. Our division was down here in the Delta, right here in Kien Hoa Province, also in Dinh Tuong, bringing a hell storm to Charlie. There were lots of patrols, wading through the paddies, foot rot, firefights where we could hardly see the enemy. The officers put the pressure on. When firing came from a tree line we would throw everything at it- machine guns, rockets, arty, gunships, even Airforce jets. It was overkill. Didn't matter if innocent villagers were in the way."

"Yeah?" asked Van Howe.

"It wasn't just that. Most of the men were good soldiers. Good guys. There were good officers too. But a few were crazy. They bought into the general's constant demands for body count. It was the constant pressure. There was killing everywhere. The brass wanted their statistics. The senior officers always talked about it. They harangued the platoon leaders and company commanders about it all the time saying, 'You're not doing your job lieutenant. If you don't want to stay out in the field forever, sergeant, you better get more dead gooks.' PFC's were given extra beer or light duty if they brought in ears cut off dead VC. There were senior officers who would even fly around in their choppers and shoot at farmers. I mean, these were Brigade commanders, colonels who were setting this kind of example. It was madness. It was crazy."

"Yeah?"

Bradford cleared his throat. "They even called the Division commander the 'Butcher of the Delta'. He was driving it all. "

"A general?" asked Van Howe.

"Yeah. He had colonels kissing his butt and doing whatever he wanted. That's all normal for us. But it got even worse."

"Oh no," muttered Van Howe.

"One day our company got orders to check out this village over the paddies, back under the trees. A patrol had taken fire from there the day before. So, we were going there to check it out. My platoon was the lead element. This chopper with the brigade commander was flying over us and going around in circles talking to the captain on the radio. We saw there were several water buffalos out in the paddies with a bunch of young boys herding them. All of a sudden, the colonel's chopper starts flyin' over them and the door gunners are machine gunnin' the buffalos. The beasts go wild and the kids wave their arms. Then the chopper starts mowin' down the kids." He paused, took a breath and sighed audibly.

"I could see the captain was yellin' into the radio handset and pointin' at the kids like he was tryin' to get the chopper to stop shootin'. Then I see him throw down the handset and scream at the chopper which was then flyin' over the village. My platoon leader heard the colonel say over the radio the kids had weapons and he was clearing out VC."

Van Howe shook his head. "That doesn't seem real!"

"It was damn real! We got up to the place where they were all slaughtered and it was just blood and shredded bodies, boys and buffaloes. There were no weapons. Some of the kids had sticks for herding. They were maybe ten or twelve years old. Most looked dead. The paddy water was red with blood. It was awful. Then it got worse."

"Oh no…," uttered Van Howe.

"Yeah, we went deep into hell that day. The platoons split off and entered different parts of the village. First Platoon on the left. Third Platoon on the right. Our platoon, the Second, went into the center. The old man was with the First. Our first squad went ahead under Staff Sergeant Wilder while me and the lieutenant checked to see if any of the boys were still alive. As we were catchin' up to them I saw one of Wilder's men toss a grenade into a bunker. A whole lot of screaming started, and this bunch of old men, women and kids popped out of the bunker and started runnin'. Wilder's troops stopped them and made them sit in the middle of the village."

"Were there any VC in the bunker?" asked Van Howe.

"No, but the grenade killed a woman and a kid. They were probably hidin' there because of the helicopter attack in the rice paddy. The lieutenant told me to get a grip on Wilder. Don't kill any more innocent civilians. Then he walked off to link up our other squads."

Bradford paused and took a deep breath. He pulled

another Lucky Strike from his breast pocket. Van Howe flicked his Zippo. The flame met the cigarette as Bradford inhaled. He held the smoke in for a few seconds and exhaled loudly.

Van Howe asked, "Then what happened?"

Bradford took another drag and exhaled slowly, his eyes searching the night. "So, I took Wilder aside and told him to watch himself. He snarled back at me with 'They're just gooks.' That's something the brass said a lot to encourage the killing. They called it 'the mere gook rule,' meaning it was OK to kill any Vietnamese, even civilians because they were not real people. Wilder liked to think he was a tough guy and smarter than anyone else. I knew he was a problem. So, I told him I didn't want that in my platoon and I would bust him down if he didn't watch it."

Van Howe shook his head slowly. "So, did that straighten him out?"

"Not at all. I think it made him worse. I went to search the village with another squad. When I came back I saw one of Wilder's detainees was laying on the ground bleeding from the side of his head. I was enraged. I got into Wilder's face and told him he was going to pay for this. He stepped back and said, 'He ain't dead but he's lucky I didn't add him to the colonel's body count.'"

"When we got back to our base camp I did some investigating and found out what happened. One of the old men, maybe a village elder, saw the dead boys in the rice paddy. He stood up from the group of detainees and started shouting at Wilder and the other men. Wilder threatened him with his rifle. The old man backed down, but he wouldn't stop yelling and screaming. Wilder lifted his rifle and pointed it at the old man's chest and waited. The old man was indignant and distraught and kept up his harangue. Wilder butt stroked the old man who dropped like a dead bird. The lieutenant and I decided to report Wilder to the captain. He was ticked off about the incident and said he would take it up with the battalion commander. The lieutenant and I thought we had done the right thing and would finally get rid of Wilder. But we were wrong."

Bradford took a deep drag on the cigarette and exhaled quickly. "The captain told us what happened. The battalion commander said the slain villagers would be counted as dead VC in the body count. He said if the captain couldn't do his job then he would find someone who could. The captain said he was so mad at the battalion commander he said, 'It's a disgrace, sir, and I don't want to serve in a unit that murders innocent civilians.' The battalion commander told him he was dismissed. The next day he was shipped out to a desk job in Saigon. If he were a lifer it would have been the end of his career but the captain didn't care. He said he just wanted to serve his county honorably and go home. He wished us a lot of luck."

"That's hellacious, man!" said Van Howe.

"Yeah. The brass came down on me too. I was up

for Master Sergeant but never got it. They put some bad stuff in my record about being uncooperative."

Van Howe just shook his head as he looked at Bradford.

"Yeah, after that me and the lieutenant had to watch our backs all the time. We were worried Wilder might try to frag us. Most of the other men were just as shocked by the incident and thought Wilder was way too crazy. We lost some respect because we couldn't do the right thing by them. We hoped Wilder wouldn't take revenge. That part got resolved soon, though. Two weeks later Wilder stepped on a mine and his leg got blown off at the knee. We evacuated him, and he left the Nam forever."

"Bad stuff," said Van Howe. "No wonder it gives you the heebie jeebies."

"Yeah. It gets to me. The whole time was bad. I tried to keep my sanity, keep from doing anything dishonorable, and protect our men from the horror. We were part of that big, bad machine and Operation Speedy Express, the general's brainchild for massacre, murder, rape, torture, mutilation and destruction of both VC and innocent civilians. In the end 11,000 Vietnamese died but we only ever recovered 750 weapons. Either a lot of VC were unarmed or a whole lot of civilians got annihilated. What we did was bigger than My Lai and a lot worse. I hate that I was there and couldn't do much about it."

"I'm sorry Brad. It shouldn't have happened like that. No one should have to go through that."

"The thing is, most of the men hated it. They didn't want to be part of killing innocent people. But, it only took a few to make it bad, especially when they were senior officers."

THE FIRST LIGHT OF THE EMERGING TROPICAL SUN was beginning to erase the darkness as the advisors departed from the outpost with a squad of wary popular force troops. They had received a message from Tho that he and his men were moving up island to meet them.

Van Howe turned and said, "Sang, tell our guys to be alert for trip wires and traps and keep a good interval." He thought, *Sang knows the drill. These troops haven't ingrained the protective habits of keeping alert for traps and staying far enough apart so an explosion won't kill a bunch of them.*

The point man moved cautiously, looking for signs of the enemy. Frequent halts allowed them to listen and observe. When possible, they used side trails to avoid traps and snipers. Thick vegetation and streams slowed their movement.

When they passed through one open area used by farmers Bradford stopped and waited for Van Howe. He remarked sardonically, "Maybe Mr. Charles hasn't booby trapped these civilian areas."

Van Howe replied, "Ha. These people are probably their supporters."

Around 1600, on a radio call with Tho, they

exchanged map positions without code, figuring that VC might have observed their locations. That information might help Charlie to decipher the code. The squad leader motioned for his men to spread out in a loose defensive circle

Van Howe turned to Bradford. "OK, Tho's comin' to us. Better make sure these guys don't shoot 'im." He pointed to the riflemen facing in Tho's direction.

They all hunkered down and waited, some kneeling, some in the prone position, rifles pointed casually outward. Some pulled out the little C-ration packets of cigarettes and lit up, like soldiers everywhere who take every chance for a smoke break.

After a half hour, they heard the password. "Whiskey" The nearest rifleman responded, "Wine." The men lowered their weapons as Tho approached.

The leaders huddled by a fallen tree. Van Howe said, "Okay, tonight we need to set up listening posts near likely enemy travel routes. If we get their direction another unit can bag 'em in an ambush." He pointed to the map. "We can form a loose perimeter here and put out listening posts, unless you have other ideas. In the event of enemy attack, we can pull back into a tight defense. Each squad can sweep an area before moving into night position." They marked routes and locations with grease pencils and nodded.

After their business was done, Tho looked up at Van Howe and Bradford. He said, "I have some good news."

"Good. What's that?" asked Bradford.

"I'm no longer Ha Si Tho."

They looked at him with surprised grins guessing what had happened.

Tho beamed, "I'm now Trung Si Tho."

"Great!" "Congratulations on your promotion Sergeant!" replied Van Howe and Bradford in turn.

"Where's your insignia?" asked Van Howe.

"No time to get that. Trung Si Nhat Tang told me just before we left on this mission. He got word from district. The captain is going to come by with my badge of rank in a few days. He sent his congratulations and said he wants to pin it on himself, that he had been pushing for this. Tang was very happy too. He has been on my side all along."

"That's good news. It's about time," remarked Van Howe.

"Well deserved!" said Bradford.

That night, the listening posts of two or three men waited quietly. They did not smoke for fear of giving away their hiding places. Each group had a vantage point concealed by underbrush, trees, anthills or terrain where they could watch likely VC movement and call in a report to their squad leader. Van Howe, Bradford and Sang teamed up with the outpost squad leader to monitor the overall situation. As night fell the mosquitoes came out. They quietly rubbed bug repellent all over their arms, legs, necks, and faces.

Bradford whispered, "I hope the stink of this stuff doesn't give us away."

"Yeah, good thing we're downwind of the mark. Better hope they don't sneak up on us." As he said this, Van Howe imagined a team of VC creeping up and tossing a grenade. In his mind's eye he saw them stealthily crawl forward, pull the pin and toss it towards them, making sure it did not bounce back off an overhanging branch. The hand grenade landed right between them with a soft thump. The startled men could hardly see it or the shocked look on each-others' faces. What would happen next? Van Howe shook the image out of his head and focused on the moment. He thought, *I hope the listening post guys stay alert.*

They waited patiently, taking turns on watch, resting in between. During the dark of the night Van Howe thought *every sound is like an alarm. I can hear every bug, every little critter in the underbrush, anything that sounds like footsteps or whisperings of approaching VC.*

The squad leaders used radios to contact the listening posts at a predesignated time with a predesignated code each hour. Three clicks of squelch from the squad leader meant report back. Two clicks from a team meant all is well. Five clicks from anyone meant danger, alert, something is up, stand by for action. One short click followed by a long one meant enemy sighted or within hearing range.

This routine went on all night. Van Howe looked at the luminescent dial on his watch more and more as the night wore on. He thought, *the hands seem to crawl at the pace of a drunken snail. This waiting makes me impatient and being tired makes it worse. It feels like bugs are crawling all around, and the dark of the night weighs me down.*

Finally, a gray light filtered through the tree tops and underbrush. They knew they had made it through the long watch, but it was too soon to move. Enemy fighters might be on the move. If they stayed still for another hour, then unsuspecting VC might walk right in front of them. It would be a lucky coup if the listening posts could identify the direction of enemy travel and unit size so other units could spring an ambush.

Time passed. The outpost squad leader was the first to stretch his arms and sigh. Van Howe stretched a leg and luxuriated in the warming muscle movement. Soon they were all stretching and limbering cold, stiff limbs. The damp night air had tightened their bodies and numbed sore muscles. It felt good to move now, but later, when the tropical heat pulled the sweat out of them, they would welcome slow movement.

Then, the radio handset sounded an urgent message. Turning up the volume the squad leader heard: "Sleeping Tiger Six, Sleeping Tiger Six, this is Sleeping Tiger Two Five" It was the platoon sergeant from the upper outpost calling his district captain.

They all gave full attention to the call:

"This is Sleeping Tiger Six." The captain spoke in a clear, calm voice.

This is Two Five. "Incoming rounds. Mortars. We are taking rifle fire from the tree line." His urgent voice was an octave higher than usual.

Van Howe thought, *this isn't the first time the upper outpost has been attacked, but with one squad out on patrol they are shorthanded. That probably accounts for the platoon leader's alarm.*

"This is Six. Are they assaulting your position?"

"This is Two Five. Negative."

"This is Six. Return fire and use your mortar to blow them away."

"This is Two Five. Roger. Returning fire."

After a few minutes, they heard "Sleeping Tiger Two Five, this is Six. Give me a situation report."

There was a long pause. Then the handset squawked again: "This is Two Five. They stopped firing before we could mortar them. No casualties here. We will check the perimeter and report back."

"This is Six. Roger." The captain's voice sounded weary.

Van Howe reasoned *that It was another harassing attack on an outpost in a long list of harassing attacks on outposts in a long, long war where outpost defenders crouched behind barricades hoping nothing would happen, that the enemy would just go away and let them get back to their farms, their families and the resting place of their ancestors.*

"Well," said Brad looking at the squad leader. Sang interpreted, "Do you think Charles knew we had left, that they were at half strength?"

The squad leader shook his head and shrugged. With a frown on his face he said, "VC no dien cai dau."

He pointed two outstretched fingers at his eyes and said, "VC biet. VC no dien cai dau."

"I think he's right," added Van Howe. "Charles had his eyes on us when we left and knew they were at half-strength. Let's hope he isn't looking at us now."

"Right," replied Bradford as he nodded at the squad leader with a tight smile.

"Let's get our guys together and get outta here," said Van Howe. "If Charlie finds us they could be dropping mortars any time."

***

THEY MOVED TO A NEW LOCATION. THE SQUADS assembled again in a rough perimeter, rifles at the ready, on half alert. They smoked, opened C ration tins, spooned up franks and beans, or whatever else the rations contained. Some aired out their feet after a long night in damp boots. The advisors and squad leaders assembled in the middle of the circle looking at maps and pointing out routes for their next patrol.

Just then, the radio squawked. It was Tho's captain from district. He sounded excited this time. Not happy excitement. Worried excitement. Tho talked back and forth with the captain several times with a worried look spreading on his face.

Almost at the same time the two advisors got a call from Clarkson back at their hooch by the ferry crossing. He sounded worried too.

"Raging Cupid Three Five, this is Raging Cupid One Seven."

Van Howe answered, "This is Three Five"

"This is One Seven. They got Cupid Six."

"This is Three Five. Say again."

"This is Raging Cupid One Seven. Charlie ambushed the jeep with Six and the prisoner. They went off the road and Charlie took the prisoner. They took Six too. Six is a captive."

"This is Three Five. Where did they go?"

"This is One Seven. They are heading up island towards you. More later. Standby for orders from district."

Tho, Van Howe, Bradford. Sang, and the other squad leader all looked at each other, eyes wide, mouths agape, heads shaking.

With a tone of disbelief, Bradford said, "They got Hoyt?"

"Yeah. We better spread our squads out in a tactical line," responded Van Howe.

"Yeah, maybe we'll be able to cut 'em off," added Bradford.

Tho nodded.

"When we hear from district we can regroup. They're probably still figuring out what to do," declared Van Howe.

THIRTEEN

Escape

Hoang Van Thiet led his NVA cell along the narrow, winding trail through the dense under-growth. The three men passed through small clearings with a few remote, thatched houses and crossed rickety bamboo bridges over deep streams cutting through the mud and lush greenery of the island. They were heading for the road between the district town and the ferry crossing. Thiet thought, *I know a good spot on the road where we can free Nha from his captors.*

Thiet walked swiftly, eyes probing the trail, ears pricked for warning sounds, AK-47 pointed forward with a light touch on the trigger. In the back of his mind he sorted through the situation. He thought, *that stupid American captain-he told Chi everything about his prisoner. He boasted that his men had caught the prisoner. He crowed and prattled on about the prisoner being a high value VC leader. He even bragged to Chi how he would bring the prisoner in to Ben Tre. He was trying very hard to impress Chi that he was a real man. She's a good one. She wasted no time to send a message about the captain's plans.*

But look at me, he reflected. *Here I am trying to impress Tu that I am worthy of her. She is always fawning over Tran Luong. She gives me little attention. I came to her homeland from the north to help the south and she gives me little thanks.* He looked at the tattoo on his arm, further up above his trigger finger. He smiled inwardly as he read 'Born In The North To Die In The South.' *I will show her how brave we are in the north. She will admire me when I save her little brother.*

The three NVA came to the edge of the tree line near the road. Thiet pointed out over a hundred meters of paddies and said, "See, the road bends near those bushes. That is a good place for an ambush."

The other two nodded in agreement and looked soberly at the road.

"We will go over the plan again. There will be two jeeps, if our spies are correct," said Thiet. "The first will have two or more government soldiers. The second will have a driver, the American captain and Nha. Maybe one more soldier."

Thiet pointed to the man carrying an RPG launcher. "You hit the first jeep with a rocket. That will stop them dead and slow the jeep behind them." He motioned to the other man who carried an AK-47 assault rifle like Thiets's, with a thirty-round banana clip and several ammunition pouches strapped to his chest. "We will shoot the soldiers in the second jeep but not the American unless he fights. We will get Nha and the American captain and go back on this trail, for a short distance. Then we will take the middle trail and head for the safe house."

The rocket man and the rifleman nodded and grunted, "Uh huh."

"Now," said Thiet, holding up his hand, "If they have a different plan and Nha is in the first jeep, we don't want to kill him with a rocket grenade. So, I will shoot the driver of the first jeep and you rocket the second jeep. But we kill all the soldiers, save Nha, and maybe take the captain prisoner. Either way we will surprise them."

He looked each of the men in the eyes and saw the burning fire of commitment. They had all traveled a long way from the north, marching long hours, enduring the hardships of mosquitoes, mud, meager rations and pounding, blazing B-52 strikes. This was a moment when they could realize their purpose and daringly strike a blow for Hanoi. Thiet said, "We are born in the north to die in the south."

Both men brightened at the familiar slogan, lifted their weapons slightly in a quiet salute, and almost in unison said, "Born in the north to die in the south!"

With that, they advanced to the road and took positions several meters apart behind covering bushes and a paddy dike. Thiet looked down the road with his field glasses. They waited quietly, making hardly any movement. The sun was halfway to its zenith. Dark clouds were beginning to form for afternoon showers. He said, mostly to himself, "This is perfect timing. They'll want to get to Ben Tre before their noon meal. They'll be along soon."

Thiet kept watching the road. His inner voice said, *time creeps by too slowly.* His stomach grumbled. He reflected that they only had a morning meal of rice and oranges. Perhaps the quick march on the trail made him hungry again. *Are my men hungry too?* He looked over and saw they were alert.

The sun climbed slightly higher in the sky. Bright sunlight beat down on the waiting NVA fighters. They hunkered down in the weeds that afforded very little shade. Drops of sweat dripped down Thiet's neck and dampened the back of his shirt. He looked back at their route of retreat. It was a good hundred meters back to the protection of concealing trees. He reasoned, *that could be a long run if we are under fire from pursuing forces or any survivors of the ambush. There can be no survivors. We have to hit hard and run.*

Soon, the faint whining of engines reached them. Thiet saw the dust trail before he saw the two jeeps. He steadied his field glasses on a hard-baked clump of mud. He observed to himself, *I count seven men in two jeeps, four in the first, and three in the second. I can feel a surge of power in my body. All my senses are alert. I am ready.* He glanced quickly at the other two. *They appear to be ready.* The nearest man smiled fiercely.

Thiet saw the four soldiers in the first jeep slouching in their seats, rifles pointing up toward the sky, looking confident. In the second jeep, the three men were dressed differently. The driver was dressed in a government uniform. The heavy man in the back seat was in American fatigues. The third man was in the passenger seat and dressed in a very worn black aobaba. He thought, *that must be Nha!* He held up one finger for his companions and said, "We do plan one."

As the Jeeps approached the RPG man already had his weapon pointed at the likely point of ambush. The other two were ready with their AK-47s. Thiet considered, *this is more than enough firepower to stop and kill these lax troops enjoying their jeep ride.*

Thiet nodded at the man with the RPG and said, "You have the first shot. We'll follow." The rocket man nodded slightly and sighted his weapon. The Jeeps were almost upon them.

Whoosh, Blam! The rocket hit the first jeep right in the engine compartment. Shrapnel exploded into the passengers. A secondary explosion of gasoline splattered over the bodies of the four men as they were hurled from the vehicle. The Jeep careened wildly around and rested crosswise to the road. The second jeep skidded to a stop almost upon the first. Its three passengers were jolted violently and struggled to keep their seats. Before they could come to their senses and grab their weapons a burst of AK rounds stitched a bloody tattoo across the driver's chest.

The three NVA rushed onto the road pointing their weapons at the two men in the back seat of the second Jeep. The American captain dropped his M16 and raised his hands. Nha hollered loudly to his rescuers, "Tot! Tot!" He quickly grabbed the captain's M16.

Thiet pointed his AK right at the captain's chest. Thoughts raced through his head. *Should I blow him away or take him prisoner? He doesn't look fit enough to move quickly. He may delay our escape. He could have valuable intelligence. We could make an example of him. It would be good propaganda. Won't Tu be impressed if I bring back a prisoner?* He eased the tension of his trigger finger and jerked his weapon up to signal that the prisoner should get out of the vehicle. "Tie his hands," he said to the RPG man. "The others are dead."

The five men walked quickly toward the tree line. Thiet said, "I don't see pursuers. This gives time to escape!"

Under the cover of trees, they looked back for a moment at the scene of destruction. Back on the road, black smoke billowed as flames engulfed the Jeeps.

"That smoke will get attention," said Thiet. "We better move fast."

They retraced their footsteps from the morning, moving at a brisk pace. RPG man went first pointing his folding metal stock AK assault rifle up the trail, RPG launcher slung over his shoulder. The other rifleman followed, pulling the American captain along with a six-foot lead rope. Nha was next, carrying the American's M-16 rifle and bandoliers of ammunition. Thiet brought up the rear. The Vietnamese moved easily through the brush, past anthills, over logs and uneven terrain. Even Nha, who had endured the abuse of torture and poor food, was able to move better than the American captain.

"This American is not used to marching quickly," observed Nha as he glanced back at Thiet. "If he's too slow we must kill him." Nha turned toward the American and said sharply, "Di! Di!"

After a half hour, they paused and listened to the distinctive whup, whup of a helicopter. Nha tensed and pointed silently in the direction of the sound. "May bay truc thang," said Thiet as he pointed up. The Vietnamese men frowned. They all knew that airpower gave their enemies a devastating advantage. It was not hard to imagine the big iron bird sweeping over the treetops, chasing them down like dogs, and spewing machine gun bullets at them as they ran. Then, they heard a second chopper. The sound came from back at the ambush site on the road.

"They are trying to find which way we are going," said Thiet.

"Yes," replied Nha. "We don't have much time. If we keep the prisoner, we will need to hide soon." Speaking with the authority of a cadre, Nha continued, "I know what we can do. Thiet, you and I can take the prisoner to the hideout. You other two," he said, pointing to the two NVA soldiers, "You will be less of a target if you separate from us and move like pythons in the jungle. Make your way back to our base with the message that I am free and we have a prisoner."

The two NVA nodded slowly as if calculating the danger in their assignment. Nha looked at each of them and said, "There are risks either way. Those in the hideout could be given away and those on the move could be tracked. With all of the experience you have gained while traveling down the Ho Chi Minh Trail, hiding from American air attacks and infantry you know how to conceal yourselves. We can be more easily seen with the American until we can hide. You have the honor of carrying an important message to our comrades."

In salute, RPG man put his fist over his heart and said, "Born in the north to die in the south." The other NVA man grunted in assent and touched his fist to his breast.

Thiet nodded and placed his fist over his heart. The two NVA turned and walk briskly away, soon disappearing in the undergrowth.

MOST HOUSES ON THE ISLAND WERE SO CLOSE TO the water level that it was not possible to dig a deep, dry hole below the ground. Luckily, the safe house was located on a slight rise on the otherwise flat and low terrain.

Woven floor mats covered a wooden trap door under a sleeping platform, hiding a meter-and-a-half deep pit with a muddy bottom from the monsoon rains. No one in the area knew of this hideout except for a few hardcore VC. It had been built during the 1945 uprising against the French. Generations of resisters who were tortured by the government had paid for the secret with their lives.

Wooden planks made from discarded government ammunition crates kept the damp earthen walls of the cellar from collapsing. Thiet and Nha sat on small crates facing their prisoner who was slumped on a board propped above the wet, muddy floor trying not to make eye contact with his captors. Nha held a flickering tin can oil lamp up to the nametag on the captain's shirt and said "Hoyt. Your name Hoyt, captain?" he said in halting English. "This your name or you take other man's shirt?"

The captain looked at Nha. "Yes, my name," he uttered.

"Where you take me in Jeep?" Nha demanded.

"To Ben Tre."

"Where in Ben Tre?"

"The headquarters."

"What headquarters?"

"The province chief's headquarters."

"Why you take me there?"

"They want to talk to you."

Nha laughed. "You mean they torture me."

"I don't know."

Angrily Nha responded, "Yes you know! You imperialist pig. You know what they do with prisoners. Many dragged in there and few come out alive. They are butchers and assassins. You let them torture and kill my countrymen. You— you pig!"

"I don't know what they do."

Nha kicked the captain in the leg. "Then you stupid, ignorant ally of assassins and murderers!"

"No. No. I didn't murder anyone."

"You murder us all. You part of American colonial machine that aids corrupt Vietnamese tyrants to ruin our country, destroy our villages, kill my people and dishonor my ancestors. You are plague in my homeland."

The captain said nothing. His chin rested on his chest and his eyes looked down at the earth.

After pausing for a minute Nha asked, "What military plans?"

The captain looked up and shook his head slightly. "I don't have military plans."

"What your mission?"

"We help the local forces be better soldiers."

"Yes, to kill my countrymen, shell our villages and ruin our lives."

"No. No."

"Captain Hoyt, maybe you Americans believe in liberty and justice?"

"Yuh."

"Why won't you let us have liberty and justice in my country?"

"We support democracy."

"No! It corrupt government now. Before that, Diem's tyranny. Also, you not help vote we promised after we defeated the French at Dien Bien Phu."

"We want to protect you from Communism, to be free."

"Oh, freedom. The French talked of liberty, equality, and fraternity, but only for imperialists like you. We defeat them and now you here in their place. How can you be so stupid to think we can't get rid of you?"

Hoyt raised his downcast eyes only a little and replied, "We…we…"

Nha cut him off. "No captain, you lie. You need reeducation but it waste time. You are no good unless you are dead, or we make example of you. You will come with us until we decide what to do with you."

They sat quietly for a while. Nha turned and said. "Thiet, my brave comrade, thank you for rescuing me. It was a daring thing to do in the full light of day."

"It is our honor," replied Thiet. "We need you for important work." He thought, *I hope your sister appreciates it.*

"Thank you, my friend. Soon it will be dark. Then we will move. The iron birds can't see us well in the dark and the government troops fear the night. We will have to be wary of an ambush, but we can avoid the likely places. Too bad we will be moving with this stumbling American. He sounds like a water buffalo on the trail."

Thiet thought for a moment. "We can take the rope off his hands and tie it around his neck. Whenever he makes a wrong move we can choke him up. Soon he will learn to move more carefully."

Nha nodded. "Let's try that. Good idea!"

LATE THAT SAME AFTERNOON, TRAN LUONG WALKED along the road to the market at the ferry crossing. He labored under the heavy yoke of baskets full of fruit. He did not carry a weapon except for the long knife hidden in the right-side basket. He thought *Tu might run into trouble and I will help her.* Leaving her weapon behind, she had taken the early morning ferry and planned to return in the late afternoon with a message from Phong.

Luong had instructed the second in command of his squad to harass the up-island outpost. He judged from the distant racket of automatic rifle fire and explosions that they had done a good job and created the desired distraction for the government troops. Meanwhile, in his longing to protect her, he went with Tu's squad to a secluded area near the middle hamlet.

A radio message said that Tu was returning from her meeting with Phong. Tu's squad hid near the trail so they would be available in case government soldiers followed her. The squad remained back in the hideout while Luong went ahead to meet Tu. He thought, *she may be angry with me for taking this risk, but she will know that I love her.*

He mused, *will she recognize me in this disguise? I usually wear these black pajamas but not this big conical hat. These baskets make me hunch over so I do not stand as straight as usual. When she sees my face, she will surely know me.*

Luong smiled inwardly, *the government troops seem very busy. Helicopters have been whirling around for half of the day. They fly in wide circles over and over again. If they go around like angry hornets, they must be mad about something. They might be looking for my fighters who attacked the upper outpost, but even more likely, they are searching for Thiet's NVA cell.*

He wondered, *has Nha been rescued? Did they run into trouble? Did they get away? Were they just now being hounded as they run through the jungle? No. If the helicopters are still flying they haven't caught Thiet. If the government is still looking they haven't found them! Maybe Thiet was successful in freeing Nha. Tu will be joyful. Maybe Thiet and his men are only fleeing from a botched attempt. No. The hornets would not be buzzing so much to chase a few VC. They must have lost their prisoner.*

I see Tu, he observed. *Her round face framed by shining black hair looks beautiful under her conical straw hat. Her black pajamas flow attractively over her slender frame. She would not wear her white ao dai on this mission. It would attract too much attention. She must appear to be a local villager visiting a relative or looking for some special goods.*

She smiled guardedly when she first recognized him, but the smile quickly turned to a concerned frown. When they met she asked, "Luong, what are you doing here? This is dangerous!"

"I was worried about you. I will risk anything to make sure you are safe."

"Oh Luong," she replied softly and affectionately as she touched his arm. "We must go before we are suspected."

He paused, thinking, *I have two baskets full of fruit.*

If I turn around now it will look odd. I should be taking them to the market. Maybe I can say I bought them at the market. It is too much fruit to say I am buying it for myself. I will say I am buying it to share in my village. I hope no one asks what village.

Tu had already started to walk away from the market. Luong hurried to catch up with his yoke of fruit baskets. They walked about a kilometer and were passing by the far edge of the middle hamlet when Tu glanced sideways and said, "Watch! Two men walking out from the hamlet."

With a furtive glance, Luong saw them on a well-beaten side trail through a mostly open area with only a few coconut palms. The men were at least fifty yards away. Luong noted that the short one carried a Thompson submachine gun with the usual long, straight magazine full of .45-caliber ammunition. The taller man carried what appeared to be an M14 American rifle. Luong knew that it fired heavy 7.62mm NATO rounds from a twenty-round magazine and was accurate at a long range. "Keep walking. Maybe they won't notice us. They are only local defense forces."

After a tense half minute of hurried walking Tu turned and made a pretense of picking a fruit from one of Luong's baskets. In that moment, she saw one of the two hamlet defenders pointing his hand directly at her with a stabbing motion. The other man unslung his M14 and held it in one hand by his side. They turned to follow Tu and Luong.

"They follow us," said Tu in an urgent tone.

"Walk quickly. Around that bend ahead, we disappear."

"What do you mean?"

"You'll see," he said.

They reached the bend in the trail after a long fifteen seconds. Luong grabbed her hand and said, "Come with me. Hurry!"

They ran between a few palm trees, ducked and pushed through underbrush over a faint trail and were enveloped in a shaded, cave-like thicket. Fighters emerged from the surrounding shadows and greeted them in low voices. They were the part of Tu's squad that had accompanied Luong.

Looking at her comrades, Tu held a finger over her mouth and held the other hand up palm outward in the 'halt' signal. She swept both hands in front of herself and whispered, "We are being followed! Go into the shadows, but don't shoot unless they see us."

The squad quickly dispersed and blended into the deep shade. Luong and Tu laid flat behind a tree where they could see out past the lower stems of the plants. The two hamlet defenders came around the bend and stopped. They held up their hands to shade their eyes and squinted. The tall man raised the M14 rifle to port arms. They walked a few steps further down the trail and stopped again. The tall man shrugged his shoulders. The other shook his head. They looked in Luong's direction and stared hard at the undergrowth. They looked in the other direction and saw a small trail leading off into the bush. "Ahh," said the tall man. The man with the

Thompson submachine gun relaxed his grip on the weapon and nodded.

———

THE MOON WAS A BRIGHT CRESCENT DIMLY illuminating the trail ahead. The three men moved slowly along a faint trail in the undergrowth. With keen night vision and knowledge of the landscape Nha led the way. The heavy man in the middle lurched several times, clumsily bashing into bushes and trees. He groaned and gasped as he bumbled and scraped along.

Nha jerked the rope around Hoyt's neck, yanking him down to the ground where he crashed and rolled flat on his back. Nha bent down with one knee on his prisoner's chest and held a long, sharp bayonet against the fat skin of his throat. "Clumsy oaf. You make too much noise. You sound like a water buffalo in the bushes. Stop it or we slit your throat and leave you to die."

"Ughhh. Okay, okay!" gasped Hoyt, his wide eyes pouring torrents of fear.

Nha jerked Hoyt up and the three went on. They moved slowly and carefully, making sure not to snap branches or sticks or trip over ground clutter. Suddenly, Nha froze and held up his hand. They all stood stock still, peering through the darkness. Nha motioned for them to get down. They hunkered in a squatting posture as he pointed forward and then held a cupped hand to an ear.

Thiet watched Nha intently, straining to hear. He saw that the captain was listening too. His pulse quickened as he thought, *what if Hoyt yells?* He slid his hand to the long-bladed bayonet on his belt thinking, *I sharpened this yesterday. It will slit his throat quickly if he tries to alert the enemy.*

Nha turned and made a squeezing motion with his fingers as he held them to his ear, imitating someone keying a radio handset. Then he held up five fingers spread wide. He did it four times. He pointed back down the trail and made a wide sweeping motion with his arm. It was clear to Thiet that Nha had heard radio sounds and they had to skirt a unit of maybe 20 enemy.

The three men spent half the night creeping back on the trail and circumnavigating the area in a wide arc. Several times Nha lightly jerked the rope around Hoyt's neck. Each time Hoyt looked directly at Nha and quickly nodded. They paused frequently with ears pricked for any sound. Hours later they stopped to rest.

"We must be around them by now," whispered Nha. He could see Thiet's face in the faint moonlight.

Thiet quietly replied, "Yes but there might be others. They are out looking for us."

"Yes, yes. Maybe only a few at night. The soldiers in the outposts don't like to go far at night. Those we ran into must be from the ferry crossing with the advisors. We have no choice. We must go on."

"Wait, that's it," said Thiet. "If the men in the outpost are afraid to go out then we should go that way. We can go right by the outpost and steal one of their boats in the dark. We can paddle up the stream most of the way to the next safe house. Others can help us escape tomorrow across the river."

"You're right," replied Nha with whispered enthusiasm. "Let's go."

THIET AND NHA PULLED THEIR PRISONER TO THE ground at the outer perimeter of the new outpost. It was still dark, but a light grey sky and pale shadows showed that dawn was not far off. The outpost was quiet. There was no shadow of a sentry in the near tower. Nha gestured with his hand toward the stream just beyond the outer ring of barbed wire. They crouched and crept through the shadows toward the stream.

At the stream bank, they scrambled over a few coconut tree logs forming a walkway over the sucking mud. Nha pointed to one of the smaller sampans pulled up on the bank. Thiet pushed Hoyt into the middle of the boat and took a seat in the aft end. Nha grabbed the bow of the little boat and pushed it out into the stream. Too late, he saw it was tied to a flare launcher.

The night sky above them filled with the glow of the flare. Instantly, Nha jumped into the boat while exclaiming, "Troi oi! Troi oi!!" As the sampan cleared the stream bank they started to paddle furiously against the sluggish current. "Di! Di!" Nha whispered loudly in a desperate tone. "Let's go before they start shooting."

No shots were fired immediately. They heard only a

single cry of alarm from the outpost. Seconds later, it was followed by other shouts. After a full ten seconds, when the little boat had gone a short distance, Nha and Thiet heard bursts of M16 rounds zipping into the trees, the mud, and the water where they had been. Then, another burst of automatic fire sprayed nearer. A few rounds hit the little boat below the waterline.

FOURTEEN

Bloody Boat

____

Shortly after receiving the message on the capture of Captain Hoyt, the two Popular Force squads had stretched out in a line through the undergrowth. The command group and a fire support team were centered behind them, ready for action if they encountered the escaping VC and their prisoner.

"We're only covering a hundred meters with this," Van Howe observed to Bradford and Tho. "That's only a fraction of the island. They can go around us. By the time district gets its act together they'll take Hoyt and be long gone."

"You're right LT," affirmed Bradford. "Maybe we can figure where they'll go and hit 'em on the run. We could get 'em before District comes up with a plan."

Van Howe spread his map on the ground and they huddled around it. He said, "Okay, we also gotta worry about those VC that hit the upper outpost, but we do know the VC that have Hoyt won't go near the middle hamlet or the new outpost, at least not during daylight."

"Fair enough," agreed the others.

Tho added, "Yes, and we know there is a squad from the new outpost looking here during daylight." He touched the map on the other side of the island with his finger.

"Okay," said Van Howe sweeping his finger across the map. "Our best chance is going this way." He pointed to a stretch of the island offering likely escape routes.

"Looks good," agreed Bradford. "Best we can do right now."

Van Howe turned to Tho. "You lead with your squad. We'll go with the second squad. Keep in tight radio contact and be ready to change plans. Watch out for the VC squad that hit the upper outpost."

They all looked up at the sky. A distant whup, whup, whup, rolled over the treetops. Bradford pointed skyward and said, "They're searching."

"Too bad they can't see everything," answered Van Howe. "They may flush our quarry or make 'em hide. If those Charlies had the guts to attack on the road in broad daylight, they won't scare easily and they ain't dumb."

AT FIRST THE TWO SQUADS MOVED SWIFTLY. As they approached the hunting area they deliberately slowed down to watch and listen. They moved off trails and crept through thick vegetation to uncover hiding spots in remote areas. At times, they broke up into fire teams or smaller sets of two or three men, always knowing where the others were, ready to support them. They frequently paused at length in one spot and then regrouped. They listened, watched and waited.

District headquarters issued orders that changed little. They would send regional forces to block off the road to the ferry crossing so the fleeing VC couldn't double back in that direction. River patrol boats were deployed to watch the river banks and the head of the island. Middle hamlet defense forces watched their home area. A squad from the new outpost searched around their base.

It was hot work. Bradford adjusted the sweat rag around his neck and said, "It'll be tough for those Charlies to sneak through with Hoyt slowing 'em down."

Van Howe, canteen in hand, replied, "This is their turf. They know places we don't. If Hoyt's valuable, they'll keep 'im alive. Good propaganda."

The helicopters kept circling overhead. The radio traffic buzzed regular updates on troop movements, house searches, helicopter searches, patrol boat positions, suspected enemy areas and negative results. All day long it was negative results. The new outpost squad searched several houses of suspected VC sympathizers, but they found nothing. The most positive negative report was that no one had found Hoyt's body.

At one point in the late afternoon, the whole

operation seemed to grind to a halt. The squads hunkered down in a loose defensive circle, followed the radio reports, and awaited orders from district. Van Howe sat leaning against a coconut log and watching Bradford light up a Lucky Strike with his old Zippo. "Hey," he said, "you never did tell me about the seven veils of the feminine mystique. What is that?"

Bradford pulled a long drag and slowly blew out the smoke, "Ooh. That got your attention, did it?"

"How could it not with veils and feminine mystique and all that about your new lady friend? So, what's it all about?"

"Well, it's about how you treat a woman like they want to be treated. Or, what makes you worth her attention."

"So, it's not just about love?"

"Well, sure as shoot'n she won't love you if you don't get it. Not for long anyhow."

"You got my attention, so lay it on me."

"Right, so the first three veils are basic. A woman needs food and shelter. She needs a safe place to live, money, and hope for the future. Worries get in the way of love."

"Makes sense."

"Then there's the interpersonal stuff— friendship, partnership, belonging, love— a deep, personal connection."

"So, that's where the love comes in," remarked Van Howe.

"Sure, it's a high point, but it can get eroded away. That's why there are seven veils."

"Now, that does sound more like a mystery," allowed Van Howe. "What are the other magic ingredients?"

With a slight chuckle Bradford said, "The fourth thing is respect. She has to feel valued. You know, recognition or status. If women don't have a strong role in the community something is missing."

"Yeah. A lot of roles keep women down," agreed Van Howe.

"Right. You gotta see what's really going on, not be blind to the truth."

'Okay," said Van Howe. "This is gettin' interesting."

"Oh yeah, it gets fascinating." Bradford pulled the canteen out of his pack, slowly unscrewed the cap and said, "Fifth is self-respect. The kind that gives a woman self-confidence like she can handle things or be good at something. The kind that makes her an independent, strong person." He tipped up his canteen and took a swallow of water.

"Oh. That wouldn't work in some places. Actually, a lot of places."

"Right," said Bradford. "Can't keep her in the kitchen, taking care of the kids, doing the laundry, all those traditional things. Look at the woman's lib movement we have now."

"Okay. I can see that. What's the sixth veil?"

"Can't wait to find out?" asked Bradford with a playful grin.

"Hey, as far as I'm concerned the only thing that could distract me is a visit from Mr. Charles."

"Alright. The sixth veil is achievement. If she feels good about an accomplishment that's appreciated by anybody around her, including you, especially if she is interested in you. She wants your acknowledgement of her special talent and good deeds."

"Whoa. I don't know how your Australian lady can resist you."

"Well, like everything else, it's easier said than done. I'm pretty good at stepping on my own foot."

"Well yeah Brad, but I'm pretty impressed that you figured this out."

"Thanks, LT. 'preciate that. Guess I made enough mistakes. I had to figure out what's right. Got some ideas from books too."

"Good. What's the seventh veil?"

Bradford sat still. His eyes narrowed slightly as if he were looking inward to pull out a deep thought. "The seventh veil is purpose. Meaning. This's when a woman feels she is part of something bigger or higher than she is. She serves a higher purpose or finds spiritual significance. Maybe she feels like she connects with the cosmos or is near heaven."

"Yeah. That's good. So, if you relate to her like that you have a serious connection. Could be ultimate love, or something."

"Right."

Van Howe was quiet for a moment, as if taking it all in. "But, this could be for men too, right?"

"Yeah, but it's easier for men. Fewer barriers from society. With my special woman I want to make sure I connect on all levels."

Van Howe scratched his chin, "So, we need to give it more definite care with women?"

"Right. If she ain't happy, you won't be either, unless you're trying to get rid of her."

"Thanks for the wisdom. You may be the Sun Tzu of love!""

"Ha, that's a bit much."

"Yeah, but it's rings true."

"Sure. Yeah. Maybe I'll write a book about it someday."

As the sun went down on a long day of futile searching, the district chief declared the prey must be laying low in a well camouflaged hideout. He predicted they would try to move at night. All units were ordered to maintain their positions and continue to wait for signs of their quarry.

Tho organized the night defense. Initially, he pulled the two squads into a loose perimeter that covered as wide an area as he dared. He reflected on his work: *We are spread out too far. Hard to defend. Attackers could chew us up. We are hunting for our prey, but we could be the prey. They may know where we are now. We will make it harder for them.*

In the fading light of day Tho huddled with Van Howe, Bradford and Sang. In a quiet voice he said, "If someone is watching us they will see our outer positions and make plans. When it gets darker we will pull into a tighter perimeter for better defense."

Van Howe replied, "Good plan, Tho."

"Cam on, Trung uy. But, we can only dig in a little. Too much noise and too wet. Just use available cover."

"Right. I'll preplan some arty. Oh yeah, maybe Trung si Sang can team with you for the night. Easier radio talk."

"Ok, Trung uy."

Tho went off to organize the men. Van Howe searched his map in the fading light to mark artillery targets on likely enemy approaches. Then he gave Bradford the coordinates. *If I'm hit, he thought, Brad could save us all. Our channels can get arty faster than Tho's.*

Bradford stretched his arms and flexed his shoulders. "Ahh, that feels good. Too much sitting still, all tensed up."

"Yeah," uttered Van Howe. "Mr. Charles must've found a good place to hide while we're out here on alert. Now we get another night of fun with the mosquitoes."

"Well LT, look at the bright side. You already stink to high heaven with bug dope so you're ready for another night. Plus, now you got a day of sweat on you to keep the bugs away."

Van Howe looked glumly at Bradford, his right eyebrow raised. "You don't smell too good yourself." He settled down behind a coconut log and said, "Since you're so full of it you can take the first watch while I take a little snooze."

Bradford rocked his head from side to side and

grinned. He twisted around and laid prone under some brush and looked out into the deepening shadows blanketing the terrain. He remarked, "Hey LT, it would be nice if I could see something out there."

"Better listen good, then," retorted Van Howe in a fading voice, lying on his back and drifting off to sleep.

The long night wore on. Watches were two hours on, two hours off. Bradford shook Van Howe's shoulder and whispered "Your turn, LT."

Van Howe grunted "Uh huh." They swapped positions. This went on all through the night.

One time, when he was getting off watch and sinking his body into the ground Van Howe thought momentarily of Cathy and their baby. *Was that cute little baby in a crib right now? Were they nestled together in the same bed, snug and secure under cover from the surrounding night? They're on the other side of the world and I'm here crawling around in this jungle looking for Charlie. Man, I'm tired.*

On his next shift, Van Howe peered out into the gloom and saw the shadows evaporating in the pale light of dawn. His senses perked up with anticipation. His inner voice said *sharpen up! This is the time when escaping prey might make a desperate rush for shelter. They might abandon caution in a last-ditch effort to escape.* Suddenly, he heard a distant volley of shots. It sounded like automatic M16 fire from the new outpost. He thought, *somethin's up!*

"Brad, Brad," Van Howe whispered sharply. "Wake up."

"What's that?" asked Bradford.

"Rock and roll from the new outpost. Keep a sharp eye. They may run this way. That VC squad may be trying to reach 'em too."

"They might run into us," remarked Bradford as he lifted his M16 and laid prone a few feet apart from Van Howe."

"Yeah. Don't you wish?"

The two men looked intently out through the brush. The sky brightened. Shapes became clearer.

The radio, leaning on a bush between them, hissed and chattered. Picking up the handset, Van Howe heard Tho and Sang who were on the other side of their perimeter.

He answered, "This is Raging Cupid Three Five."

"Raging Cupid Three Five, this is Fighting Tiger One Seven. New outpost reports a trip flare was set off near their boats. Intruders made off with a sampan. Shots were fired but they can see no bodies. They will send a team to look."

"This is Three Five. It's daylight. We can go to the fort. Maybe we can track the VC."

"This is One Seven. Roger. My squad will lead out."

"This is Three Five. Roger Fighting Tiger. We will follow with the other squad. Over."

"This is Fighting Tiger One Seven, out."

THEY HURRIED TOWARD THE NEW OUTPOST, THO'S

squad in the lead. Van Howe's eyes scanned the ground and bushes for trip wires and punji pits. He followed right behind Bradford, keeping the usual interval.

"Hey LT, Tho's guys are moving fast. They want some action after sitting around for two nights."

"Yeah, and they're real pleased they got the word first through their channels. But watch out, Charlie could be monitoring our radios. Could ambush us."

Bradford carried the radio, handset clipped on the back. A voice called: "Raging Cupid Three Five, Raging Cupid Three Five, this is Fighting Tiger One Seven."

Van Howe grabbed the handset and replied, "This is Raging Cupid Three Five."

Sang's voice came over the radio, "We are aiming one click upstream of the fort. Might intercept target. Maybe pick up signs there."

"This is Three Five. Roger One Seven. We will move to cover your right flank. Victor Charles squad may approach from up island. If Target passes your intercept point, we can do a second intercept."

"This is One Seven. Roger. Out."

"I heard it all," said Brad. "Good plan. If Tho doesn't nail 'em, we should have 'em bracketed."

"Roger," uttered Van Howe. Even in the cool morning air sweat was beading on the back of his neck. In the back of his mind he noted, *the men in the squad are keeping a good interval. This is good. If one of them hits a booby trap we won't all get blown away. They're breathing heavily from the quick pace. We'll be there soon.*

Bradford stopped a few paces away and turned toward Van Howe. "Sang's calling again."

Van Howe squeezed the talk button, "This is Three Five. Over."

"This is One Seven. Found the stolen sampan. No one here. Footprints lead away on the other side of the canal. We will follow. Over."

"Roger," replied Van Howe. "We will cross up stream to cover your flank and cut off the target. Over."

"This is One Seven. Roger. Out."

Van Howe's mind raced. He thought, *I hope that stream isn't too deep up there. Don't want a booby-trapped bridge in Charlie country. When we crossed a deep stream, up in the Huu Dinh, Brad dropped his rifle in the water. Maybe we can do the Jungle School rope trick.*

As if reading Van Howe's mind Bradford said, "Good thing our guys have a rope."

"Yuh, the old Panama rope trick." Van Howe pictured the stream crossing. *Too deep to wade. Scary for the non-swimmers. A good swimmer could take the rope across for the others to slide across on it. Not that easy, but it really does work if you keep your balance.*

The stream was deep, but only a couple of boat lengths wide. They spread out along the bank to cover the swimmer. After he got across, a few men pulled the rope tight and tied it to a tree. Most got across. One guy panicked, almost across on the rope, started wobbling and fell in with a splash. They used a bamboo stick to pull him out sputtering, dripping wet and embarrassed. The others didn't razz him. They were too busy searching the thick vegetation, trying to find a way through. Gunshots popped not too far away.

Bradford cocked an ear toward the clatter of rifle shots. "That's an AK," he pronounced. Then he held up his index finger. "That's an M16. No! That's a lot of M16s."

The radio barked. "This is Fighting Tiger One Seven. We caught 'em. Only one firing. We'll take em. Hold our flank. Over."

"This is Three Five. Roger. Good copy. Over."

"One Seven. Roger. Out."

Bradford said, "He was pretty quick on the horn. Must be a firefight."

They listened to the exchange of rifle fire. The AK shots were mostly single, but sometimes rapid. M16s fired on full-automatic, a chorus of blazing bullets. The AK kept up a response but the deafening clatter of the M16s dominated.

Leaving the second squad to cover the flank, Van Howe and Bradford went to link up with Tho. Bradford stopped short on the narrow trail and turned his head to listen. "Hey, no more shootin'!" he exclaimed.

"Yuh," uttered Van Howe. "Let's hurry!"

They entered a small clearing and saw Tho kneeling by a man laying against a Tree. "It's Captain Hoyt," said Bradford.

Hoyt looked up with a feeble smile. He choked out, "Thank God you're here! I'm beat. They dragged me with a rope."

Van Howe looked at the bedraggled figure and said, "Take it easy boss. We'll get you back."

Captain Hoyt croaked, "Tho saved me." He put his hand on Thos's arm. "Thanks, Tho. Cam on. Cam on."

Tho responded, "It is an honor. My men are good."

"Yes," Hoyt agreed. Looking up at Van Howe, he said, "They kept him busy." He pointed to the battered figure lying a few meters away. "He was ducking bullets and forgot to kill me."

Bradford walked over to the body of the lean man in muddy, black pajamas. He looked worn and scarred. A well-oiled AK-47, still smoking, lay in front of him. Bradford crouched down and peered at the tattoo on the dead man's arm. He pointed at it and exclaimed, "This says, 'Born in the north to die in the south' in Vietnamese. I recognize it."

Hoyt sat up. "He was a brave man. When you were closing in on us, I think he told Nha he could escape better alone. He said he would use me as a hostage or kill me. He pointed to that tattoo on his arm ad told Nha to go."

"He's NVA," said Tho. "They come down here to reinforce the local VC. The VC lost a lot during TET in 1968. He's our enemy, but a brave man."

"Now we can get you back Captain Hoyt," said Van Howe. "We'll give you some first aid and then Doc can look you over and we can get you some hot chow. We'll call Clarkee and have them bring the Whaler around. It oughta be pretty safe right now."

Tho added, "My men can go to the new outpost

and take boats back. It's not far." With a gesture of his hand and a nod he signaled his men to carry the NVA's body and also assist Captain Hoyt. Then he turned and strode off across the clearing toward a small bridge where the trail crossed a side stream to the main canal.

Following the squad behind Tho, Van Howe looked forward and saw Tho stop and turn. Tho looked back at his men and his allies and smiled. Then he turned and grabbed one of the handrails on the little bridge. That was the last any of them saw Tho alive.

Blam! It was a sharp blast. Van Howe saw Tho crumple down over the wooden plank floor of the bridge. He called out, "Tho! Tho!"

They ran up to the bridge. Bradford yelled, "Don't go on it! Check it! There could be more."

After carefully looking all around the bridge they pulled Tho's body off. He almost looked like he was sleeping, except for the small holes where flechettes had penetrated his forehead and torso. His body was limp. A blood-red stain spread over his back.

The soldiers at the fort were visibly stricken when they saw Tho's body. He was one of their most admired leaders. Some said he was too good a fighter to die. Others said he was too careful to be caught by a common VC trick. There was conjecture he was so elated by his squad's success that he let down his guard. His death was a gut-wrenching, mournful blow to them all.

Trung si Khiem, the outpost commander, walked up

to Captain Hoyt. "Dai uy, I am glad you have been saved. It is terrible to lose Tho."

"Thank you. – I am sorry we lost Tho."

"Yes, Dai uy. He was number one! While you wait for your boat it would be good if Trung uy Van Howe takes Tho's body back in one of our boats. This will show his family we are deeply sorry for their loss. It will also show that Americans respect him. It will honor Tho."

"Yes, I want to do that," said Van Howe as Hoyt looked over at him. "Tho was one of the best. I liked him a lot. Brad can stay here to make sure you are okay for the ride back."

IT WAS A LARGE SAMPAN. TWO OF THO'S SQUAD members were in the bow. Tho's body lay on floorboards over the bilge. Van Howe and another squad member slumped opposite each other midships on the floorboards, leaning against the gunwales. A man in the stern steered with the long motor shaft sticking out behind the boat.

The boat wound its way down the stream from the outpost to the river. Van Howe looked at the thick vegetation crowding the riverbank and numbly thought, *after all this it must not be dangerous.* He looked down at the M16 laying across his lap, not in the usual ready position. *Mr. Charles is probably up island, anyway,* he hoped.

The boat vibrated gently with the beat of the motor as it plowed through the muddy water. Van Howe mused, *it was made to carry produce and livestock to the market. Now it has a somber mission. Now my friend, a good man, and a good soldier, lies dead on the floorboards, bleeding out from his wounds, turning the bilge water red.*

The little boat finally reached the mouth of the canal where it met the larger waterway. It pulled away from the clawing overgrowth on the banks of the stream and pushed out into the flow of the river. The men in the bow held their rifles more loosely and eased themselves against the thwarts. Van Howe thought, *now we are safer — away from the darkness and death of the jungle. Tho lies there after leading one last mission. He was victorious, but that was not enough for him to escape the clawing dragons of war.*

Van Howe gazed out across the water to the opposite river bank but at times his eyes were drawn to Tho's limp, lifeless body still bleeding across the floorboards. *How can there be so much blood?* He thought. *How can he bleed so long?*

He remembered Tho's family. Father, mother, farmers in the middle hamlet. Tho's wife, one son, one daughter. *Sometimes, they stayed in the popular force building near our hooch. Where would they be today? My stomach is tight. It's the thought of seeing them, having to tell them the bad news. How will I do it?*

Van Howe realized, *someone at the new outpost would radio a report. The word will get out. Tho's family might be at the boat landing. They might be waiting and wailing when the boat arrives. How will I console them? What if the roles were changed? A brief moment, an irrevocable moment makes a lifetime of difference.*

The familiar little voice in Van Howe's head said. *How did this happen? Why is Tho bleeding here in the bottom of the boat? He didn't die in the firefight. He could have died in the firefight. But he didn't. He died going home, crossing the bridge. An ordinary bridge. Anyone could have been first. It could have been his point man. It could have been anyone else. It could have been me. No, Tho was confident and out front when it happened. He was happy to be done with battle for the day. It shouldn't be this way.*

I'm in a morbid mood, thought Van How. *I'm angry. I liked Tho. He was a friend. He was a good man. He didn't deserve it. But, to honor him, to carry on, I have to pull myself together. It won't be good if I can't keep it together. Tho would do that. He would be compassionate, but he would be tough enough to carry on.*

FIFTEEN

Freedom Lovers

Tu and Luong approached the safe house, after travelling all the way up island. They saw Thiet's two cell members sitting outside, looking bedraggled with muddy, ripped clothing. *Oh good,* Tu thought, joyfully, *They have escaped the government search.*

Looking at the rocket man she asked, "Where are Thiet and Nha?" Before he could answer she glimpsed a figure in the doorway of the house and heard a familiar voice call her name.

Rushing over to hug her brother Tu gleefully cried out, "Nha, Nha, I am so glad to see you. I was so worried. We were all worried. Thiet did it. He freed you!"

"I am grateful," Nha replied in a mournful tone, head bowed, eyes looking downward.

Before Nha could say another word, Luong clasped his hands on Nha's shoulders and said, "What's wrong, Nha?"

"If it wasn't for Thiet, I wouldn't be here. But I have bad news. Thiet didn't make it back."

"What do you mean?" asked Tu.

"He covered my escape. He may be dead or captured."

Luong held his hands open and said, "Wait. Slow down. Start again."

Nha sat on a stool. He held one hand to his temple and then lowered it, palm out. Slowly and deliberately, he said, "Thiet and his men ambushed the government jeeps. They rescued me and captured the American captain, Hoyt, the advisor. We hid the first day and then we took off at night. We had to go around government troops in the jungle. The prisoner slowed us down, so we thought it would be better to steal a sampan at the new outpost. A flare went off and the soldiers fired at us. Some of the bullets hit the sampan and we had to plug them with bits of cloth but that didn't work for long and we had to leave the boat." Nha paused and looked down at the hard packed, dirt floor.

Tu said, "Troi oi! A difficult escape. So many obstacles."

"What happened then?" asked Luong.

"Then the government soldiers found us. They had many M16s. The bullets were hitting all around us. We hugged the ground and pulled the prisoner down into the mud. We only had Thiet's AK and my stolen M16, but we could hardly get our heads up to shoot. We fired off a few magazines over the mud bank and that kept them away for a while. We knew it was impossible to get away."

Luong uttered, "Agh. Very bad. Very bad."

Nha continued, "Then Thiet said, 'You go, you go, I will hold them. You are important for our cause. Don't take the captain. Too slow. If I can't trade him I will kill him.' "

Nha looked up, "I told him, you are brave Thiet. He just pointed to his tattoo and said 'Born in the north to die in the south.' I don't think he had a chance to trade the captain. The rifle fire got hotter. I could hear his AK put out angry bursts. And then it stopped."

"Oh, very bad," whispered Tu. "He was brave. He was very brave. We will avenge his death with the uprising."

"Yes," replied Nha. "He is a hero. He sacrificed his life so we can do our work for the big attack."

"We must not let him down," declared Tu emphatically.

Luong added, "I agree."

"I feared they would torture you in Ben Tre," revealed Tu with a pained look on her face.

"I was very worried about that." answered Nha, in a low, raspy voice. "I imagined many beatings and broken bones. I dreaded they would hook my soft parts up to field telephone wires and crank to shock me. That is painful. Most of all, I feared hanging upside down out of a helicopter with them threatening to let me fall. But I was determined not to tell them anything."

"I am very glad that didn't happen," said Luong. "I am thankful you are safe."

Tu looked at Nha and Luong with relief written on her face.

"Now we must regroup and plan our next moves," said Luong. "You each have information from Phong, so let's start with that.

Tu said, "Nha, you start because you had the first briefing from Phong. I will add what I learned."

Nha took a sip of tea. Then he placed his arms on the table and looked across at them. He said, "Right now the NVA 1st Division is ready to come over the border. The 514th VC Regiment is up in Dinh Tuong Province near My Tho, right under the noses of our enemies. There is a base in Giong Trom and one in Thanh Phu near the South China Sea. There is also one at Dong Thap in the Plain of Reeds. A regiment will move into Vinh Long. There will be others too. Phong said Ben Tre has always been seen as a leading revolutionary province so it will be critical to liberating the Delta."

He paused, then added, "Another part of this is the need for heavy attacks in the north. So, they will attack in the far north, and the central highlands, and around Saigon while we push up from here."

"It will be massive," said Luong.

"Massive," echoed Nha. He continued, "Because we are near Ben Tre City, Phong wants us to coordinate with VC in other districts of Ben Tre province. Also, we are to make ourselves known to the regiments around the province. Phong will buy more weapons and munitions from corrupt government officials in supply depots. The Americans give many supplies so they can siphon them off and make a good profit."

"Ha," Tu laughed. "We will kill them with their own weapons."

"We've been doing that for years," noted Luong.

Tu nodded and said, "In a month or two all VC squads and platoons are to start small scale attacks on outposts, roads, and government supply areas. That will keep them busy. If they suspect an attack they will think that is all there is, and they will be off guard for the big attack. Then, the big offensive will be launched."

"We have much work to do," said Luong. "We must split up to get started."

"Did Phong give any instructions on how we should do it?" asked Nha.

"No," replied Tu. "I think Luong is right. Each squad must do its part. Nha, you can go with Luong to the east, and I will go to the south. We should be able to make our contacts and meet back here in one month. Then we can be here for the attacks. Do we all agree?" They all nodded with serious expressions.

Luong said, "Finally, we will be a part of something big to liberate the south."

"Yes," said Tu, "and I have proof that the people in Hanoi know how we are fighting the imperialist invaders and their Saigon puppets. Look, Phong gave me this magazine called, 'Vietnam.' It was printed in Hanoi in 1969 and came on a long trip down the trail.

It tells about Ba Vang, a cadre in Ben Tre province. They even have her picture saying she is a model cadre. It also tells about popular uprisings, how the U.S. war of aggression is faltering, how workers in the north are growing rice and making clothing for us in the south and how other countries, like Cuba, support our revolution. It repeats Ho's appeal: 'As long as there is a single aggressor in our country, we must fight on to wipe him out.'"

"We are part of a glorious effort," said Luong. "It is good they know about us all the way down here."

"Yes. It is very encouraging," said Tu. "There is this too: Phong gave me this newspaper that arrived after two years." She held up a tattered, dirt-stained copy of a newspaper.

They gathered closer to look at it. Nha said, "Yes. It looks like it passed through many hands. I see it's called the Vietnam Courier. The date is May 12, 1969."

Luong added, "I was in My Tho just before then for many attacks on the enemy."

"Yes," said Tu. "They talk about that in this paper. I'll read it to you. '…the regional troops and guerillas of My Tho province, some 60 km Southwest of Saigon, mounted 70 actions, inflicting on the enemy 850 casualties among them 250 GIs, destroying 37 vehicles and 6 artillery pieces and grounding 14 helicopters and planes.' There is more. You can see for yourselves."

"Ah," said Nha. "It reports the actions of my unit in Ben Tre, where we fought and killed hundreds of the puppet troops."

"This is good," said Tu. "We can show these to other squads. It will fill them with courage."

"I'm ready," proclaimed Nha.

THAT NIGHT, THE COUPLE WALKED IN DRENCHING moonlight. It filtered down through the treetops into a small clearing near the safe house. A pleasant breeze blew in from the big river and gently swayed the palms.

Tu stopped and looked into Luong's eyes. "Tomorrow we must go. We will be apart again."

He looked straight at her with a long, loving look and whispered, "I will miss you. I am afraid I will not see you again."

"Oh, I don't want that to happen," she said.

"I think you know I have feelings for you," Luong replied in a soft tone.

"I think we have feelings for each other but we haven't talked about it," she said with a warm smile.

"Yes. I have been afraid to admit my feelings because it will hurt if I lose you."

"I don't think that will save me or you", she replied. "If we tell our feelings maybe that will keep us safer. We will be more cautious so we can return to each other."

"Yes," he said. "I want you to know that I want us to return to each other." He held her hand. "I want to be together…always. I love you."

"And I love you," she replied and embraced him closely.

They held their embrace for a long moment.

Luong lamented, "Why do we have to be in this war? Why can't we live a peaceful life? The tyrants and the generals are greedy for power and control and they force us into this hell."

"It has been like this for a long time," Tu replied. "We have no choice, no other way to go but revolution. We must free ourselves and our land so we can live and love and prosper."

Luong took a deep breath. "Yes, we must do that. I will fight for freedom so I will be free to love you."

She smiled. "We will fight for each other, and our homeland. But, I am sad we must part for now."

He held her hand again between both of his hands, feeling the warmth and gentle touch. He looked deeply into her eyes admiring her strong but gentle soul and knowing that after tomorrow they may never see each other again, ever.

SIXTEEN

This Whole War

"Glad to see you're ok Henry," said Captain Baker, looking up from his desk.

Baker sat back in his swivel chair, papers neatly piled on his desk, a stack of folders on the side. He was the type of administrative officer who liked things neat and orderly. He kept his clerk busy filing and refiling the continuous flow of orders, personnel records, letters, and official documents.

He looked straight at Hoyt standing by his office door. "The old man wants to see you."

"Roger. Right now?" asked Hoyt.

"Yeah, he said to see him when you recovered enough from your ordeal. The doc checked you out, right?"

Hoyt answered, "Yeah. Doc cleared me. Just a few bumps and a banged-up shin. Got some good rack time. Really appreciated getting some good chow too."

"The colonel is in his office now. You can knock."

"Thanks," answered Hoyt in a tentative tone.

Baker nodded and took a quick breath through his mouth as he raised his forefinger. "Oh yeah, I want to tell ya, your team is moving. They got orders today. Lieutenant Van Howe is getting them ready. They move out tomorrow. Truck's picking up their gear."

"How come we're moving?"

"Turns out the tactical situation may be changing. We gotta regroup. Intel says it's gettin' spooky. The regional forces are going to comb thru there while we make new assignments."

"Oh, sure," mumbled Hoyt.

"Yeah," Baker responded. "Anyway, better see the old man."

"Right," Hoyt replied as he turned to walk down the hall. A sensation of foreboding rooted in a vague feeling of guilt came over him, but he could not put his finger on the reason. Was it not avoiding the ambush? Was it the loss of the prisoner? Was it Tho's death? He knocked hesitantly on the door to Lieutenant Colonel Cartwright's office.

"Come in," boomed the clear, firm voice through the door.

"Ah, Hoyt," said the colonel as he looked up from the papers on his desk.

Hoyt stood before the colonel's desk and saluted. "Good morning, sir."

Cartwright returned the salute and leaned back in

his chair. He did not gesture to the side chair or ask Hoyt to sit down. Hoyt remained standing. Cartwright ordered, "At ease, captain."

Colonel Cartwright put his elbows on the desk and folded his hands into a tent. "I trust you have recovered from that fiasco, Hoyt?"

"Er. Yes sir."

"It didn't have to happen that way," asserted Cartwright.

"Not sure what you mean, sir?"

"It looks like you got yourself into that mess and lost our prisoner to boot. The guys in your Jeeps bought it. Got one of best PFs killed too. Sergeant Tho died saving your sorry butt."

Hoyt stiffened up, sucked in his gut and replied, "But sir, he didn't die in the firefight."

"No, but he was out chasing Charlie to rescue you. He died returning from that mission. It didn't have to be that way."

"Sorry sir. I don't understand, sir."

"Here's something for you to think about captain. Phoenix Program agents picked up your local girlfriend. What's her name, Chi?"

"Er…yes sir."

"They have been watching her for some time now. They know about your regular visits."

"Oh. What's the matter?" asked Hoyt.

"Well, she's lucky she's alive, but they interrogated her and found out all kinds of things about you. You were bragging so much she could tell Charlie exactly what you were going to do on moving the prisoner. That's why you got ambushed. That's why you got captured. And that's why Tho and your team, by the way, were out chasing Charlie to save your sad ass."

"Ah. I'm. I'm truly sorry sir," stammered Hoyt. His posture slackened, and he seemed to wobble at the knees. Hoyt's mind reeled with this new revelation. His gut churned. *It was my fault! I was stupid! I'll never outlive this. My career is dead.*

"Not as sorry as you're gonna be," asserted Colonel Cartwright. "On top of all that we lost our prisoner. That man named Nha. He was a high value captive. He probably had a lot of information. We needed that information. Intel knows something is up with the VC. Their forces are moving into the area. Our spies noticed a change in the attitude of the local population. You blew one of our best chances to find out what's going on."

"I'm sorry, sir. I'm sorry."

"Yes! You're too much of a liability. You really screwed up, Hoyt. So, I'm relieving you of your command. You will no longer be team leader."

"Yes sir," replied Hoyt glumly.

"In fact, you will no longer be in this province. If it were up to me I would send you back to the States where you can't get more good men killed. But it isn't entirely up to me. It seems the brass don't like to admit that a commissioned officer under their command is consorting with prostitutes who are enemy spies and who's blabbering operational plans to her. No Hoyt, the big green bureaucracy is going to cover up your idiotic moves, at least for now. You're going to a desk job in Saigon. I don't think you'll be doing anything that could cause further damage to the war. You may be counting paper clips, or you may be a latrine inspector, but you're gonna be on a tight leash."

Big sweat stains were spreading under Hoyts arms. He shifted his feet. "Yes, sir." He thought, *Going to Saigon isn't so bad. Maybe I can get past this? Maybe I can put up a good front? Maybe I can get away with this, after all?*

Lieutenant Colonel Cartwright continued. "But don't think you're getting away with it. By the time I get done writing you officer efficiency report, even without all the bald truth, your career will be over. You won't have a chance at promotion and no one will want to give you a slot. It's over for you, Hoyt. You can lick your wounds, hide out in Saigon, and crawl home."

"Yes sir," replied Hoyt meekly.

"Now get out of my sight and don't let me see you again in Ben Tre," snorted Cartwright.

SERGEANT FIRST CLASS BRADFORD AND Lieutenant Van Howe sat on ammo boxes outside their hooch waiting for a truck to pick up team equipment and move them to temporary assignment in Ben Tre. They watched local Vietnamese take apart their deserted hooch. When they said good-bye to Trung si Nhat Tang they had given the okay for the local people to reuse the building materials.

A small transistor radio emitted a scratchy sounding 'I Can't Get No Satisfaction' by the Rolling Stones. Bradford pulled at his olive drab t-shirt and said, "It sure is sticky. When those dark clouds build up its gonna let loose like all get out."

"Yeah, don't wanna be here when that happens. Been soaked too many times by these monsoons," replied Van Howe. "Besides, I want ta make it to Ben Tre before lunch. They've got those good burgers at the compound."

"Yeah, but I may be gettin' too short for lunch," replied Bradford with a wry smile.

"Ya got me there, Brad. How short are ya anyway?"

"Don't get jealous now, LT, but I got only thirty-four days and a wake-up. Then it's the big freedom bird for me."

"That's a long time in the Nam, Brad. Hope you make it. What ya gonna do back in the world?"

"I got a few more years in the Army, but first thing is I'm gonna do Route 66 with my Aussie lady if she'll go."

"Like that TV show a few years back?"

"Yeah, like that, 'cept I won't be driving a Vette. Could be my pick-up or maybe I'll rent one of them Mustang convertibles."

"Does she like pick-ups?" asked Van Howe.

"Says she does, but says she always wanted to ride in a Mustang too."

"If she's comin' all the way from Australia you better get the Mustang. Make her happy. Ah, since you're planning to travel, are you worried about any reaction to Vietnam Vets?"

"Nah, not too worried. They're talking about ending the draft, so a lot of college kids might quiet down. If we get a peace agreement people might wanna forget the war. But, anyway, I'll avoid trouble if I can. Grow a beard maybe. Keep quiet."

"Makes sense. Too many people are angry with this war. Some think it's wrong. Some say we failed. Others are ashamed they didn't serve. A lot of people take it out on GIs. Then, there are angry vets, too. They sacrificed. They feel betrayed – angry they were sent here by lying politicians, or angry the country doesn't appreciate their sacrifice. They need to lick their wounds. A lot of anger and conflict out there. Right now, it's sick, a big hurt. Best to keep a low profile."

"Yeah," said Bradford. "Now, I just wanna get outta here, get right, have some days where I'm pretty sure I'm gonna make it through and see the sun set. Maybe, in the long run, I'll go back to school to try and make sense of this whole thing."

"Really?"

"Yep, It's not just the Nam. It's all the history we ignore. The human race ain't gonna make it like this. That's my prediction."

"Thanks for the cheery note."

Van Howe leaned back slowly and looked up at the sky. Then he glanced at the villagers tearing down the hooch and said, "Whatcha think about these people tearing our house apart?"

"Not wastin' a thing. They got the tin off the roof, the metal stake rafters, the plywood, every scrap of nails and wire we used to hold it together. Even takin' the sandbags."

"Yeah," replied Van Howe. "Look at 'em chop up that concrete floor. It's a gold mine for 'em. I can see 'em puttin' slabs of concrete right inside their houses. Better than muddy floors with these rains."

Bradford smiled, "Yeah LT, they see us here today and gone tomorrow. We'll be remembered by the junk we leave behind. That and all the sorrows. I wonder, do they think we made things better?"

"You're kinda wistful, melancholy like, Brad, but I get your drift. Ya know, our leavin' here and leavin' stuff behind is kinda like this whole war."

"Whada ya mean, this whole war?"

"Well, right now, we're leavin' this place but we haven't finished. We're leaving the PFs behind. Tho is dead. We haven't stopped Charlie. Will the villagers live their lives without chaos and disruption, and uncertainty? The only thing for sure is we're leaving behind a lot of concrete and building materials. Like the Stones, they can't get no satisfaction. Is that our legacy?"

"Ok," said Bradford. "But, how's that like the whole war?"

"Yeah, It's the same thing on a larger scale. Peace

talks in Paris with Kissinger and Le Duc Tho. U.S. troops pulling out. The war is too long, too crazy, too much confusion, misinformation, moral problems, too many dead people and all that. And, all we're gonna do is leave behind a bunch of weapons, and materials, buildings, landing strips and whatever we brought over here."

"OK, I see your point. We're gettin' out and leavin' a mess. End of story."

"That's about it. But we don't know what happens next."

Bradford pulled out his canteen and focused on it as he slowly unscrewed the cap. He paused and took a deep draught. Then he said, "True, LT. What's gonna happen next?"

"Ok," Van Howe replied. "On this island, we got VC guerillas, maybe two squads. They come and go across the water and they still dominate the top of the island, at least at night. We haven't stopped 'em. Then, there are reports of larger units all around us, like out in Than Phu, or the Plain of Reeds near MeTho. If they wanted to take this ferry crossing they could bring in a battalion and it would be theirs pretty quick. Remember, though, we practically destroyed Ben Tre to get Charlie out in '68. If we dropped bombs and shells to destroy them, then this place would be obliterated too. I bet Charlie will keep the status quo, just nibble away until they want to do something big, like another Tet or Dien Bien Phu for the whole country."

"That worries me," said Bradford. "Think about it.

We're drawing down troops. We had over half a million back in '68 but now we're down to less than half that. We beat them in big battles, like the Battle of Ben Tre, Hamburger Hill and Operation Marauder in the Plain of Reeds. We beat 'em, but it was costly. Too many dead. Our guys were tough, but Charlie is tough too. If we didn't have air power and huge fire power, it might have gone the other way instead of our victories. With us pullin' out, can the ARVN hold up?"

"Right," said Van Howe, "The big question is *can* the ARVN win if we aren't here to help?"

"That's hard to say," replied Bradford. "A lot of these Vietnamese units are good. Good soldiers. Good leaders. All the good equipment we gave 'em. But we know some of the higher-level generals and colonels are political loyalists to the president and not seasoned commanders. That's a serious weakness in combat capacity. It could be dicey."

"So, that's why I say tearin' down this hooch is like tearing down this country. We came in thinking we could build it up, keep it safe, make it work, make it free. Turns out, we did patch work, ruined the economy, killed civilians, propped up a bad government, destroyed resources, and made them dependent on us. We're leavin' our junk behind. We're pulling out. The enemy is gonna keep coming at 'em. They could get overrun."

"Yeah," said Brad. "I'm worried about these people we know right here. I hate to see them caught up in all this."

With a frown, Van Howe said, "Sometimes I think this whole war is like the 'Charge of the Light Brigade' up the 'Valley of Death', and Armageddon too, all in one."

"Yeah," said Bradford. "We don't need more like this!"

On March 30, 1972, the North Vietnamese communists launched what they called the Nguyen Hue Campaign and what has become known as the Easter Offensive. Nguyen Hue was a heroic Vietnamese emperor with the birth name of Quong Trung. In 1789 he surprised and defeated invading Chinese forces in the outskirts of Hanoi.

The Nguyen Hue offensive was primarily an all-out, conventional force invasion fought by major units supplemented by guerrillas. The North Vietnamese marshalled 125,000 troops in fourteen divisions and twenty-six individual regiments. Tanks and artillery, mostly supplied by Russia and China, figured heavily in the attack. As discovered in captured documents and later reports, the offensive reflected a change in Hanoi's strategy from one of patient, long-term liberation to an all-out offensive.

The main attacks employed three distinct thrusts

toward the north, central and south areas of South Vietnam. The attacks in the north pushed over the DMZ and also from the west toward Hue and Da Nang. In the central area attacks struck at Kontum, Pleiku and Hoai Nhon on the coast. The main effort in the south was directed at Loc Ninh, An Loc and Saigon. A smaller thrust was directed at the Mekong Delta by the NVA 1st Infantry Division, supporting regiments, and local forces.

Although initially pushed back, South Vietnamese Forces soon regained their positions. During these critical times the Saigon government replaced ineffective, politically appointed generals with more proficient officers with combat experience. Although U.S. troop strength was less than 100,000 the U.S. Advisory and logistics networks were still in place, as well as critically important U.S. air support and naval gunfire.

Military strategists have said that "He who won the battles in the Mekong Delta would win the war in south Vietnam." The Delta contained most of the nation's population and its greatest agricultural resources. In the Delta region, the area where this story takes place, the NVA 1st Division was the largest enemy force. A major achievement for the defense was the containment of this NVA division in Cambodia by aggressive ARVN action and U.S. airstrikes. Badly weakened, it was unable to support other NVA and VC initiatives in the Delta.

One of the enemy objectives was to disrupt the successful pacification efforts of the south in places like Kien Hoa/Ben Tre, often reputed to be the "cradle of

Viet Cong insurgency." As the enemy thrust toward Kien Hoa and Dinh Tuong some of the heaviest fighting took place near the Plain of Reeds where six enemy regiments fought around their Base 470.

ARVN forces were very successful in defending the Delta against strong enemy attacks from the Cambodian border and the north west. Significantly, Major General Nguyen Vinh Nghi worked closely with his American advisor Major General Thomas M. Tarpely over several months to fend off several large-scale enemy invasions and keep the area secure. The attacks were beaten back with the intervention of South Vietnamese and American air support, including B-52 strikes, as well as tenacious and courageous performance by South Vietnamese Armed Forces, including Regional and Popular Forces.

Glossary

Ao ba ba - Everyday garment, pants, long-sleeved shirt with flaps at the waist. Work clothes look like black pajamas.

ARVN - Army of the Republic of Vietnam

Au dai - Traditional fine dress

Biere Ba Muoi Ba - Vietnamese "33" Beer

Biere Larue - Vietnamese Beer Larue

Cam on - Thank you

Chao - Hello, good bye

Chicom - Chinese Communist weapon

Chet - Dead

Chieu Hoi - "Open Arms," South Vietnamese initiative to encourage defectors.

COSVN - Central Office for South Vietnam, controlled by Hanoi

Dai uy - Captain

Di Di - Go. Go.

Dien cai dau - Crazy in the head

Con Son Island - Location of Poulo Condor Prison, known for tiger cages and torture

Ha si - Corporal

Kien Hoa - Saigon government name for province originally called Ben Tre

Lao Dong - Communist Party in North Vietnam

MAT Team - Mobile Advisory Team of five Americans and an interpreter

MACV - Military Assistance Command Vietnam

May Bay Truc Thang - Helicopter

Nuoc - Water

PACEX - Military exchange providing catalogue shopping for GIs

Phoenix Program - South Vietnamese program to neutralize VC infrastructure

Piaster - South Vietnamese money

PSDF - People's Self Defense Forces

RF/PF-Regional Forces - Popular Forces

Zin loi - Excuse me

Song - River

To Cong Campaign - Diem's Purge of Viet Minh

Toi - I

Tot - Good

Troi oi - What a surprise!

Trung si - Sergeant

Trung si nhat - Sergeant First Class

Trung uy - First Lieutenant

VC - Short for Viet Cong.

Victor Charles - Letter of the phonetic alphabet for V C

Xin Chao - Formal hello

Early struggles over Chinese and Vietnamese rule. Mongol invasion.

1858 - French fleet captured Saigon.

1883 - French controlled Vietnam by expanding their domain.

1940 - Japanese occupied Vietnam

1941 - Vietminh formed to fight French and, later, fight Japanese rulers in collaboration with the U.S. Office of Strategic Services (OSS).

1945 - August-Japanese surrendered to the Allies. OSS officers advocated U.S. Support for Vietnamese independence from France. September- Ho Chi Minh declared independence for the Democratic Republic of Vietnam. Nguyen Thi Dinh smuggled supplies to Viet Minh and helped lead an uprising in Ben Tre Province.

1946 - French reclaimed colonial control and declared Vietnam an independent state in the French Union. Vietminh clashed with French and retreated to countryside.

1950 - U.S. began to provide military and economic aid to the French in Indochina. U.S. Military Advisory Group was formed.

1954 - March-May: French were defeated at Dien Bien Phu by forces of Vo Nguyen Giap.

1955/6 - Geneva Agreement split Vietnam at the 17th parallel pending a national election to be held in 1956. French troops withdrew. Diem, Prime Minister of South Vietnam, refused national election and proclaimed the Republic of Vietnam.

1959 - Diem launched Agroville Program, unsuccessful predecessor to Strategic Hamlet Program started in 1961. It tried to relocate people from ancestral home-lands to government fortified settlements to deny VC access to population.

1960 - January - Nguyen Thi Dinh (Ba Dinh) lead an uprising in Ben Tre, considered inspiration for widening war. December - National Liberation Front (NLF) was established.

1962 - April - Robert McNamara proclaimed, "Every quantitative measurement we have shows we are winning this war."

1963 - Diem was assassinated. Gen Duong Van Minh assumed control followed by a succession of generals until 1967 when Nguyen Van Thieu was elected president.

1964 - August- Congress adopted the Gulf of Tonkin Resolution giving President Johnson power to act in Southeast Asia. There were widespread war protests in the U.S.

1965 - March- U.S. Marines landed at Da Nang to defend airfield. VC bombed U.S. embassy in Saigon. U.S. troops: 200,000.

1967 - 500,000 American troops in Vietnam.

1968 - Tet Offensive began on January 31 with North Vietnamese (NVA) and Vietcong attacking South Vietnamese cities and towns. American troops: 540,000.

1969 - COSVN issued Resolution # 9 in June citing the strategic importance of the Delta and renewing guerilla war. The 19th Plenum of the North Vietnamese Lao Dong (communist party) decided on a large offensive. COSVN issued Resolution # 14 in October to prepare for large scale offensive. Ho Chi Minh died on September 3. There was a big antiwar demonstration in Washington on November 15. The My Lai massacre (1968) become public news on November 16. Americans withdrew 60,000 troops.

1970 - On November 12, Lieutenant William Calley

was on trial at Fort Benning, Georgia for his role in the My Lai massacre.

1971 - Lt. Calley was convicted on March 29, of premeditated murder of South Vietnamese civilians at My Lai. From February to April Operation Lam Son 719 was conducted by ARVN without American Advisors to invade Laos and cut off the Ho Chi Minh Trail. The operation failed and required extensive US air support to cover the retreat. The New York Times began publishing the Pentagon Papers on June 13. American troop strength was down to 140,000 by December.

1972 - Starting in January, VC in the Delta increased small unit attacks of outposts, road routes, and also built up supplies. The Easter Offensive began in March but was defeated with the help of massive US airpower. US ground combat troops had been withdrawn by August.

1973 - Cease-fire agreements were signed in Paris on January 27. The draft ended in the US. Most remaining American troops departed Vietnam on March 29th.

1974 - January-President Thieu stated that the war had restarted.

1975 - Communist forces captured Saigon on April 30.

1979 - China invaded Vietnam in February.

D.R. Van Wye was a U.S. Army infantry officer during the Vietnam War, serving as a military advisor to South Vietnamese forces in the Mekong Delta. While on a mobile advisory team he earned the Combat Infantryman Badge, the Bronze Star, and the Vietnamese Honor Medal First Class. Vietnam Blues, like his first novel, Saving Ben Tre, conveys an historically accurate, authentic picture of what the Vietnam war was like for some of the young men and women who put their lives on the line to serve their country. He enjoys sharing his appreciation for the natural beauty of Cape Cod and surrounding waters with family and friends.